"I can't stay at your ranch overnight!"

Kara felt a bolt of panic flash through her.

"Honey, you can and you are. Okay, you're having an attack of nerves, thinking about meeting the kids. Who wouldn't? I understand completely. I didn't spare you the truth, and they are an intimidating bunch. But let's not forget the reason why you're here in Montana—"

"Yes, let's not!" Kara cut in. Paradoxically, the fear she was feeling instilled in her an uncharacteristic boldness. "I'm here to visit my uncle Will."

"It's time to drop the charade, Kara. Let's be honest with each other and cut the game-playing. You know you're here to marry me and help me raise those kids."

MARRY ME, *Cowboy*

THE WILDE BUNCH
Barbara Boswell

CONVENIENTLY *Wed*

Silhouette® Books

Published by Silhouette Books
America's Publisher of Contemporary Romance

SILHOUETTE BOOKS

ISBN 0-373-65324-7

THE WILDE BUNCH

BARBARA BOSWELL

loves writing about families. "I guess family has been a big influence on my writing," she says. "I particularly enjoy writing about how my characters' family relationships affect them."

When Barbara isn't writing and reading, she's spending time with her *own* family—her husband, three daughters and three cats, whom she concedes are the true bosses of their home! She has lived in Europe, but now makes her home in Pennsylvania. She collects miniatures and holiday ornaments, tries to avoid exercise and has somehow found the time to write over twenty category romances.

Please address questions and book requests to:
Silhouette Reader Service
U.S.: 3010 Walden Ave., P.O. Box 1325, Buffalo, NY 14269
Canadian: P.O. Box 609, Fort Erie, Ont. L2A 5X3

One

"Whatever can go wrong, will go wrong?" The Reverend Will Franklin shook his head, frowning. "I'm afraid I can't agree with you on that, Mac. It's too cynical, too pessimistic." He set down his coffee cup and leaned forward, his expression earnest. "It doesn't leave room for the power of—"

"Positive thinking," Macauley Wilde interjected. "I know, I know. I read that book you lent to me. And I tried thinking positive thoughts when Brick was expelled for a week for fighting after only one day at his new school. I tried positive thinking when Lily sneaked out of the house and stayed out all night. I tried to think positive when little Clay and his 'gang' broke into the high school and liberated all the white mice from their cages in the science lab and got himself suspended. I tried—"

"I know how difficult it's been," Reverend Will cut in. He did not want to be converted to Mac's cynical, pessimistic viewpoint. At this rate, he might well be. "Your brother

Reid's children have had an—uh—difficult adjustment to life here in Bear Creek.''

"They haven't adjusted at all," Mac said grimly. "And they don't intend to. They're maniacs, Rev. Sometimes they're blatant, sometimes they're subtle, but each child is maniacal in his or her own different way."

"I won't deny that the four of them are…uh…difficult." The reverend cleared his throat. He was aware that he was overusing the word *difficult,* but it was the most tactful adjective available to him. A man of the cloth should not use words like monstrous, heinous, atrocious. Especially not when describing children. "Anyway, I wasn't speaking of the power of positive thinking. I meant to say the power of prayer."

"Religion doesn't apply to those kids. Unless you're talking exorcism."

"I know you're only joking, Mac." Reverend Will smiled uneasily. "You've always had a keen sense of humor."

"Rev, I'm not laughing. Those kids have been with me for less than six months and something's got to give. When they arrived in June, I figured they'd have all summer to settle in and be ready for school in September. Wrong! Things became exponentially worse. Now it's mid-October and I'm desperate. We can't go on like this."

The reverend tensed. "Are you thinking of giving them up to the state?"

"Ha! The state won't take them. Since they've been here such a short time, Montana thinks they should be returned to their native state of California which says, 'oh, no, not our problem anymore.' The surrounding states—Idaho, Washington, Oregon—have already warned that their borders are sealed and not to even think of trying to dump those kids there."

"Hyperbole." Reverend Will chuckled appreciatively. "Most telling. But I understand the point you're trying to make, Mac."

"That the Wilde kids are notoriously incorrigible and have invoked terror in every child welfare worker unlucky enough to cross their path?"

"No. That you intend to keep Reid and Linda's children, no matter what. I admire your courage, Mac. I mean, your dedication," Reverend Will corrected himself hastily, his neck flushing. "Your resolve."

"They're my flesh and blood, Rev." Mac sighed. "I loved my brother and I was genuinely fond of Linda, too, even though I tended to see things differently from them."

"Most people saw things differently from Reid and Linda," Reverend Will said tactfully. "It's just too bad that you didn't get the children immediately after the death of their parents. The year they spent with your brother James and his wife Eve was quite...unfortunate. I think most of their problems stem from that—uh—difficult time."

"Amen, Rev. I know *I* wouldn't want to live with James and Eve, either. I offered to take the kids then, but James and Eve insisted they should be the ones to raise them, as they're a '*solid* marital unit.' That's how they refer to themselves." Mac grimaced. "They pointed out that since I had been a partner in a *defective* marital unit, it would be detrimental to bring children into my inadequate broken home. They considered me unfit to raise kids, until they decided they couldn't stand the little monsters. Then it was 'off you go to Uncle Mac's, even though he's divorced, defective and inadequate.'"

"James and Eve undoubtedly meant well, but they are—" Reverend Will paused to cough discreetly. "Difficult." There was that word again. But it wouldn't do for a man of the cloth to use judgmental terms like self-righteous, self-satisfied and petty to describe that solid marital unit of James and Eve Wilde.

"And you are not a failure because your marriage didn't work out, Mac. You and Amy were too young when you married, you both wanted different things and you grew apart.'' The minister shrugged. "Unfortunate, but it happens. What shouldn't happen is to let a mistake which happened long ago keep you from committing to another permanent relationship.''

"Uh-oh. Here it comes. Your semi-annual 'find yourself a nice girl and settle down' sermon.'' Mac held up his hands, as if to ward off the words.

"At the risk of sounding like James and Eve, promoting themselves as a solid marital unit, I would like to point out that having a woman in your house would certainly add some stability to the environment. Not to mention a sense of family and permanence which I think those four unfortunate children desperately need.''

"I knew you were going to say that!'' Mac stood and began to pace in front of the big granite fireplace. The head of a moose, complete with a spectacular set of antlers, was mounted above it. "And here's the kicker, Rev. I actually agree with you. I swore I was through with marriage after that fiasco with Amy, but I know I can't raise those kids alone—I need another adult in the house with me. But just when I finally decide I have to have a wife, guess what.''

He stopped pacing and stared up at the moose head. "No woman is interested in the position. Not when it means taking on my brother's kids.''

"Did you actually discuss marriage with one of your— lady friends?'' Reverend Will asked curiously.

Mac shrugged. "I didn't exactly propose, but I brought up the subject. Jill Finlay shuddered and said she wasn't inter-ested in raising anybody's children but her own. Tonya Ben-nett told me, 'Lose the kids and then we'll talk about mar-riage.' Marcy Tanner said she wanted to marry me but insisted that the kids would sabotage our chance for happi-ness and I should send them packing. Of course, if I didn't have the kids, I wouldn't need to marry any of them. I wouldn't want to. But things being how they are...''

He locked eyes with the moose. "It's hopeless, Rev. What

woman in her right mind would want to marry me and move in with the Gang of Four?''

"To think that just last year, you were voted the 'Most Eligible Bachelor in Bear Creek' at the hospital auxiliary's Valentine dance." The reverend sighed. "Well, I'm disappointed in Jill and Tonya and Marcy, but not surprised. You need a young woman of exceptional depth and commitment and those ladies do not fit the bill. But I know someone who does, Mac."

"Trying to play matchmaker, Rev?" Mac stared at the older man. "Thanks but no thanks. If I can't find my own—"

"Mac, sorry to interrupt!" A tall, tough-looking cowboy burst into the room, sounding as agitated as he looked.

Mac felt his stomach lurch. His ranch manager, Webb Asher, was not quick to panic. He never would have come to the house unless it was a genuine emergency. "What is it, Webb?"

"The fencing is down in the north field, Mac. Can't tell how it happened, but the cattle trampled it and are milling around in the direction of Blood Canyon."

"Just when I thought things couldn't get any worse!" Mac growled. "We have to repair that fence and start rounding up the cattle immediately." He glanced at his watch. "And I'm supposed to pick up Autumn at five at the Community Center when her dance class is over."

"I could ask my daughter Tricia to pick her up and drive her out here to the Double R," Reverend Will offered. "That is, if you think Autumn will get into the car with Tricia."

"I don't know." Mac started pacing again. "Autumn doesn't know Tricia very well and she has all these fears.... That kid sees danger lurking everywhere. And I've never heard anybody scream louder than she does when she's upset."

"That's the truth!" Webb agreed, injecting himself into the conversation. "First time that kid screamed, I thought a bear grabbed her and was mauling her. But she was screaming 'cause her brother was throwing water balloons at her and told her they were filled with acid. Kid thought her skin was going to peel off from acid burns.'' The ranch manager shrugged quizzically. ''Who'd think a little girl would know about stuff like acid burns?''

''Autumn specializes in the grisly and the gruesome,'' Mac said glumly. ''I think she does research.''

''The child does have a highly imaginative streak,'' Reverend Will murmured. ''A pity her imagination tends toward the—uh—morbid side.''

Mac paced faster. ''How can I be in two places at the same time? Picking up Autumn *and* working in the north field? Most of the time I feel as if I'm being pulled in five different directions at once, and I see no end in sight.''

''If you had a wife at home, she would be supervising the children,'' the pastor pointed out. ''She could help cook meals and—''

''Meals! Dinner!'' Mac slapped his hand to his forehead and groaned in despair. ''Damn, I forgot about dinner.''

''Can't Lily cook for the younger children?'' Reverend Will asked. ''I know she's taking a cooking class at the high school because my Tricia is in it.''

''Your Tricia might cook a meal for her family, but Lily will either set fire to the kitchen or poison the other kids. Deliberately.'' Mac sighed. ''Mrs. Lattimore makes us casseroles for three dinners on the days she comes in to clean, but the other four days dinner is one of my major headaches.''

''The young lady I have in mind for you loves to cook, Mac,'' Reverend Will remarked, his tone purposefully enticing. ''She's great with kids and has always wanted a family of her own. She is currently working in Washington, D.C., and from her letters, I feel certain that she's ready for a change. We could bring her to Bear Creek and—''

''Like a mail-order bride, sort of thing?'' Mac gave a hoot of laughter. ''Sounds like the plot of a romance novel, Rev.

And I don't look a bit like that blond-haired guy who's on all those covers.''

''It's no worse than advertising in the personal ads, which many people do these days,'' the reverend pointed out. ''And my plan is certainly a lot better and safer. I can personally vouch for both you and Kara and the two of you can—''

''Hey, Mac, your nephew is driving the Jeep,'' Webb exclaimed, dashing toward the front door.

''Brick?'' Mac uttered a curse. ''He's supposed to be in school. If he got himself expelled again…''

The three men raced to the front porch.

''Good Lord, it's little Clay!'' gasped Reverend Will.

For one paralyzing moment the three men watched the second-grader behind the wheel.

''Hey, Uncle Mac,'' young Clay shouted out the window of the Jeep, which was jouncing around the circular drive. ''I got sent home early today 'cause I'm infected. See how good I can drive!''

''Infected with what?'' Webb backed away from Mac.

''I'd heard the elementary school was experiencing an epidemic of chicken pox,'' Reverend Will said. ''If Clay has it, he'll miss at least a week of school. My little Joanna missed two weeks when she caught it a few years ago.''

''Good luck working the ranch *and* taking care of a sick kid, Mac,'' Webb said in a better-you-than-me tone of voice.

''A marriage of convenience is starting to look mighty tempting,'' Mac uttered. ''A sensible arrangement between two adults who know what they want and are beyond confusing fantasy with the realities of everyday life. At least we'd be spared all those falling-in-love delusions that just mess everything up. Rev, get that family-loving girl you know out here as soon as you can. At my expense,'' he added, just before making a mad dash toward the Jeep.

Kara Kirby read the letter over and over, willing the words to change. They didn't. The message remained the same.

It is with regret I inform you that, as a result of the recent decision to eliminate overstaffing in certain functions performed within the Department of Commerce, your position will be eliminated within thirty days of the date of this letter.

The letter went on, reassuring her that this was not a result of her job performance, which had been consistently excellent, but rather a necessary adjunct to the department's continuing efforts to reduce expenditures in areas which no longer occupied the same level of priority as they had in the past.

She was out of a job! Thirty days from today, she would be unemployed, her position as a statistician for the Department of Commerce having been eliminated in another round of government budget cuts.

Hot tears filled Kara's eyes, and she fought the rush of panic that surged through her. She'd held that job for the past five years! Sure, it had been dull at times—well, much of the time—but the pay was decent and she had health benefits and an annual one-week paid vacation. For the past year, she'd been able to pay the rent on her apartment in Virginia, just across the district line, without having to take roommates to split the costs.

Kara enjoyed the privacy but missed the company and the activity provided by other people. She'd always been reserved and introverted, and living with other girls forced her to socialize. But faced with moving in with strangers after her last roommate, a college friend, had married, Kara decided to go it alone. Now she shared her home and her life with her Siamese cat, Tai, who sat on the sofa across the room, watching her with his inscrutable blue eyes.

Three months ago, on her twenty-sixth birthday, Kara had sat in front of her television set with Tai and had taken stock of her life. She was twenty-six years old, living alone with her cat, her small social circle dwindling as old friends married or left the area, moving on with their lives while hers remained static.

Day after day, year after year, the same routine, same job— a comfortable quiet way of life, but one that offered no surprises, no change. The years had slipped away and she'd barely noticed. Now she was past twenty-five, entering the bottom half of her twenties and grinding inexorably toward thirty. The big three-oh! She was only four years away from it and she wasn't even dating anybody! The lonely empty years stretched before her with no man, no children. And now, no job!

She sadly faced the fact that she was not going to meet Mr. Right. With women greatly outnumbering men in Washington, D.C., eligible bachelors had their choice of outgoing, high-wage-earning beauties. Why would Mr. Right settle for someone like her—a shy office worker, average in every way?

But some indomitable deeply feminine instinct within her demanded someone to love, to nurture. She had always been one of those little girls who cherished her dolls and prayed for a baby sister or brother. But there had been no siblings, and as she grew older, her dreams were for a child of her own—and a man to father her child, a man she adored, who would love her and their baby. What a wonderful, happy family they would make!

Tai meowed and jumped down from the couch. Seeking attention, he wound his way around her ankles, his meows growing louder and more demanding, until Kara leaned down to pet the soft fur around his ears.

"Oh, Tai, what are we going to do?" It hurt to swallow around the huge lump in her throat. Never had her dreams seemed as impossible as at this bleak moment.

Tai purred loudly, oblivious to her distress, his back arched in ecstasy as she stroked him. Tai was perfectly content with their solitary existence; Kara wished that *she* were. Loneliness washed over her in waves. The future loomed dark and dismal. In nine months, she would turn twenty-seven, all alone except for her cat.

The telephone rang, jarring Kara out of her reverie of despair. She was grateful for the diversion, even though it was probably just a telemarketer trying to convince her to buy magazines or something else she didn't want or need.

"Kara?" The warm tones of Reverend Will Franklin sounded over the line.

"Uncle Will!" Kara exclaimed, thrilled to hear his voice.

"How would you like to come out for a visit, my dear?"

"Uncle Will, I'd love to, but—"

"No buts. I have a plane ticket for you. Ginny and the girls and I insist that you come to Montana. Immediately, if possible."

Standing at the gate in the airport in Helena, Mac glanced at the photograph in his hand for perhaps the hundredth time since Reverend Will had given it to him one week ago. The young woman featured in the photo was Kara Jo Kirby, age twenty-six.

He had urged the reverend to contact her last week, the day Brick had been discovered hiding in the girls' locker room with a Polaroid camera. And after chasing Clay around the house trying to apply an anti-itch lotion to his chicken pox spots, Mac had decided that a *solid marital unit* in which to raise the children was no longer an option to consider sometime in the future, it was an immediate vital necessity.

Reverend Will was delighted. "I've known Kara for years, and I can attest to her trustworthiness and high moral standards." He grew quiet for a moment. "I suppose I should tell you that I was Kara's stepfather for nearly five-and-a-half years, from the time she was three until she was past eight. Then her mother divorced me," he added flatly.

Mac gaped at him, speechless. He'd known Will and Ginny Franklin for the past fifteen years, ever since the pastor had arrived in Bear Creek. The couple and their two daughters, now aged sixteen and twelve, were the picture of domestic harmony. This was the first time he had ever heard of a previous Mrs. Franklin.

"It's no secret, although I rarely speak of my first marriage," Reverend Will said. "There is really no reason to and, well, Ginny doesn't care to recall that I was married before. I've kept in touch with Kara through the years, though I haven't seen her as much as either of us would've liked." He handed Mac the picture. "This was taken nearly five years ago. I was in Washington for a conference at the time and visited with Kara there."

Mac stared at the snapshot. Kara Kirby's smile looked forced, as if she'd been commanded to say "cheese" just as the picture was being taken. Her hair was brown and blunt-cut in a straight bob, which swung below her jawline. A light smattering of bangs—not those moussed, gel-stiff bangs that stood up like a cresting ocean wave—accentuated her large, wide-set eyes.

Her nose was small and rather elegant, her teeth white and straight, her eyes a startling red, a casualty of the camera flash. Actually, her eyes were hazel in color, according to her former stepfather. In the picture, the young woman was slender, wearing white slacks and a peach-colored shirt, although in the past five years, she might have gained some weight.

Like three or four hundred pounds? Mac swallowed. Well, if she possessed the sterling character and rock-solid virtues attributed to her by the reverend, if she were willing to commit herself to a desperate man and four disturbed kids, then he was damned lucky to get her.

Clutching Tai's travel cage, Kara deplaned and walked to the gate, her eyes flicking over the small crowd gathered to meet the flight. Reverend Will Franklin did not appear to be among them. In his carrier, Tai meowed piteously. He'd hated the flight and his constant raucous cries had earned him glares and scowls from the other passengers from takeoff until landing. The flight attendants hadn't been too thrilled with him, either—or with her for bringing him aboard.

"Excuse me. Are you Kara Kirby?"

Kara started at the sound of the deep voice. "Yes." She looked up—way up, for she was just five foot three, and the man standing in front of her was at least ten inches taller. He looked like the quintessential cowboy, wearing jeans, a chambray shirt and a pair of well-worn Western boots, one of those macho sorts featured in a beer or a Jeep commercial.

"I'm Mac Wilde." He surveyed her intently. She looked the same as she had in that five-year-old picture. Her hair was exactly the same shade and style and her big wide eyes really were hazel, not vampire red. She was slender, small-boned with a slight frame, although the parts of her figure which interested him the most were not revealed. Her breasts were concealed beneath her thick, tunic-style beige sweater, her legs well-hidden in the slightly baggy pleated gray slacks.

Her clothes were certainly tasteful if not a tad dull—and a lot shapeless. Mac found himself wondering how she would look in brighter colors, more revealing styles. He frowned at the direction his thoughts had taken. Certainly he did not expect her to dress like teenage Lily, whose flamboyant sexy outfits frequently caused him bouts of avuncular shock.

His frown deepened. He'd caught Lily in the act of sneaking back into the house yesterday shortly before 3:00 a.m. and the little conniver had refused to tell him where she'd been. Or with whom.

Kara shifted uneasily, registering the man's frown of disapproval. She guessed he'd been sent by the reverend to meet her plane—and that he was not pleased with his assigned chore. Probably not with her, either. Men who looked like Mac Wilde—who was tall and dark, but whose sharp blade of a nose and hard mouth saved him from classical masculine perfection, thereby making him even more interesting and attractive to her—men like that never noticed plain, uninteresting women like her.

Uncle Will had informed her that the distance from Helena to his home in the small town of Bear Creek was about one-hundred-seventy-five miles. That meant several hours in the company of this man, who would undoubtedly be heartily bored with her at journey's end.

Kara searched her brain for something to say, wishing that some devastatingly clever bon mot would spring to mind, but of course, one did not. She'd never tossed off a clever bon mot in her entire life.

"I guess Reverend Franklin couldn't make it to the airport and asked you to give me a ride," she said, and immediately scorned herself for stating the obvious. When it came to the dull and the bland, she always delivered!

"I wanted to come," Mac replied. Having paid for her ticket—he'd even sprung for first class—having braced himself for matrimony, he was champing at the bit to see his bride-to-be.

Kara smiled. "That's kind of you to say." She knew he didn't mean it, and she appreciated his politeness.

Mac stared at her. Her smile was completely unlike that uncomfortable grimace that passed for a smile in the photograph. This smile was genuine, lighting her face and transforming it. Mac was intrigued. That sudden flash of animation revealed a very pretty woman. For the first time he took note of her skin, luminous and smooth as ivory, quite unlike the weather-tanned skin of the locals. Would her cheek be as soft to touch as it looked? And what about her skin elsewhere? He felt a stirring in his midsection which slowly twisted lower.

Kara quickly composed her face into the placid, guarded mask she'd been wearing since they'd met. Mac's eyes narrowed. Suddenly that mask she wore interested him, too, because he knew there was another woman behind it. One whose hazel eyes sparkled with warmth when she smiled, whose mouth was wide and full and sensuous.

He allowed himself to contemplate kissing that sweet

mouth. The heat in his loins flared pleasantly. Yes, he liked the idea of kissing her. This past week, he'd finally come to terms with the necessity of having a wife. After all, a woman *had* to know more about kids than he did; women possessed the acclaimed maternal instinct to guide them. And the availability of a wife would certainly be sexually convenient for him. Having a woman living under his roof and sharing his bed meant he would not have to go elsewhere for feminine companionship. He had discovered that the concept of dating was logistically impossible with four children around. Especially those four!

As for having sex…well, he wasn't. An ache spread through his body, reminding him that there had been no woman in his bed since the children had come into his life. The long period of enforced celibacy was taking its toll on his nerves and his temper. He couldn't wait to rectify the situation with his brand-new wife!

Kara cast a covert glance at him, feeling uncomfortable by the intense, almost predatory, glint in his eye. Her experience with men was woefully at odds with her chronological age. She was suddenly tense and on edge. "Is—is it a long drive to Reverend Will's house in Bear Creek?"

"About three hours to Bear Creek and another twenty-five minutes to the ranch."

"What ranch?"

"My ranch."

"You have a ranch?" Interest replaced her vague unease. "A real Western working ranch?"

"Didn't the Rev tell you about the Double R?" Mac was confused. He'd assumed the pastor would have provided her with at least the basic facts about her new home.

Kara shook her head no. "He talked a little about his own house," she added, wondering why Mac appeared to be so perplexed. Was his ranch such a showpiece that he assumed it was the natural topic of conversation between any Bear Creek resident and visitor?

Tai chose that moment to utter an earsplitting meow which seemed to echo throughout the Helena airport.

"I can see that Autumn is going to have some competition in the screaming department," Mac murmured. Just what the household needed, a cat whose meow could shatter glass.

Kara gulped, not quite sure what he was referring to, but had no doubts that he did not appreciate Tai's no-holds-barred, executive meow. "Tai isn't a good traveler," she apologized. "This was his first flight and he's very unhappy."

Mac kept staring at her. She found his silence unnerving. "I—I'm glad that I insisted on bringing Tai in the cabin with me, though." Mac Wilde's eyes were a deep, dark brown, piercing and intent. When she felt his gaze sweep over her once again, a warm blush stained her cheeks.

"I know he wasn't too popular with the crew and the other passengers, but I just couldn't consign him to the freight area of the plane," she continued, averting her eyes from Mac. "Tai's never traveled before—it might've left lifelong emotional scars."

"A cat with emotional scars," Mac repeated. He decided her concern boded well for the kids. After all, if she had empathy for a cat, she would undoubtedly have it for four young orphans who had been uprooted for a second time after their parents' demise.

"Come on, we'll pick up your luggage. It should be in the baggage area by now. Then we'll head out to the ranch."

"I—I'd rather go to Reverend Franklin's house." Kara stood stock-still, clutching Tai's carrier. "It's been so long, I just can't wait to see Uncle Will. Oh, and—and Ginny and the girls, too," she added quickly.

Mac was not pleased, but he decided her request was not unreasonable. The pastor used to be her stepfather, and it *had* been five years since they'd seen each other. "Okay," he agreed. "But I can't leave the kids for too long." The prospect of them on the loose made him shudder, considering the havoc they managed to wreak when under supervision. "We've really got to get going!"

He headed toward the baggage area, leaving Kara to follow him. She watched his tall muscular frame stride away from her. He had children. It was inevitable that an attractive, virile man such as he would be married with children. She wondered where his wife was and why, if he didn't like leaving the children for long stretches of time, he had agreed to drive all the way to the airport to pick her up.

She thought about the way he had been looking at her. It didn't seem right for a married man to stare in that particular way. Unless she was overreacting and misinterpreting? Was she turning into a suspicious spinster who spied a slavering sex fiend in every male who glanced her way?

The notion depressed her. She'd always despised that dreadful old card game *Old Maid*; now it appeared she was turning into the personification of the losing card. Kara flinched at the thought.

Her shoulders drooping, she trailed after Mac to retrieve her luggage, with the yowling Tai announcing his arrival and issuing complaints to everyone in the airport.

"How many children do you have?" Kara asked politely as they left the outskirts of Helena in Mac's sturdy Jeep Cherokee. She'd taken Tai out of his carrier and held him on her lap, which had finally quieted him. But the cat was still tense and on guard, his blue eyes darting around the roomy interior of the vehicle.

"Four," Mac replied. Surely the reverend had mentioned the children, the sole reason for her journey out here! He glanced across the seat at Kara and saw her stealing a quick glance at him. She flushed a little, embarrassed to be caught looking at him.

"How nice." Kara continued in those same courteous, impersonal tones.

Mac noted that she was able to say "how nice" with a straight face. Exactly what had the pastor told her, anyway?

The radio was on, and an intensely romantic song pulsed over the airwaves. Kara stroked Tai's fur and tried to calm her own increasingly taut nerves. She and Mac were alone, enclosed inside, and suddenly the atmosphere seemed disturbingly intimate.

She was acutely aware of his strong masculine presence. She couldn't keep her eyes from straying to him. His big hands on the wheel, his broad shoulders, the wide powerful chest—Kara took inventory of them all. As if of its own volition, her gaze abruptly dropped lower to glide over his long, muscled legs, though she was careful to avoid the button fly of his jeans.

She was ogling him! Kara was shocked by her own blatant—and completely inappropriate—behavior. She had never actively ogled a man in her entire life and her first chosen target was a married man, a father of four!

It must be jet lag. Kara quickly strove to remedy her appalling lapse.

"How old are the children?" she asked, toying with Tai's orange-and-black collar. Tai owned twelve different ones and Kara changed them monthly, the color and motif of each coordinating with whatever holiday or activity was associated with that particular month. Orange and black were for October and Halloween.

Mac frowned. This was not going as planned. In the scenario he'd envisioned, Kara arrived in Montana knowing all about her future family, as told to her by her former stepfather. Or was Kara Kirby simply playing dumb, trying to break the ice by asking questions to which she already knew the answers?

The sexy, smoky sounds of a sax filled the car, conjuring up images of a couple moving in rhythm to its beat. His eyes traveled to the curve of Kara's slender neck where the skin looked as silky soft as her slightly flushed cheeks. He found himself wondering about the taste and feel of her mouth.

"What are the children's names?" Kara asked a little frantically, her voice rising. He didn't seem inclined to talk to her, but he was definitely not ignoring her, not when he kept looking at her in that dark, disturbing way. How well did Uncle Will know this man he'd sent to fetch her? she wondered nervously. What if he were one of those seeming pillar-of-the-community types with a hidden Dr. Jekyll alter ego?

"You want to know about the kids." Mac sighed. "Well, it wouldn't be fair to sugarcoat it, so I'll give it to you straight. Lily just turned seventeen. She's manipulative, sneaky and rebellious, and those are her good points. Brick will be fourteen on New Year's Day and when he doesn't find the trouble he's looking for, he creates it. Autumn is ten and a little ghoul who sees danger in everything and is obsessed with crime and disaster. And finally, Clay, the youngest, is a seven-year-old hellion who lives by his own rules and sees no reason to follow anyone else's. Needless to say, living with that crew has not been easy."

Kara gulped. "I suppose not." Perhaps he was just having a bad day and was venting steam? She decided that that must be the case and tried to come up with some diplomatic comment to offer. "The children's names are interesting. Rather different."

"Yeah, rather different," Mac agreed grimly. "Like they are. Their parents—my brother Reid and his wife, Linda—wanted their names to be something besides a name. They wanted their names to be attached to the earth and be part of nature and the planet or something like that."

"I think I understand," Kara murmured. *They're not his children?*

Mac was pleased. She hadn't condemned the kids nor scoffed at Reid and Linda's hug-a-tree philosophy of life. Kara seemed nonjudgmental and tolerant, exactly what they needed. Relief surged through him. He had made the right decision, bringing her out here. The sooner she moved in, the better for all of them.

"And the children are staying with you now?" Kara tried to put the pieces together.

"They're living with me permanently. Their parents were killed in a car accident in a chain-collision pileup on one of the L.A. freeways nearly two years ago."

"How tragic!" Kara was horrified. "Those poor children."

Mac nodded. "It's been rough. At first, Linda's mom moved in with the kids but she barely lasted three months. She couldn't handle them and was only too glad to escape to her retirement village condo, where kids under twenty-one are banned—even as visitors."

"Oh, dear," Kara murmured.

"Next, my brother James and his wife, Eve, decided it was their duty to take the kids. That arrangement lasted one miserable year."

"The chemistry wasn't right between the children and their aunt and uncle?" Kara surmised, her voice warm with sympathy.

"You could say that." Everybody else, himself included, had said a lot more about the kids' incorrigibility and James and Eve's repressive rigidity. *Not the right chemistry.* Now that was putting a benign spin on an impossible situation! Mac liked her lack of negativity. She was going to need it, living with those four young terrorists.

"And after things didn't work out, you took the children?" Kara prompted.

"They've been with me since June. I'm the first to admit that I don't know much about raising kids. Aside from being one myself a long time ago, I haven't had any experience with children." Mac cast a sidelong glance at her. "It's become clear to me that I'm not cut out to be a bachelor father."

He was not a married man. Kara felt a peculiar heat suffuse

her. She was dealing with the ramifications of having ogled a bachelor when Mac reached for the car phone.

"I'm going to call the kids and tell them we're on our way."

Ten rings later, he debated whether or not to hang up. "Why doesn't someone answer? Where are they?" He glanced at his watch as the phone rang on and on. "It's five o'clock, they should all be home from school by now."

"Perhaps they—uh—were detained after school," Kara suggested. *Assigned to detention.* Given Mac's description of the kids, the possibility of punishment could not be ruled out.

Finally a small scared voice came over the line. "Hello?"

"Autumn, it's Uncle Mac." Mac breathed a sigh of relief. "What took you so long to answer the phone?"

"I was in my room and I pushed the dresser in front of the door, so it took me a while to move it," Autumn whispered.

"What were you doing barricaded in your room, Autumn?" Mac braced himself for the answer. "And where are the other kids?"

"I was watching TV, Uncle Mac."

"In your room? You don't have a television set in there."

"I do now," Autumn said rather proudly. "I dragged the TV from the living room into my room. Uncle Mac, do you know that bad guys in jail try to get pen pals? And if you write to killers in jail, when they get out they'll come and find you and try to steal your money or kill you."

"Autumn, I told you that you weren't allowed to watch any more of those tabloid news shows or talk shows, either," Mac said sternly.

"Everything else is a rerun," whined Autumn.

"And you are *not* to move the TV from the living room. I want you to put it back," Mac ordered, then paused. "You never did say where the other kids are, Autumn."

"They're gone," Autumn said gloomily. "I don't know where, they just left. Uncle Mac, what if one of those killers who got out of jail is on his way to kill his pen pal and sees Lily or Brick or Clay and—''

"That's enough, Autumn," Mac cut off her morbid speculations. "Don't you have any idea where the kids are?"

"Not Lily or Brick, but Clay said he was going to ride that big black horse."

"Blackjack?" Mac choked. "The stallion? God almighty, Autumn, you have to—''

"Uncle Mac, someone's knocking at the door!" Autumn shrieked into the phone. "Knocking real loud and hard like a murderer!" She let out a bloodcurdling scream audible to everyone in the Jeep.

Tai dug his claws into Kara's thighs and growled a warning.

"Is she all right?" Kara asked with concern.

"Autumn!" Mac shouted her name a few times before finally reclaiming his niece's attention. The screaming ceased.

"He says he's Webb Asher, Uncle Mac. He says he has Clay," Autumn reported. "He says to open up the door. I'm not going to, though. I think it's someone pretending to be him. A killer from jail who's pretending to be Webb," she concluded dramatically.

"Autumn Wilde, you open that door and put Webb on the line, *right now!*" Mac commanded.

A few terse moments later, Mac hung up the phone. "My ranch manager caught Clay in the stallion's pen tossing cookies at Blackjack, trying to make friends so he could get a ride. This is a wild-tempered stallion who could've killed him with just one kick. If Webb hadn't gone down there when he did…'' Mac's stomach lurched. "I've got to get back there immediately. Lily and Brick are God-knows-where, and I can't leave the two little ones home alone. I told Webb to stay with them till I got back, but his tolerance for children doesn't go far.''

Kara glanced at her watch. "How much longer till we're in Bear Creek?"

"We're not going into town. I'll take another road that will bypass Bear Creek and get us to the ranch faster."

Kara swallowed her disappointment. Under the circumstances, she could hardly demand that Mac Wilde take her to the Franklin's house in town before going to his ranch to check on his recalcitrant nieces and nephews.

"I'll call Uncle Will as soon as we get to the ranch and ask him to pick me up. Then you won't have to leave the children again to drive me into town."

Mac frowned. "Can't you wait until tomorrow to see him? You've had a long trip, and there's no need for the reverend to come out to the ranch after dark."

"Wait till tomorrow?" Kara echoed. "That's impossible. I—"

"Let me put this another way. Nobody is going anywhere tonight. We'll talk about getting you into town to visit the Rev tomorrow."

"I can't stay at your ranch overnight!" Kara felt a bolt of panic flash through her.

"Honey, you can and you are. Okay, you're having an attack of nerves, thinking about meeting the kids. Who wouldn't? I understand completely. I didn't spare you the truth, and they are an intimidating bunch. But let's not forget the reason why you're here in Montana—"

"Yes, let's not!" Kara cut in. Paradoxically, the fear she was feeling instilled her with an uncharacteristic boldness. "I'm here to visit Reverend Will Franklin."

"It's time to drop the charade, Kara. Let's be honest with each other and cut the game playing. You know you're here to marry me and help me raise those kids."

Two

Kara gaped at him, stunned into speechlessness. Mac's words seemed to hover tangibly in the air between them. Once again, she felt the heat of intensified color turn her cheeks a scalding pink.

"If—if this is your idea of a joke, I don't appreciate it." Kara finally found her voice. She wished she sounded less anxious and more sternly forceful. She had never felt so off-balance in her careful quiet life. "Uncle Will bought my plane ticket and he—"

"No, he didn't. I paid for that ticket. If the Rev told you otherwise, he was—well, lying." Mac shrugged at her shocked look of outrage. "Hey, the man is only human, after all. 'Let he who is without sin' and all that…"

"Do you honestly expect me to believe that Uncle Will would invite me here, *implying* that he was paying for my ticket," she emphasized the word, for Will hadn't come right out and said that he'd bought it. "That he would be part of some plot to get me out here to m-marry you without ever mentioning you to me? That's right, he never even mentioned your name, let alone this—this crazy notion you seem to have about—''

''It's not the way I would've handled things myself,'' Mac said, frowning his disapproval. ''I thought the Rev would be up-front with you. After all, he was the one who came up with the idea in the first place.''

''He wouldn't do such a thing!'' Kara cried. ''Not Uncle Will.''

''Listen, baby, Uncle Will dreamed up the whole thing. I didn't even know you existed, until the Rev told me. He knew I was having trouble with the kids, and we both knew I needed a wife to help me with them. He suggested that you might be willing to come out here and marry me. When you accepted my ticket, I assumed you'd accepted the—uh—position.''

''Ohhh!'' Kara covered her burning cheeks with her hands. ''This can't be true!''

''But you know it is.'' Mac's voice was firm.

''No!'' Kara closed her eyes, fighting a crushing urge to burst into tears. ''I came out here to visit my uncle—''

''He's your stepfather,'' Max said bluntly. ''The Rev told me all about his marriage to your mother. I was surprised to hear it. I don't think anybody in Bear Creek knows he was married before or has a grown stepdaughter.''

''Ex-stepdaughter,'' Kara corrected tightly. ''Ginny, his wife, made the *ex* very definite over the years. When I was still a little girl, she told me that I wasn't allowed to call him Daddy anymore, that he had daughters of his own and I was not to think of myself as one of them.''

''Ouch.''

''Yes, it hurt. He told me to call him Uncle Will, instead. I did as he asked, but for a long time afterward I still thought of him as my dad. My real father died shortly after I was born, and Will was the only father I'd ever known.''

''So he placated his wife at your expense?''

"He had no choice," Kara loyally defended her former stepfather. "A husband does what he has to do to make his wife happy."

"Let me rephrase that for you—a wimp caves in and lets the woman have the upper hand," Mac said scornfully. "And it's always a big, *big* mistake."

"One you'd never make, I'm sure," Kara murmured, because she simply could *not* let his chauvinistic remark go unchallenged.

"That's right," Mac agreed proudly. It seemed he'd interpreted her challenge as a compliment. He shook his head, bemused. "None of this sounds like the Rev and Ginny I've known for the past fifteen years."

"Uncle Will was heartbroken when my mother left him for another man. So was I." Kara's voice grew bleak, remembering that sad time. "Mom always claimed he married Ginny on the rebound and Ginny knew it. That's why she resented Will's relationship with me so much. I was a reminder that my mother, and not Ginny, was the great love of his life."

"It's hard to imagine the Rev in the role of romantic lead," Mac said wryly. "And even harder to picture Ginny as a possessive shrew, nasty to little girls. She's always been so helpful and upbeat."

"I doubt that even the most helpful, upbeat woman likes to think of herself as second best when it comes to love. Women always found my mother a threat because she was—and still is—a very beautiful woman."

Kara felt Mac's eyes upon her, assessing her. Doubtlessly trying to imagine how a very beautiful woman had managed to produce such an ordinary daughter. It was not the first time she'd been confronted with that particular puzzle.

"Unfortunately, I look nothing like my mother. From the pictures I've seen, I take after my dad's side," she felt compelled to explain. "Average in every way."

"There is nothing wrong with the way you look," Mac said gruffly.

Kara shifted uncomfortably and turned her attention to her cat, kneading his fur with gentle fingers. She had never discussed herself or her past so frankly with any man, and she suspected she'd sounded downtrodden and filled with self-pity. Which she was not! She felt a surge of anger at Mac Wilde for putting her into this unholy predicament.

Mac reacted to her silence. "Are you waiting for me to counter with a feature-by-feature rave of your face and figure?" He heaved an impatient sigh. "Look, I've never been one of those touchy-feely types who ooze syrupy compliments and pour on the charm. And I—"

"Obviously not," Kara cut in tartly. "You seem extremely practical with no time or patience for anything dealing with emotion or sentiment. I guess that falls into the dreaded touchy-feely department? Well, has it occurred to you that there might be a direct correlation between your hardheadedness and your need to—to attempt to buy a wife?" She had never been so caustic or outspoken in her life, but somehow Mac brought it out in her.

Mac arched his brows. "At the risk of sounding redundant—ouch!"

He lifted his hand from the wheel to run one long finger along the length of her arm, from her shoulder to her fingertips. "The lady has claws, hmm? Just like her kitty."

Kara shivered. Though well-protected under the heavy cotton of her sweater, her skin tingled along the path that he'd traced. "Don't patronize me," she growled.

"Whatever you say, sweetie." He flashed a teasing grin.

A quivering spiral of tension coiled in her stomach. When he smiled like that, he was devastating. A fact he probably well knew, lectured a stern little voice in her head. Some cautious feminine instinct warned her that Mac Wilde was not averse to turning on the charm, should it serve his purpose.

Silence descended between them. Kara's nerves felt stretched to the screaming point as she reviewed this decidedly bizarre situation. Mac Wilde had footed the bill for her journey and in return expected her to marry him and help him raise his four unruly nieces and nephews.

What a preposterous idea! Was he dreaming? Perhaps she'd fallen asleep on the plane and when she opened her eyes, the flight would be landing and Uncle Will would be waiting eagerly at the gate for her.

Mac, on the other hand, did not seem affected by any tension whatsoever. "This is one of my favorite songs," he announced cheerfully. He turned up the volume and drummed his fingers on the steering wheel in time to the beat. "Merle Haggard. 'That's the Way Love Goes.'"

It did not go well, according to the lyrics. And Kara knew this absurd idea of his was just doomed to fail.

"I'll repay you for the cost of my plane ticket, of course." Kara gulped, wishing she could appear cool and controlled, but failing utterly. "I—I'm terribly sorry about the misunderstanding. This is all so embarrassing. No, it's beyond embarrassing. It's absolutely mortifying!"

"I don't want to be reimbursed. I expect you to honor the terms of our agreement and marry me."

"But we have no agreement!"

"I bought that ticket in good faith and assumed you'd accepted it and the terms offered in the same good faith." Mac slid a glance at her.

He was surprised at how well he was able to read her already. She was confused and aghast, the better to fall for this legal spiel he was spinning. "Maybe you're scamming me," he accused. "Using my money for a free visit to Montana? Who can guess how much more cash you planned to wring out of me. Maybe the Rev is in cahoots with you. Find a sucker, promise him a—"

"How can you even think such a thing!" Kara cried, panic

lacing her voice. "This is all just a—a terrible misunderstanding."

"That's what you said before. I'm not buying it, honey. I think you and the Rev tried to con me," Mac said rather gleefully.

"We did no such thing!" Kara stared at him. That gleam in his dark eyes, that note of triumph in his voice suddenly alerted her to the possibility that Mac Wilde might be improvising. Masterfully. "You have no reason to suspect any conspiracy or wrongdoing. Or any proof, either," she added succinctly.

"Don't I? Then answer this question for me, Kara. If Ginny Franklin regards you as a thorn in her side, if she sees you as an unpleasant reminder of an era she is determined to forget, then why would she suddenly allow her husband to invite you to stay at their home and to pay for your ticket out here?"

Kara opened her mouth to speak, then abruptly closed it. She'd asked herself that same question when Uncle Will had first extended the invitation. But she had been so happy to be invited, she hadn't probed any deeper. Had it been pure wishful thinking on her part, that she would at last be accepted into the Franklin family?

"You've never visited them out here before," Mac went on. "The only times you've seen the Rev have been when he was traveling on church-related business, without Ginny and the girls. Am I correct?"

Kara gave a grudging nod.

"From the time you were a child, Ginny made it plain that she didn't want you and your ex-stepfather to maintain your ties," Mac continued. "The Rev told me himself that he wasn't able to see you as much as you two would've liked. That was because of Ginny. Well, why should Ginny have a sudden change of heart at this late date? I happen to know that she's not suffering from a terminal disease so she isn't trying to set things right before she meets her Maker. The truth is, Ginny Franklin is not expecting you to stay at her house. If she even knows about your visit to Bear Creek, she's been told that you will be with me at the Double R. As for that fantasy you concocted about the Rev buying your plane ticket—ha! Only over Ginny's dead body.''

Kara swallowed hard. "You're using the information I gave you against me."

"All's fair in love and war, baby."

"Well, this isn't either one. Stop this car!" Kara commanded impulsively. "I'm getting out."

Mac laughed at that. "You plan to hitchhike back into Helena? With your luggage and that caterwauling cat?''

"Yes."

He raised one dark brow. "Are you sure? The sun is going down and it gets pretty scary out here at night. Bears and cougars and wolves prowl along the highway. Your cat could end up being their appetizer while you serve as the main course."

Kara tried to ignore the apprehensive chill that rippled through her. "You're deliberately trying to scare me. I think I'm in greater danger from you than any animal predator out there. And if you don't stop this car right now, I—I'll jump out."

Mac abruptly steered the Jeep off the highway, onto the wide shoulder of the road.

Kara trembled. It seemed he was about to grant her wish and let her out. A cold lump of fear settled in her stomach and expanded to fill her throat. How was she going to get back to Helena? This interstate was going in the wrong direction—she would have to hitch a ride or walk to the next exit and then make her way to the eastbound portion of the highway to hitch or walk back to the city. Tai emitted a miserable meow, and Kara stifled a sob of her own. What if there really were dangerous wild animals on the prowl out there?

"You'd better put the cat back in his carrier," Mac advised.

Kara nodded dumbly. Tai did not go gracefully back into his hated carrier. She practically had to wrestle the cat into it, while he hissed and tried to claw her. Finally, after he was safely locked inside, Mac placed it on the back seat.

Kara reached for the door handle. "I'll get my luggage out and take Tai last," she said stiffly.

"That won't be necessary." Mac moved as swiftly as one of those animal predators he'd warned her about.

Before she realized what was happening, he'd outmaneuvered the armrests and the seat belts which restrained them, and took both her hands in his. Their knees touched, their faces were very close.

"What are you doing?" Kara's voice rose to a squeak. She tried to snatch her hands away but his grip was too firm for her to break.

"I'll tell you what I'm *not* doing. I'm not abandoning you and your cat on the highway. I would never expose you to that sort of danger, Kara."

Kara's heart was thundering in her chest. She was in danger right here in the Jeep! She tried frantically to recall the self-defense tips she'd heard in that lecture she had attended last year with some women from work. It had been given by a police officer who'd designed a program to teach women street smarts and safety.

Now Officer Murray's number one piece of advice came back to her and roared in her ears. *"Don't get into a car with anyone you don't know."* Well, she'd already blown that one. Officer Murray would be chagrined at her stupidity.

"Relax," Mac said softly. "I can feel you trembling. I'm not going to hurt you."

"Then let me go. Right now!" Was she supposed to plead for mercy or issue a command? Kara tried both, the plea followed by the order.

"You don't have to be afraid of me, Kara."

"Then why are you doing such a good job of scaring me? You let me think you're dumping me out on the highway and then you g-grab me."

"You demanded that I stop. You even threatened to jump out if I didn't," Mac reminded her. "I wasn't about to call your bluff. Dealing with hysterical women has never been my strong suit," he admitted wryly. "Just ask my ex-wife."

She was immediately distracted. "You've been married?"

"Once. It lasted three years. We split up nearly nine years ago, so it falls into the realm of ancient history. Don't look so shocked, Kara. Most men don't reach the age of thirty-five without experiencing the unholy state of matrimony at least once."

"Unholy state," she repeated. "Since you feel that way, then why—"

"I already explained. There are four compelling reasons why."

Tai chimed in with another commanding meow.

Mac rolled his eyes. "I led you to believe I was going to put you out of the car because I wanted that furball with claws back in his carrier so we could talk. I didn't want him distracting you, and he's easier to ignore in his cage."

"Much to his outrage. Poor Tai." Kara's fear had already begun to dissipate, but the nervous excitement pulsing through her had heightened and intensified. She felt his thumb glide over the sensitive skin of her wrist, then move upward to stroke her palm. The small gesture was sensual and provocative and her whole body responded to it with a strong swift surge of desire.

"You agree that we do need to talk before we go any farther?"

She drew a sharp breath. "I—I agree," she murmured, trying to regain her bearings. "I'm terribly sorry for the inconvenience and expense you've had to—"

"Forget about that," Mac ordered. "Let's cut to the chase, Kara. I know this whole situation is a bit unorthodox. I mean, out West mail-order brides have gone the way of the Pony Express and the Wells Fargo Wagon, yet here we are...."

"Mail-order bride? Is that what I'm supposed to be?" She could not suppress the bubble of laughter welling up inside her.

"Yeah, I know. It sounds ridiculous. I laughed too, when the Rev first suggested it." Mac smiled wryly. He sobered almost instantly, his dark eyes intense. "But I've come to believe it's a damn good idea." His eyes slid over her. "Now that I've met you, it seems like an even better one."

"Oh, please!" Kara swept an agitated hand through her hair, tousling it. "It's bad enough that you think I'm so desperate for a man that I would hightail it out to Montana to marry a stranger who paid for my fare. Don't make things even worse by pretending to be attracted to me."

"Who says I'm pretending?" His voice grew deeper. "I am attracted to you."

"You're playing some kind of role. Saying things you think I'd like to hear." Kara swallowed hard. Depressingly enough, she realized that she liked hearing him say he found her attractive, even though she knew he couldn't mean it.

She straightened her spine, holding her head high, as she steeled herself against his insidious virile charm. "You must think I'm downright pathetic if you expect me to believe that you could possibly—"

"Enough about me," Mac cut in. "Let's talk about you. I think you're attracted to me, too, Kara. A little scared of me, maybe, but definitely attracted." With one deft move, he slipped his hands to her waist, and gripping her, easily lifted her out of her seat and onto his lap. "So let's work on eliminating the fear and heightening the attraction."

Kara gasped a protest. "No, Mac!"

Mac grinned, settling her more deeply into his lap, his arms fastening around her like steel bands. "Let's work on changing that into, 'Oh, Mac!'"

He held her fast against the hard male planes of his body,

making her fully aware of his muscular strength. And of
something else. There was no mistaking the blatant arousal
of his body. Kara's stunned eyes locked with his intense,
knowing ones.

"I told you I was attracted to you." Mac lightly touched
his mouth to hers.

"I—I'm not as gullible as you seem to think," Kara whispered. It was difficult to talk and even harder to think. His
lips were nibbling at hers, their breaths mingling. "I know
I'm not the type to inspire instant lust—"

"You're not?" Mac traced the shape of her mouth with
the tip of his tongue, until she unconsciously parted her lips.
"Well, I don't see anyone else here but you, baby. You know
what that means, don't you?"

"Probably that you've been in a—a state of deprivation
and that any woman would turn you on." Kara squirmed on
his lap and made a feeble effort to free herself. Her cheeks
burned with shame. She was well aware of how very slight
her attempts to escape from his lap actually were.

"Don't underestimate yourself." His voice was husky and
hypnotizing. "You're the one who inspired my case of instant
lust. You, Kara."

His warm hand closed over her breast. There was nothing
alarming or demanding in his touch, no heavy-handed possession. He caressed her gently, as if it were the most natural
thing in the world for him to touch her there, to learn the
feminine shape of her body.

Kara's breathing became deeper and heavier. He was seducing her and she knew it. Knew it, and was falling hard
and fast. She'd never been exposed to an experienced man's
advances. Her dates had been with quiet young men as unsure
and reserved as she was; passion had never been a remote
possibility. In D.C., confident, good-looking, assertive men
like Mac never gave her a second glance, let alone gazed at
her with intense dark eyes while murmuring how sexy she
was. Never had she been lifted onto a hard male lap while

his mouth and hands aroused this hot, melting sensation that made her close her eyes and wriggle closer to him, helpless in the mounting throes of ardor.

Mac let his mouth wander to her cheeks, then along the curve of her jawline to her ear, where his teeth nipped sensuously on the lobe. "Your skin is so soft," he marveled. "Beautiful and creamy soft." He was nibbling on her neck now, and his hand made a bold foray under her sweater. "I want to see more. I want to taste you, feel you."

With a slow, sure touch he slipped his hand inside her bra, his fingers gliding deeper into the cup to caress her already taut nipple.

"Mac, no!" Kara cried frantically, unnerved by the flooding warmth surging through her body. The sensual heat spread like wildfire through her veins, from wherever his lips and fingers touched her. The most secret intimate part of her felt unaccustomedly swollen and achy and embarrassingly wet.

"No?" Mac reluctantly removed his hand from beneath her sweater. "Am I going too fast for you, sweetie?"

She pressed her thighs together, trying to suppress the too-exciting pleasure he had evoked.

"W-Way too fast. After all, we just met." Yet she couldn't summon the willpower necessary to get off his lap and return to her own seat. Her fingers dug into his shoulders, making her achingly aware of his powerful muscular strength.

"True. But we're not bound by any stupid traditional courtship rules." Mac's hands slid down her back to cup the roundness of her bottom, his fingers kneading the firm softness there as he lifted her still closer.

"That's what's so great about this whole deal, honey. We're spared the getting-to-know-you games, the who's-going-to-make-the-next-move strategies, the is-it-too-soon-for-sex conundrum, the commitment worries. We're already beyond all that, even though we just met. We know what the outcome is—we're going to be married. There is no purpose in holding back—or holding out.''

His voice was soft and warmly reassuring. As he talked, his hands grew bolder and more insistent. He caressed the backs of her thighs with long sweeping strokes, the tips of his fingers moving toward her inner thighs with leisurely smoothness. Instinctively, her legs parted, and he began to trace erotic circles, his fingers moving higher toward the place that burned and throbbed for him.

Kara's pulse was racing wildly. The raw sexuality of his caresses blitzed her natural inhibition and reserve and common sense, the three hallmarks of her personality. She was reeling with pleasure, unable to control the shooting streaks of desire burning through her.

''Kiss me,'' Mac growled huskily, but he didn't wait for her to comply to his sensual command. He cupped her chin in his hand, angling her mouth to meet the hot hard slant of his.

There was nothing hesitant or tentative about the way his mouth took hers. His lips parted hers easily and his tongue penetrated the moist hollow of her mouth, as he moved to secure her more firmly against him. One hand fastened in her hair to hold her head, the other continued to glide over the curves of her body with slow enticing strokes.

The kiss deepened and grew longer, more intimate. She had never been kissed with such mastery, such fierce hunger. Dazed and dizzied, Kara had neither the control nor experience nor sophistication to hold back her response. She was throbbing everywhere, her whole body flushed and heated with the sensual fire Mac had kindled and set blazing.

Kara felt as if she were drowning in a wild, thrilling whirlpool of sensations. She moved restlessly, clinging to him and trying to get even closer. She was aching with an urgency and an emptiness she had never before experienced, a force which could not be ignored. Sensuality pumped through her body like a potent drug; she felt as high as Montana's Big Sky.

And then suddenly, unexpectedly and most unwelcomely, the sharp ring of a telephone sounded, blasting through the sensuous cocoon enveloping them, with the force of a gunshot.

"Damn!" Mac muttered, lifting his mouth from hers. His hands stilled on her body. "This is the downside of car phones. Back in the good old days, you couldn't be reached when you decided to do a little parking."

The car phone rang again. The sound offended Tai who had momentarily ceased his meowing, and he voiced his protest with another screeching cry.

Kara whimpered softly as Mac set her away from him. Her body roiled in a turmoil of frustration and thwarted need. It was as if she had become instantly addicted to his touch and was now undergoing the physical deprivations of withdrawal.

"Yes, this really is Uncle Mac, Autumn," Mac said into the phone. "No, I'm not some bad guy pretending to be him. It's okay that you called me, Autumn. That's why we have the car-phone number written down beside the phone, so you can get in touch if you need to."

Mac's voice filtered through Kara's shell-shocked haze. As she began to slowly regain her composure, she noticed that Mac appeared to be quite collected. He seemed to have pulled himself together with remarkable haste. Embarrassingly remarkable haste.

While her mind was still awhirl, unable to form coherent thoughts, let alone phrases, Mac was conversing with his young niece as if nothing out of the ordinary had just occurred.

Maybe it hadn't, not for him.

The nasty possibility seemed too obvious to ignore. Maybe a heavy make-out session in his Jeep was strictly routine for him. While she had lost her head, made mindless and helpless under the potent spell of his sexual expertise, he had re-

mained in complete control. He couldn't have recovered himself so quickly and so completely if he'd been as far gone as
she, Kara was certain of that.

"She *what?*" Mac's voice rose to a shout. "Autumn, put
Webb on the— He what? Oh, great!" The way he said it left
no doubt that he considered the opposite to be true. "Just
great!"

Kara dared to glance at him. He didn't appear collected
now; he was clearly agitated.

"Autumn, I'll make a deal with you. If you and Clay sit
quietly in front of the television set until I get back, I'll order
you whatever you want from the toy catalog. "Yeah, the
Christmas Wish Book. One thing apiece. But remember, for
the deal to be valid, you and Clay can't fight and neither of
you can move from in front of the TV."

He replaced the receiver and restarted the engine, flooring
the gas pedal. The Jeep roared back onto the highway in a
burst of speed. Mac was scowling. There wasn't a trace of
the sexy, seductive lover evident in his grim expression.

Kara nervously twisted her fingers. She felt as if she were
on an emotional merry-go-round—first up, then down, going
round and round, giving her no time to adjust or maintain
any sort of equilibrium.

The silence was getting to her. As long as it was quiet, she
was free to reflect on her shockingly abandoned response to
Mac. And that, of course, led to thoughts of his response to
her. He'd been hungry and impassioned, but turned cool and
controlled immediately, as if a switch had been thrown. The
implications of that made Kara cringe.

"I guess…something's going on at the ranch?" she ventured. "With the kids?" Talking to Mac was better than sitting here agonizing over their earlier hot scene.

"Something's always going on with those kids," Mac
growled. "Autumn called to tell me that the sheriff picked
Lily up in a bar just outside Bear Creek, a place called the
Rustler. There's a pool table and darts and a jukebox there.

The patrons are hardworking, hard-drinking cowboys who don't mind a good fight when things get dull.''

"And women aren't welcome there?"

"Oh, there are women who go to the Rustler. But they're either good ol' gals or women who are not looking—'' He paused and cleared his throat.

"For a committed relationship?" Kara asked tactfully.

A slight smile creased Mac's face. "Something like that. It is definitely not a place for seventeen-year-old schoolgirls," he added, his expression turning dour. "My ranch manager drove over there to bring Lily home. That means Autumn and Clay are alone again."

"Thus, your bribe."

"You don't approve of bribing kids?" Mac demanded testily.

"Well, I—"

"I can't risk trying out any fancy child-rearing theories from this distance. I have to rely on what works. And promising toys and candy is the most successful ploy I've got. It's also the only one," he added glumly.

"If you bribe the two little ones with toys and candy, what do you use to bribe the older kids?" Kara asked.

"Nothing. You can't buy them. Brick and Lily do as they please." Mac heaved a groan. "Sometimes I think it's too late, that they're already destined to be future career-criminals. I mean, the kids have always been brats. Their parents considered themselves free spirits, who 'didn't believe in restraining kids' natural curiosity and exuberance with rules and restrictions.' That's a direct quote from my sister-in-law, Linda. I heard her say it so often, it's emblazoned on my brain. And my brother bought into that, though we certainly weren't raised with the complete freedom Reid and Linda were determined to give their kids."

"It seems to me that children want some limits," Kara murmured. "Complete freedom would be terrifying. There should be certain boundaries to make kids feel secure."

"I agree with you completely." Mac smiled, his relief evident. He reached over to lay his hand on her knee. "We're going to be a good team, I can tell. Have I thanked you for coming out here, Kara? I am so grateful that you're willing to—"

"I don't want your gratitude," Kara interrupted quickly. "I haven't agreed to anything, yet." She deliberately crossed her legs in an attempt to dislodge his hand. He took the hint and removed it.

His words stung her. His gratitude seared even more deeply. He was grateful she was here to rescue him from the solitary burden of dealing with his nieces and nephews. He was so grateful to her that he was willing to pretend an attraction to her, to kiss her and arouse her...

Was that his plan? Throw some sexual crumbs to the desperate old maid and she'd be so thrilled and appreciative that she'd be unable to resist him and his plans for her? Kara winced.

Mac tried to interpret her expression. Stubborn, sad or mad? Or a little of each? He wished he knew her better, wondered if he should keep pushing or back off. After some consideration, he decided to give her the space she seemed to want. For a while.

He decided a neutral topic of conversation would be in order.

"Tell me about your job," he said conversationally. "The Rev said you work for the—uh—department of...um..." He racked his brain but couldn't come up with the name of the department. He had not been particularly interested in her place of employment, which would soon be in her past. "The government," he amended.

"I'm a statistician with the Department of Commerce." Kara didn't bother to add that she had less than thirty days left before her position there was terminated, that she was taking her vacation this week rather than lose it.

She hadn't told Uncle Will about her pending unemployment, either, not wanting to spoil their time together with her job woes. Now she was inordinately relieved she hadn't said anything. Let them believe she was too dedicated to her career to be a proper mail-order bride.

"A statistician?" Mac mulled that one over. "Then you must be good with numbers."

"I—uh—always did well in math," she confessed rather reluctantly. She well remembered that females with a prowess for mathematics were hardly the romantic ideal, at least not among the young men she'd known through her school years.

"Great!" exclaimed Mac. Was he unaware of the stigma against numerically gifted women? "You can do our taxes. That's my annual nightmare. And then there's the matter of the children's trust funds, set up for them by their parents' insurance policy…another numbers headache I'll gladly cede to you. And you can do the books for the ranch and handle the budget."

"I—"

"Oh-oh, there I go again. Making presumptions." Mac tried to look penitent. "I mean, of course, if you decide to stay, you'll be taking over those chores." He tried to sound as if he wasn't sure she would be staying on as his wife.

Kara eyed him. That smarmy tone of his reminded her of the fairy tale where the Big Bad Wolf tried to convince the hapless Little Pigs on the other side of the door that he was harmless and innocent.

"I'm going to take Tai out of his carrier," she announced. The cat's vocal protests over his confinement were a welcome diversion to her, a note of reality in this astonishingly unreal scenario she seemed to have landed in.

"Good idea," Mac agreed amiably. He was smiling, lost in his own thoughts. For the price of a one-way plane ticket, he was getting a sexually desirable wife, a caretaker for the kids and a math whiz! A very good return on his initial investment, despite the presence of the noisy spoiled cat as part of the package.

"Nice kitty," he murmured, reaching over to pet the cat who'd settled himself on Kara's lap with a disgruntled meow.

Tai tried to bite his hand.

"He's nervous around strangers," Kara half explained, half apologized.

"Not to worry. He'll have plenty of time to get to know me." Mac would've liked to rest his hand on her leg, perhaps even link his fingers with hers. It seemed a romantic gesture that she would like, and it would set the possessive aura he wished to convey.

But Tai's less-than-amiable disposition and sharp white teeth precluded that.

"Did I mention that Reverend Will's oldest daughter, Tricia, is severely allergic to cats?" Mac asked casually. "The reason I know is because the Rev and Ginny bought her a cat for her birthday several years ago, and poor Tricia ended up in the hospital emergency room with a serious allergy attack. The Rev pleaded from the pulpit the next Sunday for somebody in the congregation to please give the cat a home because the Franklins couldn't keep it. There were several offers and a happy ending to the story. The cat got a new family and Tricia got a pet bird."

"You're making that up!" Kara accused.

"Now why would I do that? I was just providing you with some essential information."

"You're implying that Tai won't be able to stay at the Franklins' house with me!" Kara's hazel eyes widened with apprehension, despite her doubts about his credibility.

"Oh, he won't be. That's a given," Mac assured her.

What if it were true? It occurred to Kara that she hadn't asked Uncle Will if she could bring Tai. She'd assumed he would know the cat would be coming along with her. After all, her former stepfather was well aware of Tai's existence; she mentioned him several times in every letter she wrote. There were times when Tai and his feline antics were more interesting than anything going on in her own life!

"But I want you to know that Tai is welcome to stay at the ranch, even if you decide to stay in town with the Rev," Mac offered, sounding for all the world like a Boy Scout bent on doing a good deed. "Of course, leaving him by himself in a strange place with a household of strangers could definitely be traumatic for such a sensitive cat. He might suffer long-lasting emotional scars."

"As if you care!" Kara flared. "You just want to make me—"

"Yeah," Mac cut in, a devilish grin lighting his face. "That's right, I do."

It took Kara a moment to catch on, her experience with suggestive banter being practically nonexistent. She flushed scarlet and fell silent.

For the remainder of the drive, conversation was desultory and always initiated by Mac. There wasn't much to see in the darkness, but Mac commented on the terrain, the mountain peaks towering to the sky and promised a view of breathtaking fall scenery during the daylight hours. He told her a little about the history of the area and some Wilde family history, as well.

The Double R Ranch, whose brand was two *R*'s back-to-back, had been owned by the Wildes for four generations, passing from father to son.

"It was an easy tradition for the first three generations because each family had only one son, along with some daughters who were not eligible to inherit the ranch," Mac explained. "Then my dad and mother had three sons, Reid, James and me. Crisis! Who'd get the ranch? It ended up being me because I loved the place and wanted to stay here. Reid headed for Southern California, and James to the world of academia. My dad signed over the ranch to me ten years ago, not long after Mother died. Dad lives in Scottsdale, Arizona now and is the sought-after bachelor in senior citizen circles."

Kara listened attentively. "So you got the ranch and your

brothers got nothing?'' She had no siblings of her own but could imagine the hard feelings such partiality must engender.

Mac nodded. ''Reid didn't care, he'd married into money. James was resentful. He thought Dad should give him some sort of cash equivalent, but Dad refused to even consider it. He told James that he'd paid for his education, that James was earning a comfortable living as a college professor and the ranch was for the Wilde son who'd live and work there. End of story.''

''Does James still feel cheated?''

''Of course. James thrives on collecting injustices done to him. Reid's kids made a major contribution to his collection. Don't count on him or Eve coming out for our wedding,'' he added dryly.

Kara was not about to touch that bait. ''Well, I think it's terribly unfair that all the Wilde daughters were automatically cut out and not even given a choice if they wanted to live and work on the ranch,'' she said instead, in defense of her own sex. ''It's downright medieval.''

Mac nodded. ''Yeah, my aunts weren't too pleased. Neither were their aunts. But that's tradition for you.''

''No, that's stupid, sexist tradition for you,'' Kara retorted. ''If I had a daughter—''

''Hopefully, we will,'' Mac interjected. ''Along with the requisite Wilde male heir, of course.''

Kara ignored him. ''If I had a daughter, she would split any inheritance evenly with her brother. There would never be a single doubt about that.''

Talking about her and Mac's hypothetical children was entirely too provocative a subject. She felt edgy and belligerent, needful to keep him at bay.

''We're jumping the gun here, honey,'' Mac drawled. ''After you meet Reid's kids, you may opt for immediate sterilization.''

"They can't be as bad as you say," Kara insisted, feeling the need to disagree with anything he said.

"You're right—they're even worse." Mac turned off the main highway, onto a dirt road. "The house is a few miles ahead. Prepare yourself for the onslaught."

Three

The headlights of the Jeep lighted the gravelly road leading to the ranch house. Kara saw clusters of tall, thick evergreens horseshoed on three sides of the house—to protect it from the sweep of blustery winter winds, according to Mac. The house itself was a sprawling stone-and-wood one-story structure with a wide porch spanning the front.

Lights blazed from every window, illuminating the landscaped bushes, shrubs and small ornamental trees surrounding the paved stone walk leading from the circular drive to the front door.

"Home, sweet home," Mac said drolly. "I can hear the welcoming cacophony already."

He was exaggerating, of course. From the confines of the car, Kara could hear nothing at all. The apprehension that had been gnawing at her for miles erupted into a surging force. She was in the middle of nowhere, miles from the only person she knew in the state of Montana! And she was about to face a tribe of brats, so monstrous that their own blood

relative was willing to marry a perfect stranger in an attempt
to cope with them.

She turned to Mac, feeling as desperate as he must have
felt when he'd shelled out the money for her plane ticket.
She couldn't spend the night in his home! The idea of such
intimacy sparked a nerve-tingling anxiety that was one part
fear and three parts excitement. Oddly, the excitement was
more disturbing than the fear.

"Mac, please, I—I can't do this. Please, please take me to
Uncle Will's tonight."

Mac studied her face, which was a picture of distress. Her
enormous hazel eyes were filled with tears, her lips were
quivering. "You make me feel like a rat," he murmured.
"Scaring a pretty young woman, making her cry. Damn, I
am a rat!"

He reached out to trace the sensual curve of her warm full
lips. Remembering the feel of that sweet mouth under his and
remembering her immediate and passionate responses to him
caused a tightening ache in his loins.

"I—I'm not crying," Kara protested, but her voice qua-
vered. She lifted her hand to remove his from her mouth. His
touch was unsettling, exciting. She craved it as much as she
feared it.

Mac succeeding in interlacing her fingers with his. She
watched, wide-eyed, as he brought her hand to his cheek and
held it there. His skin was slightly stubbled and sensually
abrasive to her already overcharged senses.

Her heart jumped. She had to get away from him before...before... Kara trembled. "I—I just want to—"

"I know, I know," he soothed. "You've been very brave,
considering the way you were caught off guard by—uh—the
plan. You've been a helluva good sport, Kara. I'm sorry
you're upset. Damn, I'm worse than a rat, I'm a flea on a rat
for upsetting you."

"It isn't really your fault," Kara acknowledged charitably.
"Uncle Will should have told me the whole story right from

the start. Then we would have been spared this unfortunate mis—''

''—understanding,'' Mac chimed in.

Their eyes met and they smiled at each other. Once again, her smile had a peculiar effect on him. Mac felt a possessive urgency shoot through him. He wanted her. He certainly hadn't expected to be aroused by his mail-order bride, but for the children's sake—and his own—he'd been prepared to be a proper husband. It was a wonderful surprise to find himself attracted to her.

And it bolstered his determination to proceed with his plan.

''I'll take you into town to the Rev's place,'' Mac said silkily. ''But first, I'd like to check on the kids. See if Webb's back yet. He ought to be by now. See if they've killed each other yet. Will you come inside while I do a body count?''

Relief flowed through her. There was no reason for her to be anxious and fearful, Mac was not going to force her to stay. He was a reasonable man, not a threatening one. Her fears had been for naught. *A body count?* His sardonic edge made her grin.

Calmer now, she had no problem granting his very reasonable request. ''Of course I don't mind waiting while you check on the children.''

Mac smiled his satisfaction. He had no intention of driving her back into town, though he didn't know how he was going to get out of it, having just promised to do so. Well, he'd cross that bridge when the time came. Right now, he was elated that she'd agreed to come into the house. That was a major victory. Forcing her inside definitely would've been a tactical error.

He gazed into Kara's warm, trust-filled eyes. She'd wholeheartedly believed his promise to take her into town. Had he called himself a flea on a rat? Mac decided that he was something even lower, which would probably make him a plague-carrying flea on a rat.

"Thank you, Mac," Kara said warmly. "And don't worry, I'm sure the children are getting along just fine."

"I bet you believe the weather predictions in the *Farmer's Almanac,* too."

She chuckled appreciatively. "Meanwhile, I'll call Uncle Will and tell him where I am and when I'll be arriving at his house." She made no reference to his claim regarding Tricia's allergy to cats; she still wasn't sure she believed him on that one. It was just a little too convenient for his purpose.

"Good idea. Call the Rev." Mac got out of the Jeep and came around to open the passenger door for her, every inch the chivalrous gentleman. He even took her arm and helped her climb out. His fingers lingered, rubbing from her shoulder to her elbow, then sliding along to take her hand. He raised it to his lips, lightly brushing her fingertips. "Welcome to the Double R, Kara," he said, smiling into her eyes.

Kara's knees felt strangely weak. She was lost in his deep, dark eyes.

"Shall we bring the cat inside?" Mac asked solicitously.

It took a moment or two for his words to penetrate the dreamy cloud enveloping her. "Y-Yes, maybe he'd better come in. Even a few minutes alone out there would be too terrifying for Tai."

"My thoughts, exactly." Mac dropped her hand and reached for the cat carrier.

He and Kara walked onto the porch, Tai's meows announcing their every step.

The door was unlocked. Mac pushed it open and Kara followed him inside.

They entered a room-size entry hall, its hardwood floor well-scuffed by foot traffic. The walls were painted a creamy beige, rather dull but functional. At the end of the vestibule, the hall narrowed to a passageway, leading to other parts of the house.

Kara looked around her. To the left was a closed door. A bit farther down, on the same side, she caught a glimpse into the dining room. A massive breakfront and long rectangular table almost filled the room.

To the right was an enormous room, a combination living room and den, dominated by a big granite fireplace. Above the fireplace was mounted the head of a moose. A baseball cap hung jauntily from one of its antlers. There was a wall of windows which undoubtedly offered a spectacular view during the daylight hours, although all that was visible now was the vast blackness of the night sky. The other walls were paneled with a dark wood, giving the room the feel of a rustic, oversize cabin.

A young boy and girl lay on big bright floor cushions in front of a large-screen television set. Neither child looked up when Mac and Kara entered. Not even Tai's indignant howls drew a glance from them.

"There are Clay and Autumn," Mac murmured. "They love TV. It's the one thing that can keep them occupied for hours. I bought a satellite dish after they moved in so they could *always* find something to watch. We've seen everything from Mexican soap operas to rugby meets in Australia."

He'd bought a satellite dish after the kids had arrived to keep them entertained? Kara pondered that one. Though she made no claims as an expert in child psychology, incessant TV-watching didn't strike her as an ideal way to spend a childhood. What about reading and playing indoors and out, what about activities with other kids?

But Mac sounded sincerely proud of his efforts to keep the children happy. She didn't have the heart to tell him that round-the-clock viewing, however diverse, might not be in their best interest.

"What are they watching now?" Kara asked, wondering which nation could be held accountable for the pandemonium currently roaring on the screen.

A number of very scantily clad young women were running in circles screaming, while a gang of menacing young toughs in black leather terrorized them. It was a veritable festival of blood and mayhem, and Clay and Autumn watched raptly.

"Hey, kids, what's on?" asked Mac.

"A really good movie," young Clay replied, without turning his attention from the set. *"Biker Vampires Go To College."*

"Ah, an educational film," Mac remarked dryly.

"The biker vampires got into the sorority house and hid in the attic till nighttime," Autumn explained. "When I go to college, I'm keeping a cross and some holy water right beside my bed, just in case. Ohhh!" She hid her face in the pillow as one particularly graphic scene flashed across the screen.

"Won't that give them nightmares?" Kara murmured. "It's so gory, it's sort of making me queasy."

"It's just fake blood," Clay piped up reassuringly. "There aren't any real vampires."

"Sometimes real killers pretend to be vampires and drink people's blood, though," Autumn interjected with relish.

Mac winced. "Turn that off and come here and meet Kara. She's a—uh—a friend of mine."

When neither child moved to do his bidding, Mac crossed the room and switched off the set. Two small scowling faces turned to Kara. Clay's was covered with drying, crusting lesions which had been swabbed with some pinkish lotion.

"Did I mention that Clay is recovering from chicken pox?" Mac asked a little too heartily. "He was out of school all last week, and will probably have to miss most or all of this week, too."

"And you need someone to stay with him while you're working," Kara surmised. No wonder he was desperate! Poor Mac had been cooped up with a sick child for a week and was facing the prospect of still another. She was beginning to understand his impulsive action in sending for a wife candidate. She felt genuine sympathy for his plight, but that was certainly not grounds for marriage!

"I'm not much of a nurse," Mac admitted. "Of course, Clay isn't much of a patient, either. The itching drove both of us nuts."

"I was terrible!" Clay agreed. "I scratched all the time, even when Uncle Mac paid me not to."

"You *paid* him not to scratch the pox?" Kara asked, incredulous.

Mac shrugged uncomfortably. "Nothing else worked. Not lotion or medicine or even threats about having pox scars for life. The kid likes money, so I gave it a shot."

"I'm pretty rich now," Clay confided. "But I still scratched sometimes."

"There's a cat in here!" Autumn exclaimed, walking over to investigate Tai's carrier. "Oh, she's pretty. What's her name?"

"He is a male and his name is Tai," said Kara. "He's very upset, he's had a long trip." She felt obliged to explain as Tai continued to meow at the top of his feline lungs.

"Poor kitty!" Autumn crooned. "Can he come out of that cage?"

"I don't think we'd—" Kara began, but Autumn moved with the speed of sound and had unlatched the carrier door and opened it before Kara had even finished speaking. Tai leapt out like the springing figure in a jack-in-the-box and took off, running around the room before disappearing into the entry hall.

"He likes it here!" Clay cried delightedly. "He wants us to play hide-and-go-seek with him!" He ran out of the room, seeking Tai.

"I saw him first, Clay!" Autumn bellowed. "I get to find him first! I get to play with him first! Me, not you!" She charged out of the room, screeching her demands.

Kara and Mac exchanged glances.

"Just like a heartwarming scene from one of those feel-good family flicks, hmm?" Mac's grin was nothing if not sardonic. "Is there anything more charming than kids and animals together?"

"Biker vampires on the loose in a sorority house runs a pretty close second," Kara murmured.

Mac gave a shout of laughter. Kara felt ridiculously pleased she'd made him laugh.

The children's voices echoed down the hall, but there were no more meows to be heard. Apparently Tai was hiding out from his enthusiastic pursuers and was not about to reveal his whereabouts.

"Mac! Thank God you're back!" The deep male voice, filled with unmistakable relief, drew their attention to the far side of the room.

"So you made it back, Webb," called Mac. "Where's Lily?"

A tall, tanned man with sunbleached blond hair had passed through a swinging door to join them. He was wearing old boots and faded jeans and an equally faded plaid shirt, untucked. "I've got your hellcat of a niece tied up in the kitchen, Mac."

"Uncle Mac!" called an indignant, feminine voice. "Help!"

Mac strode briskly across the room and disappeared through the swinging door. Kara, for lack of anything else to do, followed him. The tall blond cowboy, in turn, followed her.

The tiled kitchen was big and airy and distinctly modern with every kind of appliance, from an electric can opener to a microwave oven. It seemed at odds with the rustic Western decor in the sprawling living room-den, except for the head of an elk sporting an amazing set of antlers, which was right in keeping with the hunter-trophy theme.

A curved bench was built into one wall and an oval table stood in front of the bench. There were four captain's chairs grouped around the table, and sitting on one of them—tied to one of them!—was a very pretty, raven-haired, dark-eyed teenage girl.

Kara's eyes widened in astonishment. This had to be Lily, Mac's oldest niece. It occurred to her that, except in film, she had never before seen anyone tied up. It was a jarring sight. The young girl's arms were pulled in back of the chair and her wrists were secured together with rope. Each of her long, slim blue-jean-covered legs was tied to one of the chair's thick wooden ones. She was rocking back and forth, tilting the chair precariously, but not actually getting anywhere.

"What's going on here, Webb?" Mac demanded, glaring at his ranch manager.

"The sheriff told me to pick her up at the Rustler, or he'd take her to the jail house and hold her in a cell till you came for her," muttered Webb. "I should've let him throw her in jail. She's more trouble than—"

"Tie me up, Webb," Lily interrupted mockingly. "Tie me down. You're a guy with real kinky tastes, huh? I bet what you'd really like to do would be to tie me to your bunk." She was wearing a tight, ribbed blue sweater and she arched in the chair, displaying full, rounded breasts.

"What I'd really like to do is gag you," growled Webb.

"Oooh! Like I said, kinky," Lily teased, provocatively running the tip of her tongue over her lips. "How do you feel about blindfolds, Webb?"

"Oh, jeez!" Mac groaned.

Since neither of the men made a move to untie the girl, Kara took it upon herself to do so. She went to Lily's side and knelt down, attempting to undo the formidable knots binding her wrists.

"Thanks," Lily said with a smile that didn't reach her steely brown eyes. "Whoever you are."

"I'm Kara Kirby, a…a friend of Reverend Will Franklin's and his family."

"Well, you made a wrong turn somewhere," Lily said

coolly. "This asylum is about as far from the perfectly perfect Franklins as you can get."

Kara had once been a Girl Scout, and the skills she'd learned to earn a badge involving knot tying automatically kicked in. After loosening the bonds on Lily's wrists, she went to work on the ones binding her ankles to the chair.

"Hey, you're really good at that," the ranch manager said with genuine admiration. "Usually, nobody can untie my knots, but me."

When Kara rose to her feet, her work completed, the cowboy extended his hand and said respectfully, "I'm Webb Asher, Miss Kirby. I'm pleased to meet you."

"Any friend of the Rev's is a friend of yours, huh, Webb?" Lily shook off the ropes and sashayed over to Webb Asher. Suddenly, unexpectedly, she made a fist and attempted to sucker punch him in the solar plexus. But Webb Asher was remarkably fast and caught her hand before she could strike, twisting her arms behind her back and holding them there.

"You'll have to be quicker than that to pull a fast one on me, little girl," Asher snarled.

"Lily, you can't go around punching people," Mac exclaimed, exasperated.

"Not even after he tied me to a chair?" Lily struggled in Webb's grip. "Tell him to let me go, Uncle Mac."

"You have to promise not to take a swing at him again, Lily," Mac admonished.

Lily abruptly stopped her struggles and cuddled back against Webb Asher's tall rangy frame. "On second thought, maybe I'll stay just where I am. I like having a hard man to lean on." She arched her brows and flashed a sensual challenging smile. She wriggled provocatively against him.

Instantly, Webb Asher cast her away from him with such force that she went crashing into Kara. Face-to-face, Kara gazed into the younger girl's gleaming brown eyes and realized at once that Lily Wilde was in full control of this scene and taking great pleasure in making both men feel uneasy and inept.

"I'm getting the hell away from that conniving little witch," snarled Webb. He stormed from the kitchen.

"Dammit, Lily! All I need is to have my ranch manager decide to quit on me!" Mac snapped. He strode out of the kitchen, too, presumably to placate his irate ranch manager.

Lily turned to Kara with a shrug. "What can I say? The guy turns me on."

"You're just kidding, aren't you?" Kara asked uncertainly. "You don't really have a crush on Webb Asher?"

"A crush? How juvenile! I haven't had one of those in years." Lily laughed. "But I'm definitely hot for Webb's incredible, muscular body. You should see him without a shirt on— Wow! And he's so strong he can pick me up with one arm. He carried me out of the Rustler tonight. It was so cool, so macho! Just like in the movies," she added exuberantly.

"But he's so much older than you are," protested Kara.

"It's not like he's ninety or something. He's thirty-four."

"That's twice as old as you are," Kara said pointedly.

"What are you—a human calculator? Anyway, who cares about years with a man like him?" Lily suddenly scowled at Kara. "Of course, if you're a friend of those prissy Franklins, you probably think I should be dating someone from school or something dull like that."

"Does your Uncle Mac know how you feel about his ranch manager?" Kara asked curiously.

"Oh yeah, right!" Lily jeered disparagingly. "Like Uncle Mac and I sit around having heart-to-heart talks about my love life! Or his lack of one."

"He doesn't have many—um—dates?" Kara felt a twinge of shame for pumping Mac's teenage niece for information about him, but it wasn't strong enough to stop her from doing it.

"Try none! Hey, if you're new in town, why don't you

take up with my uncle? I don't think the poor guy has had sex since me and my brothers and sister moved in.''

"He hasn't?'' Kara's heart started to beat like a runaway train. Well, there was the definitive but disheartening proof that Mac's instantaneous response to her earlier was merely a result of his sexual deprivation rather than any real attraction to her.

Lily shook her head no. "From what I've heard, Uncle Mac was Bear Creek's major hunk, with girlfriends falling all over themselves to get to him—and into his bed,'' she added wickedly, her brown eyes gleaming. "Then the four of us arrived. Bam, his partying days were over! He turned into an instant family man and the party girls of Bear Creek didn't like it. They sure don't like us kids, either!''

"Are there many…party girls in Bear Creek?'' Kara asked, chewing her lower lip thoughtfully.

"Enough, I guess. And if you believe in gossip, my uncle has had them all, at one time or another. But not since June. It's looking like Uncle Mac's never gonna get it.''

Once again, Kara remembered those tempestuous moments in the Jeep when Mac had taken her in his arms and kissed her into a sensual daze. She felt an unwelcome surge of color sting her cheeks.

Oh, yes, she could believe the Bear Creek gossip about Mac Wilde and his party girls! To make matters worse, her sexual experience was as lacking as his was plentiful. She wondered if he'd been able to tell, then decided of course he had. He'd probably been secretly laughing at her lack of expertise; he probably considered her surrender pitifully inevitable.

"What's with all these questions about my uncle Mac?'' Lily asked shrewdly. "Are you hot for him or something?''

Mac reentered the kitchen, glancing from Lily's amused face to Kara's anxious one. "Quit harassing Kara, Lily,'' he ordered.

"She's not," Kara replied quickly. "She was just telling me about...about some of the citizens of Bear Creek."

"Yeah," Lily agreed. "And I didn't even get to her friends, the Franklins, yet. I have lots to tell about them. Prim Miz Ginny who smiles when she doesn't mean it, and icky-sweet Tricia who pretends to be everybody's friend, but has never seen a back she didn't want to stab."

"That's enough, Lily," Mac warned. "I'm sure Kara doesn't want to hear you bad-mouth her friends. Anyway, I happen to like Ginny and Tricia."

"Well, that doesn't count for much," retorted Lily. "You like all kinds of strange things—fly fishing, watching golf on TV, Mrs. Lattimore's putrid casseroles. Of course you'd like Ginny and Tricia Franklin!"

Clay and Autumn came charging into the kitchen. "We can't find the cat!" Autumn wailed. "It's like he just disappeared! Like he was kidnapped by aliens and flew away on their spaceship."

"What cat?" asked Lily. "Autumn, is there really a cat or is this another one of your weird paranoid fantasies?"

"No, there's a real cat," insisted Clay. "*She* brought him." He pointed a stubby finger at Kara. "Me and Autumn are playing with him. Except he's not playing with us! Tell him to come out and play with us," he ordered Kara.

"You can't tell a cat what to do, cats do exactly as they please," Mac explained. "Maybe if you two quiet down and stop running around yelling, he'll decide to come out on his own. But you'll never make friends with him by carrying on like a pair of maniacs. Go and watch some TV."

Clay and Autumn got into a shoving match while trying to beat each other through the swinging door.

"Don't put that vampire thing back on," Mac called after them. "Why not watch the tape of the *Little Mermaid* I bought you?"

That stopped them dead in their tracks. The two youngsters, allies again, whined their protests.

"Okay, then watch *Beauty and the Beast,* instead," Mac compromised. "You can pretend the Beast is a biker vampire and the Beauty is a sorority sister."

"Uncle Mac, that is so geekful," complained Autumn.

"Thanks, Autumn. I lay awake nights trying to come up with geekful ideas, and your heartfelt words make it all worthwhile." Mac turned to Kara. "Well, you've met three of the clan. Now all I have to do is to locate Brick. Lily, where is your brother?"

"How should I know? Brick goes where he wants, when he wants and he sure doesn't run it by me." Shrugging, Lily turned her attention to Kara. "Are you really going to visit the Franklins?" she asked, her dark eyes assessing Kara with unnerving scrutiny.

Kara nodded her head. "In fact, I should call him now and—"

"That is so incredibly cool!" Lily squealed in delight. "You look so harmless and sweet but you're really a stealth witch."

Her tone indicated that this was a compliment. Kara stared at her askance. "I don't understand."

"Oh, that's perfect!" chortled Lily. "You sound so innocent. Even that old bat Ginny will have to believe you when you say it like that." She laughed merrily. "Taking a cat with you to visit the Franklins! Super! Is your plan to put that snotty Tricia back in the hospital? How diabolical! I love it!"

"You know all about Tricia Franklin's allergy to cats, too, hmm, Lily?" Mac asked casually.

"Anybody who knows the Franklins, knows the story about Tricia being rushed to the hospital because she was so allergic to her new kitten she couldn't breathe," Lily said. "I think it was the highlight of Tricia's boring life. She works it into the conversation five minutes after you meet her. Like anyone cares!" she added caustically.

Kara's knees felt oddly, suddenly weak. She slipped into

one of the chairs and clung to the armrests for support. So it was really true; her pseudo-stepsister really did have a serious allergy to cats. Lily's unsolicited collaboration of Mac's story was convincing proof. And if Ginny Franklin had no part in inviting her to Bear Creek, as Mac had claimed, Kara could only imagine the reception accorded to her by the woman if she arrived on their doorstep bearing a yowling feline allergen—a dire threat to her daughter's health!

"I honestly didn't know about Tricia's allergy to cats," she murmured. "What am I going to do with Tai?"

"Turn him loose in Tricia's room," Lily said enthusiastically. "Rub her pillow all over his fur."

"You could always leave him here," Mac offered a more humane alternative. "Autumn and Clay would love that."

Kara thought of poor Tai, hiding somewhere in this ranch house terrified by this overly enthusiastic reception. Tai had never met a child in his life, and those two were a rather unnerving introduction to the species. She imagined leaving her cat here while she went to stay in town with the Franklins—with Ginny Franklin who had never liked her and probably still didn't, but who would be forced to take her in at Uncle Will's command. It was not the sort of week's vacation she'd imagined upon accepting the invitation.

One scenario after the other tumbled through her mind, each one more unpleasant than the next. It was nearly impossible to keep a reasonable perspective, try as she might. "I—I'd like to call Uncle Will, if you don't mind," she said softly.

"Of course. There's the phone." Mac pointed to the cordless telephone resting on its base on a corner stand.

"*Uncle* Will?" Lily echoed. "Reverend Franklin is her uncle?"

"I'll explain later. Let's give Kara some privacy while she makes her call." Mac took his niece's arm and propelled her through the swinging door, out of the kitchen.

Reverend Will Franklin answered the phone on the second ring.

"Uncle Will, this is Kara."

"Kara!" he repeated jovially. "Are you all packed? Tomorrow's the big day! I can't wait to see you, my dear. I'll be right there at the gate, waiting to meet your flight. I thought we could have a nice dinner in Helena and then drive to Bear Creek."

Kara was confused. "Uncle Will, I'm already here. I arrived today."

"What? Here? Today?" The reverend sounded totally flummoxed. "But how could that be? I wrote down the time and date of your arrival. Yes, it's right here in my personal calendar. You're to arrive tomorrow."

"Who told you that?" Kara asked, suspicion dawning. "Was it Mac Wilde?"

"Why, yes," the reverend confirmed. There was a pregnant pause. "Uh-oh," he muttered glumly.

"Yes, uh-oh. That about sums it up, doesn't it?"

The pieces were fitting together with startling clarity. Mac, who had purchased her ticket and therefore knew her scheduled time of arrival, had fabricated a different one for Reverend Franklin. But why?

"When were you going to tell me about Mac Wilde and this—this plot to marry me off to him, Uncle Will?" she asked tightly.

"You've met him? He told you everything?" Reverend Will's tone was morose.

"Everything," Kara confirmed.

"Marry?" Lily exclaimed on the other side of the kitchen door. She and Mac were both pressed against it, listening, though Mac periodically tried to push Lily away, in the direction of the TV set. She refused to leave. "Uncle Mac, are you going to marry her?"

"Go ahead, tell me how much you hate the idea," growled

Mac. "I assume you'll pull out all stops and try to wreck the plan."

"Actually, I think it's a good idea for you to get married, Uncle Mac. Autumn and Clay need somebody to mother them, and I bet you wouldn't get so grouchy if you had a woman to—"

"Be quiet!" Mac hissed fiercely. "And get away from this door. You shouldn't be spying on Kara."

"Okay, I'll leave that job to you," Lily said archly. "I wish you luck with her, Uncle Mac. You're sure going to need it. From what I've heard so far, you botched it big-time."

Truer words had never been spoken, Mac thought grimly. Lily wandered away, to join Autumn and Clay. He remained fixed to the spot, eavesdropping on Kara's conversation with Reverend Will.

"Why didn't you tell me, Uncle Will?" Kara demanded. "You led me to believe you'd bought my ticket because you wanted me to visit you."

"I do want you to visit, my dear. I've been so looking forward to seeing you. I've missed you so much over the years, Kara. That's why I immediately thought of you as a...a mate for Mac. It seemed like the perfect solution for all of us. Mac needed a wife to help him raise the children, and you sounded so lonely and lost in the big city. I know how much you've always wanted a family, and here was a ready-made one for you."

Kara drew in a sharp breath. She'd always tried to make her letters to Uncle Will light and witty; she had never written the words "lonely" or "lost" in a single one of them. But it seemed he had read between the lines and thought her pathetic and desperate, with no hope of ever getting a steady boyfriend, let alone a husband and family. She was humiliated to the bone!

"If you married Mac, you would be living on the Double R, close to Bear Creek." She tuned back in to hear Reverend

Will continue wistfully. "I could be a part of your life again, watch your children grow up. I know I should have told you, but it seemed so awkward to do it over the phone." He had the good grace to sound ashamed. "I thought if you came out here, I would introduce you to Mac, he could court you and things would proceed naturally."

"And I would've never known it was actually an arranged marriage. I would've been deluded into thinking it was a love match."

A flare of anger scorched through her at the idea of such deception. She felt both disillusioned and betrayed by this previously unrevealed manipulative streak of Uncle Will's. At least Mac Wilde had been upfront and open on the subject. His honesty and unwillingness to hoodwink her was definitely a point in his favor!

"You should've checked with Mac, Uncle Will. He would've never agreed to the pretense of a courtship. He loathes the very idea. He expects an immediate return on his investment without any foolish pandering. He thought you'd filled me in on all the details, and he wanted to avoid— Oh!" She jumped as the kitchen door swung open with such force that it hit the wall.

Mac was back in the kitchen, his expression thunderous. "I'd like to speak to the reverend, right now."

Kara was certain that whatever he was about to say to the older man wouldn't be pleasant. She did not like confrontations. Her quiet life had been devoid of them—until now. Now she feared a confrontation of nuclear proportions between the man she'd loved like a father and the man...

She stared at Mac. The man who had tricked the reverend out of coming to the airport to meet her, the man who thought the price of a plane ticket was enough to buy her as a wife. She swallowed hard. He was also the man who'd made her laugh, the man who had kissed her and touched her as if she were the passionate, attractive woman she'd always wanted to be. The man who had nobly taken in his brother's kids and was trying his best at child-rearing—even though he seemed befuddled by the task. Though her own experience with children was limited, she knew satellite dishes and bribery were questionable methods, however well-meaning. His mail-order bride scheme fell into the same realm.

One thing she had learned about Mac Wilde in the short time she'd spent with him: he was good-hearted but impulsive and aggressive. Sometimes those traits could clash, causing trouble. Like now.

Kara put the phone behind her back, to keep it from him. "You should wait and cool off before you talk to him, Mac. You're liable to say something you'll regret."

"It's very generous of you to want to protect the Rev and me from ourselves," Mac murmured huskily. "And very sweet."

He had moved closer to stand directly in front of her. So close that she could feel his breath rustle her hair, could feel the heat that his body generated. She was heart-stoppingly aware of how well his shirt fit his muscled torso, how his jeans molded to his powerful thighs and gloved his sex.

Kara tried to breathe and couldn't. Her breasts were suddenly full and aching, and she could feel the phantom touch of his hands on them, cupping them, teasing her taut nipples, like he'd done earlier tonight. The realization of how much she wanted him to do it again shocked her out of her state of dazed immobility.

She took a step backward. Mac moved a step forward to eliminate the small space between them, his dark eyes glittering. His smile was pure male sensuality.

The phone dropped from her nerveless fingers and hit the tiled floor.

"Mac," she said, using his name as an admonishment, holding out her hand, trying to literally keep him at arm's length. She touched his chest, feeling the hard warmth of him beneath her fingers. Lily's words were ringing in her ears. *"Girlfriends falling all over themselves to get to him—and into his bed.... My uncle has had them all at one time or another...."*

"Kara." He used her name as an endearment. His hands gripped her, his thumbs rotating over the blades of her hip-bones, drawing her lower body nearer, closer to the throbbing male heat of his.

She felt herself melting, moistening in response. "Mac," she whispered. This time his name was an incantation. The sight and the sound and the feel of him combined forces to block out Lily's voice in her mind. Her senses were too filled with Mac to have room for anything or anyone else.

"Hello!" Reverend Will's voice sounded from the telephone receiver, lying forgotten on the floor. "Kara? Mac? Hello? Is anyone there?"

Mac groaned. "Ignore him and maybe he'll go away," he muttered hopefully, then gave the phone a light kick, sending it skittering across the floor.

"Hello! Hello! What's going on?" Reverend Will's disembodied voice sounded loud and clear and rather eerie, coming from the opposite corner of the kitchen.

Kara blinked, once again, emerging from the power of Mac's sensual spell. "Uncle Will!" She pulled away from Mac and hurried over to pick up the phone.

"Tell him you're staying here," Mac ordered softly.

"I—I..." She averted her eyes from the intensity of his commanding dark gaze. "Uncle Will, is Tricia allergic to cats?" she heard herself ask stupidly, in a breathless voice that sounded nothing like herself.

Uncle Will was silent for a moment, clearly perplexed by the non sequitur. And then: "She certainly is! On her eleventh birthday, Ginny and I bought her a kitten because she'd been badgering us for months for one..."

He went through the whole story, not leaving out a single detail. Kara tried not to look bored, but she was. It was a very long, very dull story, though Uncle Will tried to give it dramatic flair, at times.

Mac sank into one of the kitchen chairs, his shoulders shaking with laughter. "You asked for it," he murmured wickedly. "Now you're getting it—the unabridged trials of Tricia."

"We found the cat!" Clay burst into the kitchen, his poxy little face flushed with excitement. "He's on top of the beams in your bedroom, Uncle Mac, right above your bed."

"Naturally," Mac drawled. "Where else would he be? Has he gotten sick on my bed, yet? I'm sure he has a nervous digestive tract and will hurl everything he's eaten within the past twenty-four hours. Probably right on my pillow."

"Cool!" Clay exclaimed happily.

"Uncle Will, I have to go now," Kara said quickly into the phone. "I—I'm staying here at the ranch tonight. I'll talk to you tomorrow."

She hung up quickly and followed Mac and Clay down the narrow hall into a dark wood-paneled bedroom, dominated by a king-size bed which was covered by a thick goose-down quilt. There was a fireplace on one wall—granite, like the one in the living room but not nearly as large—and above it was the mounted head of a ram with a magnificent set of curled horns and shiny, accusing coffee-brown eyes.

Kara winced. At least the moose and the elk had blank stares, seemingly resigned to their fates. The ram looked furious. Vengeful, even. "Are there heads of dead animals in every room?" she asked uneasily. She found it a disconcerting decorating scheme.

"There's a mountain goat in my room," boasted Clay. "He's cool!"

"My room has a bear," Autumn, who had just joined them, piped in. "I tried to pretend he was Smokey but he looks so mean! I was scared of him so Uncle Mac put a blanket over its head."

Kara thought a similar cover was in order for the ram's head. Who could sleep with such blatant ill-will directed at them?

"Grandpa was a big game hunter," Mac said dryly. "And he left future generations of Wildes plenty of souvenirs."

"There's Tai!" Clay pointed up to the ceiling where Tai was crouched on top of one of the exposed, polished beams, gazing down at them with a ferocity matching the trophy ram.

Clay hopped onto the bed and began to jump up and down, trying to reach the beams with his outstretched arms. Autumn joined him in his efforts. Though neither of them came close, Tai considered them bothersome enough to hiss threateningly.

"I could lure him down with some food," Kara suggested. "He must be hungry, he hasn't eaten a thing all day. I packed some cans of his favorite food in my suitcase. I'll have to be alone with him, though," she explained to the bouncing kids on the bed. "He's very shy around strangers."

"So am I," Clay announced.

"Strangers are dangerous," Autumn said solemnly. "I'm scared of them."

"Let's not get started on stranger danger again, Autumn," Mac soothed. "You know I'll always protect you and not let anything happen to you." He scooped Autumn up under one arm and Clay under the other. "Kara, we'll leave you alone to deal with the cat. Take all the time you need."

He left the room with a shrieking, wiggling child under each arm.

It was strange, being in Mac's bedroom. After Kara had spooned some minced ocean-fish feast onto a plate and placed it on the floor to lure Tai down from the beams, she glanced around the room. There were no photographs on the nightstand or bureau, no books or knickknacks or any other personal touches to distinguish this as his own particular turf.

Her eyes kept straying to the bed and images of him lying on it, under that thick down quilt, filled her mind's eye. She wondered what he slept in. Pajamas? Underwear? Nothing? The provocative melting warmth between her thighs grew hotter as she mentally stripped him.

Kara sank down onto the big bed with a moan of despair.

What was happening to her? She had never had such thoughts about any man in her whole life! How was she going to hold strong against his demands for a marriage of convenience when she was almost in thrall to him after only a few hours' acquaintance?

She didn't know how long she sat there, nervous and preoccupied, yet dangerously excited, filled with a wildness and a hunger she'd never dreamed had been lurking within her. Every time she tried to plan her imminent departure from the ranch, she was sidetracked by imaginary erotic scenes of Mac Wilde kissing her, touching her, tumbling her back on this mattress and doing things to her she'd only read about, had only seen in R-rated movies!

Kara gripped her head with her hands. She was exhausted, that had to be it. The time difference had caught up with her, along with her lack of sleep the night before. She wasn't thinking clearly and so these unknown, unwelcome thoughts had infiltrated her previously cautious, well-ordered mind.

"I see Tai has decided to climb down and have his dinner." Mac's voice was low and quiet, so as not to disturb the cat, who had indeed left his refuge in the rafters and was on the floor, chomping on his favorite meal.

Kara's head jerked up and her eyes met Mac's. He was standing in the doorway, watching her with a sexual intensity that made her leap to her feet and move swiftly away from the bed.

The house was amazingly quiet, compared to the noisy chaos earlier.

"The two younger kids went to bed. Lily turned in, too, after finally confessing that Brick is spending the night at his friend Jimmy Crow's house." Mac sighed. "The team of Brick and Jimmy are notorious in Bear Creek for such adventures as the 'photos in the girls' locker room' marketing scheme and the deflating of the tires of every car in the teachers' parking lot, to name only a couple."

"You do have your hands full with the kids," Kara said

quietly. "Taking them to live with you must've turned your whole life upside down. I admire you for taking the responsibility, Mac. Lot's of men wouldn't.''

Mac shrugged. "Don't make the mistake of believing I'm some kind of saint, Kara." He crossed the room to stand beside her. "I assure you that I'm not. I'm just a man." He slipped his hands under her arms and pulled her closer.

Kara gulped. She kept her arms straight at her sides, fighting a temptation to slide them around his neck. "According to Lily, you're a man who hasn't had sex since the kids moved in. And you're not accustomed to such long periods of…going without. You're the type who's had girlfriends falling all over themselves, hoping to get into your bed."

"Don't believe everything you hear, especially not when Lily is the one telling the tales," Mac said, holding her eyes with his.

"Naturally, you'd say that," Kara said shakily. "I'd hardly expect you to brag about your…your…" She sought a tactful word to describe his bedroom adventures.

"My exploits? My conquests?" Mac grinned, his dark eyes teasing. "What makes you think an alleged stud like me wouldn't flaunt my scorecard or even embellish it? Haven't you seen all the notches on my bedpost? I keep a penknife handy so I can carve in my latest success, moments after the act."

He trapped her head between his hands. "Aha! I caught you! You were surreptitiously trying to sneak a look to see if the bedpost really was carved."

"You don't have a bedpost." She knew he was making fun of her, making fun of himself, as well. Part of her wanted to smile along with him. Another darker, jealous part wanted to retaliate in fury at the thought of him with any other woman.

But being Kara, she did neither. Instead, she replied with prosaic calm, "You have a rectangular headboard that doesn't have a single mark on it."

"And doesn't that tell you something?" Mac asked huskily. He rubbed his bristly cheek against her soft smooth one, sliding his hands along the curvy length of her.

"It tells me that you're adept at twisting the conversation around until I'm so confused I'm not sure what we were talking about to begin with."

"We were talking about the past, which is irrelevant." Mac eased her into his embrace, bending his head to press his mouth into the sensitive curve of her neck. He kneaded the small of her back with firm, strong fingers. "What matters is right now, Kara. And the future we're going to have together."

Delicious shivers ran through her body. He was doing it again, seducing her with his words and his caresses, his husky voice as potent as his big warm hands. It would be so easy to succumb to this sensual heat he aroused in her, to yield mindlessly to his rampant masculinity. Temptation surged through her. Did she dare?

"Forget all about that girlfriend nonsense, Kara." Mac scooped her up into his arms, lifting her off her feet with the same ease as when he'd hoisted the two children under each arm. "You're going to be my wife."

He carried her over to the bed and sat down on the edge of it, holding her on his lap. "You're so sexy," he breathed, his mouth brushing hers. "So beautiful. I want you so much, baby."

Four

Kara froze.

"What's wrong, honey?" Mac asked solicitously. One moment she had been snuggling against him, soft and warm and pliable, the next she sat straight and rigid as a cattle prod. His hand slipped to the nape of her neck to massage the taut muscles there.

Kara leapt up, as if she'd been ejected by a spring, and headed for Tai, who was lapping water from a dish. Mac watched her, bemused. Perhaps she had some sort of hang-up about making love in the cat's presence. Though he had no such aversion himself, he was certainly willing to accommodate her own particular quirks. "Should we put the cat in another room?" he offered.

"The cat can stay here if he wants. But *I'm* going to another room," Kara announced, walking to the door.

Mac rose slowly to his feet and followed her. "Will you at least clue me in on what happened to make you change your mind?"

Kara paused in the doorway and stared out into the narrow, darkened hall. "You told me I was sexy and beautiful."

"And that turned you off?" Mac was baffled.

She whirled around to face him. "Yes. Because it was such an obvious lie. Not to mention one of the most laughably generic compliments ever!"

"Generic?"

"You tell every woman you want to take to bed that she's sexy and beautiful, don't you? You say how much you want her and call her *baby*." Kara's hazel eyes flashed. "You were making a pass by rote, using the same words, the same phrases you use every time with every woman, I could tell. And it's insulting!"

"That's not true!" Mac protested, indignant. Was it? He scanned his memory. Those particular phrases did have a familiar ring. But who could remember what was said at certain crucial moments? And who cared, anyway?

Kara obviously did. She stalked into the hall without looking back. The floor plan of the ranch house was atypical and confusing, having been added to over the years by various generations of Wildes. The children's bedrooms were off to the left, down a side corridor. She did not take that turn but headed straight toward the lighted vestibule, instead.

She had no idea what she was going to do. Tai was still ensconced in Mac's bedroom and she had no transportation into town. Even if she managed to get there, she had nowhere to stay.

Mac was suddenly behind her. He put both hands on her shoulders, and though his touch was light, she felt the strength in his fingers, anchoring her in place.

"You've got to be hungry," he said, before she had the chance to try to break away from him. "I know I'm starving. We didn't stop to eat dinner, which was definitely an oversight on my part. We should've gone to a restaurant in Helena and—"

"You were in a hurry to get back to the kids," she reminded him. Mac's big hands were cupping her shoulders, his fingers gently stroking. Kara quivered. For one who claimed not to be a "touchy-feely" type, Mac Wilde certainly did a lot of touching. In this one brief evening they'd spent together, he'd touched her more than any man ever had. As for feeling…

She blushed at the wayward direction her thoughts were taking. It was past time to derail this latest seduction attempt of his, if that's what it was. "Anyway, from your point of view, why bother wining and dining a sure thing? You assumed that I was here to marry you, so who needed to waste time with anything remotely resembling courtship behavior?"

She stepped away from him, but putting physical distance between them did not dispel the lingering warmth of his hands upon her. She could feel the effects of his touch spread through her like a fever.

"I think I've been firmly put in my place," Mac remarked dryly. "No doubt deservedly so. But since you're stuck here tonight, can we call a truce and get something to eat? Mrs. Lattimore was here today and left—"

"One of her putrid casseroles?" Kara quoted Lily. She felt exceedingly lightheaded, probably the result of an empty stomach and an overexcited nervous system. And the dizzier she felt, the more outspoken she seemed to become. "I think I'll pass."

"I won't tell Mrs. Lattimore you said that. Come on, we could both use a heaping plateful of her notorious ground meat surprise." He took her arm and guided her into the kitchen.

Kara let him because she really was hungry, and because there was no point in running away from him. She was stuck here tonight. A truce was the sensible, adult course of action.

She sat at the kitchen table while Mac heated the casserole in the microwave. Her eyes flicked to the cordless phone which stood upright on the small corner table, and she thought of tonight's rather disjointed conversation with the reverend. "Why didn't you give Uncle Will the correct date of my flight?" she dared to ask.

"I figured he'd show up at the airport and I didn't want to share you with him. I wanted your first hours in Montana to be spent with me."

"That sounds like another line." Kara spoke her thoughts aloud. "What is the *real* reason?"

"Well—" he flashed a sudden grin "—I do admit to having some qualms about meeting my future bride in the Rev's presence. It might've been awkward if we'd taken an instant dislike to each other and he was right there trying to play Cupid. On the other hand, if we hit it off immediately, I didn't want a chaperone interfering."

Kara resisted the urge to ask for his reaction to the first sight of her. She'd been there, she already knew. Although he hadn't found her unspeakably repulsive, he had been less than impressed, resigned to what he considered to be his fate. He wouldn't admit that, of course. He would make up some fairy tale about being smitten from the moment he'd set eyes on her. A queer little pang of longing flickered within her. It was depressing that she wished the fairy tale was true.

"I've thought about it, and you do have a point," Mac said, putting a handful of silverware on the table. "I'm not too original when it comes to—" he cleared his throat "—certain compliments. But in my defense, I truly mean what I say when I'm saying it."

Automatically, Kara arranged the silverware into two place settings, one for him and one for her. She knew without asking exactly what he was referring to. "So when you make love to a woman, you really believe she's sexy and beautiful?"

"Of course. Why would I want to make love to somebody I consider a troll?"

"Why, indeed?" Kara hid a smile.

"I'm sorry if I offended you. It certainly wasn't my intention to insult you with a pack of *generic* adjectives."

"Your intention was to get me into bed because you wanted me so much, because I'm so sexy and beautiful," Kara said drolly.

"I don't know why you find that so difficult to believe," Mac growled. "Remember earlier tonight in the Jeep when—"

"I don't want to talk about that," Kara cut in quickly. She remembered "earlier tonight in the Jeep," too well, and she'd already thought about it way too much. "Our truce includes no references to—to that."

"Who set the terms of this truce?" Mac put the steaming casserole on the middle of the table with a large serving spoon. "Suppose I insist on including references to *that*?"

He was teasing her; he seemed to delight in it. But teasing him back would involve the kind of sexually charged exchange which was not her forte. Nervous, Kara decided to respond in the way she knew best. "What is the surprise in the ground meat surprise?" she asked blandly. When it came to the dull and the bland, few could match her, she thought rather glumly.

"If I told you, it wouldn't be a surprise. But it goes great with some cold Mad Cougar Malt." He took two cans of malt liquor out of the refrigerator and handed her one.

Kara studied the rabid-looking cougar on the label. "I've never heard of this, uh, particular brand."

"It's the ranch hands' favorite brew." Mac grinned. "Pure liquid fire. But you'll need it to get past the taste of Mrs. Lattimore's casserole."

"I think I'd rather have water, if you don't mind."

"Not at all. You can have one of Lily's bottles of designer water or get it straight from the tap as we uncultured proletarians do."

She opted for tap water, and they proceeded to eat Mrs. Lattimore's casserole, which was chock-full of ingredients one usually wouldn't expect to find in the same dish. Nonetheless, it was edible, not putrid.

"I put your bags in the spare bedroom," Mac told her as she rinsed the plates in the kitchen sink. She'd taken on the cleanup chores while he sat back in his chair, sipping from the Mad Cougar can. "Of course, the invitation to share my room still stands."

"Tai and I will take the spare room, thanks." She loaded the dishwasher and put the remains of the casserole back into the refrigerator. "I brought a bag of litter, and if you have a cardboard box, Tai will be all set."

"I'll find a box." Mac studied her thoughtfully. Anyone who carried kitty litter and cat food in her suitcase to provide for her cat certainly knew the meaning of responsibility. It stood to reason that such a woman must be enormously gifted with the hallowed maternal instinct he was seeking for the kids.

"I couldn't expect Uncle Will to run around town shopping for cat necessities," she explained, looking sheepish. "I know you must think I'm weirdly compulsive or—"

"I think you're very conscientious." His eyes traveled over her. She was also passionately responsive and seemed to grow prettier and more desirable by the minute. Not that he dared tell her so, not at the risk of incurring another lecture about making generic passes.

He found a useable box and helped her move Tai to the spare bedroom, which was connected to his by a bathroom with two doors, each providing access. The room was sparsely furnished with only a bed and an old mahogany highboy in desperate need of restoration. The inevitable animal's head was mounted on the wall. This one was a gentle-eyed deer, a doe who did not possess the spectacular antlers of the other trophy heads. No doubt that was why the poor thing had been banished to this little used, seldom seen room.

"I see your grandfather didn't spare Bambi's mother." Kara's eyes were compulsively drawn to the doe staring down at them.

"I get the feeling you don't approve of hunting?"

"I never gave it a single thought until I came here. Now I don't know if it's hunting or all those heads that gives me the creeps. This place is a taxidermist's dream."

"When you marry me and move in, you can do some redecorating. Replace the heads with some nice pictures of flowers or fruit or something. I'm sorry about this room," he continued quickly, before she could reply to that provocative offer. "It's small and cold, but it's the only available room in the house. Believe me, you would not want to sleep in one of the kids' rooms, and you've made it clear you won't sleep in mine. You can lock yourself in here if you're worried I'll make another pass by rote."

His self-mocking smile made her grin in response. "I'm not afraid of you," she said, meaning it. What scared her was the way he could make her go warm and weak inside with just a glance.

"Good," Mac said gruffly.

They would have to share the master bathroom, which was large and rather luxurious with double sinks, a shower stall and a big old-fashioned bathtub. The proximity and intimacy would've unnerved her an hour earlier. Right now she was too tired to summon any anxiety.

Mac gallantly insisted that she use the bathroom first, and after completing her nightly ablutions and slipping into her nightgown, a demure ankle-length pink cotton one with a yoke neck and long sleeves, she climbed into bed. Tai curled up at the foot of the bed, as was his habit at home.

The mattress was very soft and seemed to envelop her. There was a chill in the air that required more warmth than the woolen blanket and cotton-ribbed spread provided. Kara thought longingly of that thick goose-down comforter on Mac's bed and tried to wrap the covers more tightly around her.

Still, she shivered from the cold. If she couldn't get warm, she would never be able to fall asleep. Maybe if she got up and put on a pair of socks and a sweater—

"Kara?"

She heard Mac's voice from the other side of the room. He'd entered through the bathroom door which she hadn't locked. Though the room was dark, her vision had adjusted enough to allow her to see a tall form moving slowly toward her.

Her heartbeat took off at an alarming rate and she sat up, clutching the covers around her. "W-What do you want?" she asked, barely able to speak around the lump of fear in her throat. As if in a trance, she watched Mac approach the bed.

His chest was bare, his corded strength and rippling muscles fully revealed. Her eyes flew to the dark mat of hair which arrowed lower, beneath the waistband of his loose-fitting boxers. Those shorts were the only thing he was wearing! She stared at the long, powerful lengths of his thighs and the unmistakable, thick bulge straining against the cotton material.

Her jaw dropped, agape. He was so big, so strong. And she was all alone in this dark, isolated room with him.

"I brought you some extra blankets." Mac's voice was deep and low. "It's cold tonight, I'm sure you'll need them."

"Oh." The violent surge of anxiety was making her feel sick. Or perhaps it was the aftermath of Mrs. Lattimore's casserole surprise. She hadn't even noticed the blankets he carried, so focused had she been on his body and the threat it presented.

She watched him drape the three heavy blankets over the bed, on top of Tai who was sleeping so deeply he never even twitched.

Having completed the task, Mac stared down at her. Moonlight streaked into the room through the slats in the old-style venetian blinds, illuminating her face. She looked lovely—and absolutely terrified.

He sat down on the edge of the bed. "I thought you weren't afraid of me," he said softly, reaching out to touch her lips. "So how come you look scared to death, like I'm a biker vampire who just flew into your room at the sorority house?"

She tried to smile but her lips were trembling. "It occurred to me that I've been very stupid," she murmured breathlessly. Her mouth felt oddly swollen as her lips moved against his caressing fingertips. "I've put myself in a very vulnerable position."

"True," he agreed. He bent his head to nuzzle her neck. "Which is why you need a husband to take care of you." His hands drifted under the covers to her breasts. He gently cupped them. "I'll look after you and won't let you get into trouble—or vulnerable positions, either. Except with me, of course."

Kara was stunned and scared by the pleasure searing her as he touched her breasts. They had become excruciatingly sensitive. He lightly stroked around her nipples with his thumbs, coming close to the taut centers but not touching them. Oh, how she wanted him to! She gulped for breath, shocked by her wicked longing. "Mac, please, I—I—don't…we—we can't…"

Her voice trailed off as her mind splintered. The pleasure was so intense it was interfering with her thinking, with her breathing! It was as if she'd been conditioned to his touch, beginning earlier tonight and continuing to this moment, readying her body for him.

"We can, but we won't," Mac corrected huskily. "Not tonight, anyway. Now kiss me good-night and I'll get out of here."

A shuddering sigh ripped through her as he claimed her mouth with his. He thrust his tongue boldly between her lips, which had instantly parted for him. A deep growl rumbled in his chest as he plundered the moist sweet warmth of her mouth, probing the softness of her inner cheeks and persuasively enticing her tongue into a sensuous duel with his. He was making love to her mouth, and she moaned with sensuous pleasure.

Hot tendrils of desire ribboned through her and when his hands found her breasts again, she pressed herself against his palms. His fingers continued to excite her by drawing erotic concentric circles around the ultrasensitive aureoles of her nipples. A dizzying liquid pleasure flooded her. She wriggled against his clever, masterful hands. If he didn't touch the tips of her nipples, she would surely explode.

He eased her back onto the mattress, and she clutched at him, threading her fingers through the dark springy thickness of his hair. Her nipples thrust seductively against the confinement of the thin pink cotton of her nightgown. Mac's eyes narrowed and he lowered his mouth to one tempting plump curve.

Kara felt his warm breath against her, then his mouth, hot and damp, closed over hers. The tip of his tongue found the hard pointed center, and she arched reflexively, crying out his name. Somehow, the buttons on the yoke of her nightgown had become undone, allowing him to push the material aside, baring her to him. His lips fastened around the taut pink bud, drawing her into his mouth. He suckled strongly, sending shock waves of primitive pleasure crashing through her. She twisted against him, clinging to him, wanting more, more...

And then abruptly, it ended. He sat up, his breathing harsh and heavy. "We're stopping now or we won't stop at all." His features were taut with strain, his dark eyes glittering.

Kara lay on the bed, every nerve in her body crackling with a combination of fierce arousal and a frustration that was every bit as intense as the desire sizzling through her. There was a throbbing ache between her thighs that pounded in rhythm with the pulsating fullness of her breasts.

She had never been so out of control, had never dreamed she was capable of feeling so passionate, so wild and wanton. It was as if her body had turned into a stranger, a traitorous one, who was eager to betray her sense of what was right and proper, who listened to Mac's sensual demands rather than her own commands.

Kara couldn't lie to herself. If Mac hadn't stopped her of his own accord, she wouldn't have stopped him. She closed her eyes, unable to face him.

"Good night, baby," Mac rasped, leaning over her once more, his weight braced on his arms. He kissed her mouth briefly, firmly, then in an unmistakable show of possession, he moved his head lower to nuzzle the cleavage between her breasts. "Sleep well."

He knew he wouldn't. His whole body was aflame and pulsing with need. He walked out of the room, his legs unsteady, the swollen ache of unslaked arousal affecting his gait.

Kara did not call him back, and he didn't turn around to look at her. He didn't care. If he were to see her, lying there, soft and sensual and exposed to him, he would crawl into that bed with her and not leave it until they were both exhausted from their spent passion.

He could've been doing that right now, he admonished himself. He could've taken her and she wouldn't have even tried to stop him. She had been too far gone; he'd recognized all the signs of imminent surrender.

Mac heaved a groan. Was he crazy? He'd had a hot willing woman eagerly writhing beneath him in bed, and he'd called a halt to what would've inevitably progressed to intercourse. Just the thought of plunging deep into her sweet softness brought a fine sweat to his skin. Despite the cool night, he lay on top of the quilt. He felt like a human furnace, radiating therms of heat.

The problem was, when he'd recognized her loss of control he had also realized something else. That she was too inexperienced to control the sensations his kisses and caresses had aroused in her. He'd made her want him, set her afire with need and she did not have the experience to hold back or control her responses to him.

So why hadn't he taken her? Mac scowled into the darkness. It wasn't as if she were going to be a one-night stand; he planned to marry her. That made his intentions strictly honorable, so what was the harm?

Mac determinedly put his inexplicable behavior from his mind. He was not an introspective type, and he had little time or patience for self-analysis. Tomorrow he would continue his campaign to keep her here, he promised himself, and he would pull out all stops to win. That meant no stopping when passion flared between them. He knew it would flare, too, because she wanted him as much as he wanted her.

He closed his eyes and his mind drifted, the events of the past twenty-four hours tumbling through his head in kaleidoscope fashion. This time last night, he'd been worried, tossing and turning and wondering if he'd lost his mind for even considering the Rev's mail-order-bride scheme. Tonight, he was tossing and turning for an entirely different reason that had nothing to do with worrying and everything to do with the desire churning through him. For his mail-order bride.

Tai sat in the middle of the small bedroom and emitted a bloodcurdling yowl that jerked Kara awake, out of the deep dreamless sleep she'd finally fallen into shortly before dawn.

He meowed again, protesting either his confinement to this one room or homesickness for the apartment back East. Kara sat up and reached for her watch, which she'd placed on the floor beside the bed. It was nearly nine o'clock. The lateness of the hour shocked her. As she had not yet adjusted to the time-zone changes, that meant she'd slept till almost eleven, eastern standard time. Later than she'd ever slept in her entire life!

She felt decadent and slightly disoriented. The house was quiet except for Tai's complaints, and she showered and shampooed her hair as quickly as possible, taking care to lock both bathroom doors. But Mac did not attempt to enter and there were no sounds at all from his adjacent bedroom. Kara dried her hair and dressed quickly, pulling on jeans and a soft lilac blouse. She dared to peek into Mac's bedroom, but it was empty except for the ram's head which glared accusingly at her. Kara quickly withdrew, feeling guilty for trespassing.

"You look pretty!" Autumn greeted Kara enthusiastically the moment she stepped into the hall.

Kara jumped, startled. Obviously, Autumn had been there waiting for her.

"Lily said I couldn't bother you till you came out," Autumn said chattily. "Where's the kitty? I heard him crying."

Tai dashed out of the room and charged down the hall, as if he were being pursued by an invisible gang of marauders. Or perhaps he was pursuing them.

"Want a breakfast burrito?" Autumn offered. "I can defrost one for you in the microwave."

They walked down the hall together, side by side. Kara noted that Autumn was wearing her nightgown, and her long dark hair streamed wild and uncombed around her shoulders. It crossed her mind that this being a Tuesday, the child should have been in school. Perhaps the schools were closed for some local holiday? Autumn was certainly the picture of health, far too lively to be sick.

"It's okay to defrost stuff in the microwave if it's already cooked," Autumn prattled on. "But you can't cook raw chicken in the microwave 'cause it doesn't kill all the germs. You could get food poisoning and die. You can die from hamburgers in restaurants, too. My mom and dad are dead," she went on without missing a beat. "But they didn't get food poisoned. Their car crashed. I told Brick he was going to get killed in a car crash, too, but he just laughed. Boy, is Uncle Mac going to be mad!"

"Did Brick drive a car somewhere?" Kara asked, trying to sort out the most current of the jumble of facts provided to her. Autumn jumped from past to present to future with dizzying speed.

Autumn nodded. "He drove Jimmy Crow's mother's car

out here this morning to get some stuff. He and Jimmy are going camping in Yellowstone.''

Kara stared at her, aghast. ''Autumn, do you mean that your brother and this Jimmy Crow are driving to Yellowstone Park right now? Does your Uncle Mac know?''

Autumn shook her head. ''He wouldn't let him go. Not on a school day.''

''Not to mention that Brick is only thirteen years old and is driving!'' Kara was gripped by fear for the boy, though she'd never laid eyes on him. ''Autumn, we have to tell your Uncle Mac, right now.''

''Okay,'' Autumn agreed. ''Where is he?''

''I was hoping you knew.'' Kara was dismayed. ''Maybe Lily does. But I suppose she's at school. We'll call her there.''

Autumn laughed merrily at the very idea. ''Lily's not at school. She said she was going to—'' she paused, trying to remember. ''Paradise?''

Kara's concern escalated to full-blown anxiety. Was this ''Paradise'' another sleazy roadhouse like the Rustler, from which the girl had been evicted yesterday? Now it appeared that both Mac's nephew and his niece needed to be retrieved. She simply had to find Mac!

''Lily said I didn't have to go to school today 'cause I didn't want to. She said you'd take care of me and Clay,'' Autumn confided.

Clay! Kara's heart turned a somersault in her chest. ''Where is Clay?'' she asked apprehensively. The silence in the house boded ominously for Clay's whereabouts.

''He went to see his horse,'' said Autumn.

''N-Not Blackjack?'' Kara remembered Mac's description of the horse as *''a wild-tempered stallion who could kill him with just one kick.''*

''Yeah, Blackjack, the pretty big black horse,'' Autumn affirmed. ''Clay loves him. He wants to ride him.''

Kara felt like a triage officer at a disaster scene. Three

young Wildes needed aid, but little Clay was in the most immediate danger. He was also the most accessible. "Autumn, you have to show me where that horse is. We have to get Clay, right now."

Autumn responded to the urgency in her voice. "Okay. Should I get dressed first?"

"There isn't time. Just put on your shoes and coat. We have to hurry!"

Moments later, they were running along the driveway, hand in hand, with Autumn leading the way. Kara prayed the little girl knew where she was going, that they would reach Clay before the stallion could do him any harm.

"There's the horse barn," Autumn panted, leading Kara to the big wooden building which looked freshly painted. "Maybe they're in there."

Working together, the two of them managed to slide the huge door open. Inside, the barn was spacious, well-kept and thoroughly modern. Wide stalls lined each side of the center aisle, and the horses within were beautiful animals, sleek and strong and obviously well-cared for.

"I don't see a black horse." Kara scanned the stalls. "Or Clay, either." She called his name but there was no response.

"There's the striped cat, though." Autumn pointed, as a big gray-and-black striped cat dashed up the thick rungs of the wooden ladder leading to the hayloft. "He's one of the barn cats. Uncle Mac said he doesn't have a name, so I call him Stripe. I wanted him to come live in the house but Uncle Mac said 'No, he's not a house cat.' Do you think Tai would like to be his friend?"

Kara was so worried about Clay, she paid scant attention to the girl's chatter. "Autumn, where else could Clay and the stallion be?"

"Maybe outside in one of the pens. Let's go get Stripe and bring him into the house to meet Tai." Autumn headed for the ladder.

Kara caught her and turned her around. "We have to find

Clay before we do anything.'' She deliberately did not mention the unhappy fate which might befall him, though she was somewhat surprised that Autumn, a self-appointed barometer of danger, seemed to have missed the inherent threat of a strong, temperamental horse. ''Show me where the pens are.''

Luckily, they weren't far away. Behind the barn, a short distance down the road, was rolling green pastureland divided into corrals by a network of sturdy fences. In the horizon, majestic mountain peaks towered over the landscape piercing the cloudless blue sky. The tops of the mountains were rocky and gray, the slopes covered with trees whose leaves were a spectacular riot of fall colors—oranges, yellows, reds and browns. Mixed among them were evergreens in vivid, varying shades of green.

It was breathtaking scenery and Kara wished she had the time and the inclination to be awed by it. Unfortunately, her attention was concentrated on locating one small boy who was trying to befriend a stallion with a decidedly unfriendly reputation.

Kara spotted Clay before Autumn did. He was sitting on the fence, watching the magnificent black stallion race around the pen, snorting and occasionally rearing up on his hind legs. Clearly, Blackjack was not charmed by his young admirer.

''Come on, Blackie! Here, boy! I got something you're gonna like!'' Clay called, extending his hand toward the horse. Blackjack, increasingly perturbed by the intrusion, whinnied angrily and pawed the ground.

Kara's heart pounded against her ribs. Clay was acting as if the horse were as tame and lovable as Lassie. He seemed oblivious to Blackjack's equine dislike of him.

She ran over to the child and lifted him down from the fence. He was barefoot and wore cotton shorts and a T-shirt. His bare arms and legs were cold to the touch, for despite the bright sun, it was a chilly, brisk fall day. She remembered that he was still recovering from chicken pox, and winced.

"Clay, you have to stay away from this horse," Kara said shakily. She noticed that he held a bag of sugar in one hand and in the other was a sweaty fistful of the stuff which he'd been offering Blackjack as a lure. "He is a wild, dangerous animal and he could hurt you very badly."

"Blackie could kill Clay?" Autumn gasped. "I didn't know that horses killed people."

Kara could see her adding horses to the murderous demons who haunted her world. Poor little girl. Her parents had been killed in a car accident and now she looked for danger everywhere, expecting to find it, determined never to be caught unawares again. As one who valued control, Kara understood Autumn's need to have at least the illusion of it.

"Horses don't usually hurt people, but Blackjack is an exception," Kara tried to explain. She walked between the children, following the road back to the house.

"I wanted him to be my friend," Clay said gloomily. "Like in that movie *Black Beauty* me and Autumn saw on TV."

"About a jillion times," Autumn added dryly. "He wanted to watch it every time it came on."

"Maybe you should think about getting a pet," Kara suggested. He definitely needed a diversion from his pursuit of Blackjack. "Something smaller and friendlier."

"Like a dog?" Clay brightened. "When can we get him?"

"We're getting a puppy! We're getting a puppy!" squealed Autumn.

"I always wanted a puppy," Clay confided, tucking his hand into Kara's. His spontaneous gesture touched her, and she gazed down at him. He seemed so small, so innocent and trusting. His dark eyes were glowing, his dark hair, straight and thick, reminded her of Mac's. The familiar resemblance between the two was striking; Clay looked like a pint-size edition of his uncle Mac.

"I love dogs!" Autumn enthused as she skipped along beside Kara. "Mom and Daddy said we couldn't have one, and of course, Uncle James and Aunt Eve said no. They always said no to everything! But Uncle Mac said no, too, 'cause nobody was home during the day to take care of a puppy.''

"But you'll be home, right, Kara? Lily said so," Clay insisted.

Kara was temporarily tongue-tied. How had her innocuous mention of a pet snowballed to her living there and caring for a puppy? Neither Clay nor Autumn pressed her for an answer; they seemed to have already taken Lily's word as confirmation.

Back in the house, she went to each child's room and found warm clothes for them to wear. Clay was safe, but Lily and Brick remained unaccounted for. She wondered where Mac was and how to summon him. Inspiration struck when she entered the kitchen and saw the phone.

"That's why we have the car-phone number written down beside the phone, so you can get in touch if you need to," Mac had said when Autumn's phone call had interrupted their...tryst. Kara's cheeks burned. Calling Mac with that particular memory searing her was unnerving, but she really had no choice. She dialed the number written on the tablet beside the phone and waited while it rang, hoping that Mac was within hearing distance of the Jeep, wondering and worrying about what to say to him.

Many rings later—so many that she was ready to give up and hang up—Mac picked up the phone.

"Yeah?" he said warily.

After their adventure this morning, Kara understood why he was wary. When this phone rang, it was likely that the news was not going to be good.

"I hate to bother you," Kara began apologetically, and immediately reproached herself. She wasn't bothering him, she was doing him a favor. Brick's and Lily's whereabouts were *his* responsibility, not hers. Yet somehow, somewhere between yesterday and this morning, she had come to feel that she was responsible, too.

"Uh-oh." Mac made a sound that was a combination of a groan and a sigh. "What's wrong?"

She decided to spare him the tale of Clay—that was already old news—and relayed Autumn's message about Brick's camping trip. Mac did not take it well. He ranted and raved, and Kara listened quietly, making no comment. She thought he was entitled to be upset that the two thirteen-year-olds had blithely taken off for Yellowstone—the world of school, adults and driving laws be damned!

Mac finally wound down. "I'm over in the south pasture repairing the fencing and it'll take me at least an hour, maybe longer to get back to the house." He sounded thoroughly dispirited. "If you'll stay with Clay, I'll drive straight into town and talk to the sheriff. He's a buddy of mine and I think he can get the boys picked up without having them arrested. Autumn and Lily should be coming home from school around—"

"Autumn is home," Kara cut in.

"Why?" His voice rose in concern. "Is she sick?"

"No, but she's here. Don't worry about her or Clay, I'll stay with them," Kara promised.

Mac was so upset about his nephew that she didn't have the heart to mention Lily at the Paradise. It seemed kinder to let him believe that the girl was in school, so he could devote his full attention to retrieving Brick.

"Kara, I'm sorry I wasn't around this morning. Usually, I have more flexibility with my schedule, but today is Webb's day off and I knew he was planning to spend it away from the ranch. That means I cover for him. I looked in on you when I got up shortly after five, and you were so deeply asleep I didn't have the heart to wake you."

The thought of him watching her as she slept made her flinch with embarrassment. Suppose she'd been snoring or something equally unspeakable?

"You looked so soft and sweet and tempting that it took all my willpower not to climb into bed with you." His voice was warm and intimate and seemed to trap her in a web of sensuality. "Some morning soon, that's the way it's going to be, Kara. I'll stay in bed beyond the crack of dawn and you'll be there with me."

Kara drew a jagged breath. She could imagine the scene all too well...the two of them lying in bed...Mac reaching for her....

Her body was already heating, quivering in sensual remembrance of his caresses, his kisses. Her imagination stoked the fire higher. An achy, restless throbbing pulsed deep inside her. She felt paradoxically both swollen and empty as a voluptuous hunger surged through her. Kara knew she was in dire trouble when merely the sound of his voice could produce such a fevered response.

She struggled to get a grip on herself. "You have to find Brick," she said huskily, pushing the potent combination of fantasies and memories aside.

He laughed softly, as if he knew what she was trying to do. And why. "Don't worry, I'll find him and bring him home." His voice lowered a notch, to a velvet growl. "I'll see you later, baby."

Five

The call had ended, the connection was broken but Kara sat in the chair, clutching the receiver and staring into space. She tried to remind herself that she was offended he had called her baby again, that overused, oversung generic term, but she could summon no indignation. He made her feel hot and sexy and desirable, so different from the woman she had always been. After all, no one in the Commerce Department had ever claimed her as his baby.

A terrible, otherworldly screech jarred her as effectively as a thorough dousing with ice water. Kara dropped the phone and charged through the swinging door into the adjacent living room den. Her eyes were drawn immediately to the source of the wild feral howls. Tai was crouched on top of the moose head, his back arched and his tail bristling like a porcupine as he sounded his battle cries. On the floor below sat the striped barn cat, his back and tail equally raised for war, though he was staring up at Tai in something akin to wonder.

"I don't think they like each other," murmured Autumn. She and Clay stood on the cushions of the wide black leather sofa, watching the cats who were a clear-cut case of feline incompatibility.

Tai inched forward toward the antlers, his eyes slitted with outrage and yowled another threat to the intruder from the barn.

"We have to get Stripe outside and back to the barn," Kara said with commendable calm. "Preferably before Tai launches himself from the moose head like a grenade."

"I'll chase him out," Clay volunteered, climbing to the arm of the sofa. He launched himself into the air like a human grenade, propelling himself in the direction of the barn cat.

The cat took off with a wild screech. Kara ran to the front door and opened it and after a few laps around the house, with Clay running a distant second, the cat found his way to the open door and ran outside, heading for the barn without a backward glance.

"We did it!" Clay exclaimed and slapped her palm with his in a victorious high five. Kara grinned. It was the first time she'd ever participated in that particular ritual.

They walked back into the living room. Tai remained on top of the moose head, growling at Autumn who was trying to sweet-talk him down.

"I guess I shouldn't've brought Stripe in," Autumn admitted wistfully. "But I wanted Tai to have a friend. It's hard to be someplace new and not have any friends."

Kara put her arm around Autumn's shoulders. She had a strong hunch that the little girl was talking about more than Tai's solitary state. "It's okay," she said softly. "Tai likes being the only cat around, in fact, he prefers it. He isn't at all like people."

"He can still be the only cat when we get our puppy," Clay interjected. "Because a puppy is a dog."

Kara didn't allow herself to be diverted. "Autumn, why didn't you want to go to school today?" she asked.

Autumn shrugged and stared at the floor. "They're picking groups today to work on the Halloween party. I knew I'd be the last one picked, so I decided to stay home. I'll get assigned to a group 'cause I'm absent and that's better than standing there, not getting picked till the very end."

Kara's heart ached for the child. She knew how it felt to be an outsider. Shy and unsure of herself, she'd spent most of her own life wishing she belonged somewhere, with someone. "It must be hard moving to a new school, especially one in a small town where everybody's known everyone else forever."

"It's not hard for me," Clay chirped. "Everybody likes me. I have lots of friends."

"That's 'cause you're in second grade," Autumn said disparagingly. "Little kids are friendlier. In fifth grade, they're not."

"Taken as a whole group, it must seem that way," agreed Kara. "But maybe if you tried to make just one friend." She tried to remember herself as a fifth-grader; she'd had a best friend, and having just one friend could make all the difference. "Ask a girl in your class if she'd like to do something with you—you know, go to the movies or to the mall or come over to your house after school."

"There isn't a mall in Bear Creek but there is a movie theater," Clay offered helpfully.

"I used to have friends over when I lived in California with Mommy and Daddy," Autumn reminisced. "Not in Ohio with Uncle James and Aunt Eve, though. I didn't want anybody to know I lived with *them!*"

"Do you feel that way about living here with your Uncle Mac?" Kara asked curiously.

"I love Uncle Mac," Autumn said, chewing on a piece of her long hair. "But it wouldn't be any fun for a friend to come here. Clay would hang around and pester us. It would be like babysitting."

"Yeah," Clay agreed. "There isn't anybody around to tell me not to bother the girls, like Mom used to do."

"Uncle Mac is always working and if Brick or Lily are here, they just tell us to shut up when we fight or complain," Autumn added. "Why would I bring a friend here for that?"

Obviously, Autumn had given the matter some thought and decided that friendlessness was preferable to revealing the chaos at home. Kara felt a swell of sympathy, both for Autumn who was lonely and sad, and for Mac who didn't understand the dilemma of being a ten-year-old girl who felt her family was hopelessly different from everybody else's.

Clay wandered over to the television set and turned it on. Autumn joined him. Tai, observing that all was quiet, ventured from the moose head to the mantel below it, then permitted Kara to lift him down.

Kara's stomach rumbled, reminding her that she hadn't eaten. She glanced at the children who were sitting in front of the screen, glaze-eyed and slack-jawed. It was tempting to let them sit there, quiet and still and out of trouble. This morning they'd already chased after stallions and lured untamed barn cats inside, and it wasn't yet noon. On those grounds alone, she understood Mac's desperate satellite dish purchase to keep the children inert but safe.

But Kara felt guilty, watching them sit there mesmerized by a manic game-show host. She didn't understand why, but she felt guilty just the same.

"I have to make some phone calls, but afterward, I'd like you two to show me around the ranch," she heard herself say. "Then we'll make some cookies."

There was no reaction from either one. They were too absorbed in the show. Nevertheless, Kara's plans for the day were set. She had a quick breakfast of toast and coffee while studying the phone book, looking for listings of "Paradise" anything, be it lounge, room, bar and grill, or worst of all, motel. If only she could track down Lily, get her out of the

Paradise and the inevitable trouble lurking there. Convince the girl to come home before Mac arrived.

But the word Paradise did not appear once in the directory, not in any form. Wherever Lily was, it wasn't within dialing range. Which meant she'd either lied to her little sister or Autumn had gotten the name wrong.

It was nearly five o'clock when Lily finally came home. She paused in the doorway of Autumn's room where Kara and Autumn were surrounded by boxes of toys and clothes. Kara was startled by her outfit, a gauzy flower-print baby-doll dress worn over tight bicycle shorts with black boots. Only a girl as beautiful and shapely as Lily could pull off that unlikely ensemble!

"Hi, Lily!" Autumn called, waving to her. "Kara is helping me fix up my room, so it won't look stupid, anymore."

"We made cookies," Clay announced. He was sitting on the floor, leafing through a comic book while he chomped on a thick sugar cookie. "We're getting a puppy, too."

"Cool." Lily smiled benignly and drifted into the hallway.

Kara followed her. "Lily, I know you weren't in school today," she said bluntly, deciding to tackle the issue head-on.

She trailed Lily into her room, which was smaller than both Autumn's and Clay's, and painted a startling deep purple. An enormous fish was mounted in its entirety on the wall, something of a change from the animal heads but not much of an improvement, Kara thought distractedly.

Lily lay on her bed, propping her head on her hand. "I learned much more where I was today than I ever would've learned at school."

Kara studied her. The girl's mouth was swollen, her smooth cheeks and neck red as if brush-burned. Her long, silky raven tresses were tousled, her makeup was almost completely rubbed off. Kara gulped. Even to her own inexperienced eyes, Lily looked like a sultry, satiated woman who had spent the day engaging in riotous sex. She felt totally out of her depth with Mac's precocious niece, who was watching her with amused dark eyes.

"Autumn told me you'd gone to a place called the Paradise and I looked in the phone directory but there isn't a single listing for anything named Paradise," Kara said, trying to sound matter-of-fact and not accusatory or condemning.

Lily sat up, her face lighting with a smile of delight. "You thought I was at some place called Paradise and tried to call there? Oh, that is soooo cute!"

Kara was taken aback. She wasn't certain how to react to being called "cute" by someone nine years younger than herself. "I—I was worried about you, Lily. I didn't tell your uncle Mac you weren't in school because he was so upset about Brick's trip, but I don't know if I did the right thing by not saying anything."

"Thanks, Kara." Lily sauntered across the room and gave Kara a quick sisterly hug. Or perhaps it was a coconspirator's hug? "You don't have to worry about me, I know what I'm doing and what I want. And you're right not to say anything to Uncle Mac. There is nothing he can do, and he has his hands full with the kids and the ranch and all. Why make him crazy? Now, what's this about Brick going on a trip?"

Kara explained about the Yellowstone adventure.

Lily was both amused and admiring. "Brick is a free spirit, and so is Jimmy Crow. It's great they found each other. Although I guess the Bear Creek school district, Jimmy's mother and Uncle Mac might not think so," she conceded.

"You're not going to tell me where you were today, are you?" Kara asked her.

"I was in paradise, small *p*. And it's not exactly a place, more like a state of…bliss." Lily arched her dark brows provocatively. "That's really all I can tell you for now. But maybe when you're sleeping with Uncle Mac, we can exchange tips on how to drive a man wild in bed."

Kara was certain Lily meant to shock her. Well, she had been supremely successful.

Suddenly, Kara felt like the high school girl she'd been years ago. She had known some girls like Lily back then—girls who'd carried condoms in their purses and dated men in their twenties and were blatantly, terrifyingly sexually fast. Even the perky popular types like the cheerleaders and the homecoming queen and her court were subdued around those girls.

It was disheartening to realize that years later, she could still be intimidated by the teenage Lilys of the world.

"I'm going to take a nap," Lily said, yawning. She put her arm around Kara's shoulders and walked her to the door. "I had the most incredible day, but it was absolutely exhausting. Thanks for watching the kids today, Kara. You're an angel." She gave Kara a gentle shove into the hall and closed the door behind her.

Kara wandered slowly down the hall, trying to gather her scattered thoughts. The sound of a car in the driveway stopped her in her tracks. She heard the engine cut off, doors slam, footsteps on the wooden porch.

Moments later, the front door was flung open and Mac strode inside. Kara's heart went into overdrive at the sight of him, strong and tall and vibrant with muscled masculinity. He was wearing jeans and boots, a dark brown shirt and a denim jacket, and even from this small distance she could feel the effect of his powerful charisma. It tingled along her spine, making her warm and flushed.

Her mouth went dry. She felt dazed, almost disoriented. She'd spent the day here with Autumn and Clay, and had quickly, comfortably grown accustomed to the three of them together. Mac's presence introduced an entirely different element into the atmosphere, a charged sexual tension that made her want to run for cover.

Instead, she stayed rooted to the spot. Mac strode toward her and pulled her into his arms. "I am so glad to see you," he rasped, and his warm hard mouth settled over hers.

Kara's eyes snapped shut as an intense surge of pleasure

swept through her, wiping out any thought of resistance. His lips moved over hers and his tongue probed for entrance within. She felt overwhelmed and exhilarated by his heat and rampant sexuality and she sank against him, her arms locking around his neck. Desire exploded in her like a fireball, burning hot and bright.

He kissed her deeply, urgently, with mind-shattering absorption, as if he couldn't get enough of her, as if he was as hungry for her as she was for him. Her body ached and tingled with the pleasure and excitement he was rousing in her, with the building need to have more of him.

When Mac finally lifted his head, his dark eyes were intense and heavy-lidded as he gazed into hers. A small whimper escaped from her throat. She felt helpless, wanting to pull his head down to hers for another one of those deep, intimate kisses, yet fighting an equally strong urge to twist away from him, to lock herself in the small bedroom until her mind had cleared and she was able to think again.

Before either could speak or move, a rather cheerful young voice sounded behind them. "I hate to break this up, you two, but we have company. And you're not going to believe who it is."

"Company?" Mac echoed, scowling. Kara was lying limply against him, her breathing shallow and fast. "Talk about lousy timing...."

Kara pulled out of his arms, her legs trembling, her whole body aflame with an unnerving mixture of desire and embarrassment. She kept her eyes averted from Mac, only to lock gazes with the boy standing to the left of him.

"You must be Kara." The boy stepped forward to present himself. "I'm Brick. Uncle Mac said that you were the one who told him about me and Jimmy driving to Yellowstone."

Kara wasn't sure how to respond. Brick was staring at her, but did not appear to be either hostile or accusing, merely curious. He had longish, wavy brown hair and brown eyes, both lighter in shade than that of the other Wildes. He was short and wiry, with a smattering of freckles across his nose, still just a kid despite his deeds. The hormonal testosterone surge which transforms a boy into a man had not yet occurred.

"I'm glad to meet you, Brick." Kara extended her hand to his. "I hope you understand that I had no choice but to tell your uncle."

"Yeah, I know." Brick shook her hand for a split second, then shoved both his fists into the pockets of his jeans. "But I'd like to zap Autumn into another dimension. If she hadn't blabbed, me and Jimmy would be in Yellowstone right now." He turned to his uncle. "I'm going to my room. I'm not gonna stick around out here to hang out with that pest Joanna Franklin."

"The *Franklins* are here?" Mac grimaced.

"Comin' up the walk. Don't let them near me, especially not Joanna!" Brick dashed down the hall and turned the corner to the kids' wing of the house.

Through the partially open door, Mac and Kara watched Reverend Will Franklin, his wife Ginny and their two daughters approaching the front porch.

Kara tensed at the sight of them. Her eyes—wide and hazel and wary—flew to Mac's. Immediately, he moved to stand beside her, slipping his arm around her waist.

"Kara, my dear!" Will Franklin exclaimed when he saw her. Pushing the door fully open, he stepped inside. His wife and daughters, their arms laden with covered dishes, followed him.

Kara's first reaction was to throw her arms around her former stepfather, just as she'd done when she was a little girl and he had been her daddy. She instantly stifled that urge. She was not a child, and the reverend was neither her daddy nor her stepfather; he was not even her uncle. Plus, he was flanked by his family, who were not *her* family. Ginny Franklin had succeeded in making that fact painfully clear.

Kara's gaze flicked to Ginny, whom she'd last seen years

ago, shortly before the Franklins moved to Bear Creek, Montana. She was trim, attractive and looked younger than her age, which Kara knew to be in her midforties. Tricia, the older daughter who had been a baby then, was now a pretty blond teenager. Kara recognized Tricia and her younger sister Joanna from the annual Christmas card photo she'd received every year with The Franklins stamped in red on the bottom of the card.

"Hello, Reverend Franklin," Kara said politely. Considering Ginny Franklin's attitude toward her, she didn't know what, if anything, Tricia and Joanna had been told of their father's relationship to her. "Hello, Mrs. Franklin, Tricia and Joanna. It's very nice to see you." If she was a skeleton rattling around in Uncle Will's personal closet, she intended to stay put.

Mac glanced from Kara's smiling polite mask to Reverend Will. He saw the pain flash in the reverend's eyes at Kara's rather stilted greeting.

Well, how else could she possibly have greeted them? Mac felt suddenly, fiercely protective of her. Kara had been deliberately kept on the periphery of the Franklins' lives all these years. If the Rev had expected a heartwarming father-and-child reunion, he had been foolishly deluding himself.

"Goodness, let's not be so formal," Ginny interjected gaily. "It's Will and Ginny, of course. Kara, Mac, you both look wonderful."

"We brought you some dinner to welcome you to Montana," said Joanna, the younger daughter, a plump seventh-grader with short curly blond hair. "I made the lime Jell-O salad with pears and cream cheese." She held up a shimmering green gelatin ring.

"And we have fried chicken and hot potato salad, coleslaw, rolls and pumpkin cake for dessert," added Ginny. "Shall the girls and I take everything into the kitchen?" She addressed Kara, as if she were already the woman in charge of the house.

Kara glanced at Mac to find him watching her intently. Her cheeks pinked. "I—I guess so," she murmured. She was intensely aware of his arm around her, of the pressure of his big warm hand on the hollow of her waist.

Ginny and her daughters, apparently familiar with the layout of the house, headed toward the kitchen, leaving Kara, Mac and the reverend standing in the vestibule.

"I tried to call earlier in the day but there was no answer, Kara," Reverend Will said, breaking the awkward silence. "I couldn't imagine where you were because I knew you had no way of getting into town, especially not with Mac off fetching Brick."

"So the word is already out on Brick's and Jimmy's adventure?" Mac groaned.

"All over town," the reverend confirmed. He turned back to Kara. "I was going to drive out this afternoon, but when there was no answer here, I decided against it."

"That must've been when Autumn and Clay were giving me a tour around the ranch," replied Kara. "We walked to the bunkhouse and saw the mess hall and the ranch manager's trailer. We saw the horses and the cats in the barn and Autumn's least favorite place—the chicken coops. She's convinced there is a salmonella outbreak just waiting to happen there."

"Not on my ranch," Mac disputed. "So the kids showed you around?" He looked pleased. "Tomorrow I'll take you out in the Jeep to see the outer buildings where we sort and brand calves. You'll want to see the pastures and the creek, too. This place extends much, much farther than you could ever walk."

"I hoped you would spend the day in town with us tomorrow, Kara," said Reverend Will. "I would like to show you around the town, have lunch with you at our house and hopefully, convince you to stay with us. We have an extra bedroom that—"

"Daddy, there's a cat in the kitchen!" Tricia Franklin

came racing through the hall at breakneck speed. "A nasty-tempered Siamese. He is sitting on top of that elk head, hissing at us. My eyes started to water and I sneezed twice. Mama said to come out here right away, she and Joanna will finish setting up. We have to leave immediately, of course."

"The cat is on the elk head?" Mac repeated, incredulous.

"Siamese cats like heights," explained Kara. "Tai discovered that those trophy heads offer an ideal vantage point." To observe menacing enemies like Stripe the barn cat and Tricia Franklin.

"I'd better let some fresh air inside to counteract the pollutants in here." Tricia proceeded to open the front door and hold it open, despite the chilly shaft of wind that blew into the house. "I can't be exposed to cat fur, I was taken to the hospital—"

"There's no question about where Kara will be staying, Rev," Mac cut in, ignoring Tricia. "It's here."

"We can discuss that later." The pastor dismissed him to focus exclusively on Kara. "Let's make our plans for tomorrow right now, Kara. I'll be more than happy to pick you up tomorrow morning—or, better yet, you can come back with us this evening and we—"

"No, that won't be possible," Mac said firmly. "Kara is going to have to take a rain check on your kind invitation."

Kara felt his grip tighten on her. She stole a glance at him, saw the implacable set of his jaw, the hard gleam in his eyes. He was answering for her without giving her a chance to even voice her opinion. Her lips thinned into a straight line. If she wanted to spend some time in Bear Creek with the Franklins, she most certainly could.

"I would love to see Bear Creek and—" she began.

"Clay still has chicken pox and he can't go back to school, yet. Kara can't leave him alone to go running all over Bear Creek," Mac interrupted abruptly. "There'll be plenty of time for her to see the town later on—it's not going anywhere."

His arrogance sparked Kara's temper. She was not a prisoner here, and she could speak for herself. But before she had a chance to point out those two crucial facts to Mac, Ginny and young Joanna joined them, carrying the now empty plates and dishes.

"We transferred the food to your own plates and containers," Ginny explained. "It's all set up for your dinner. We hope you enjoy it."

"Is Brick here?" asked Joanna. "I want to tell him we brought fried chicken. I know he loves it. He ate twenty-two pieces at the Church Lawn Fete in August. It was a record!"

"Brick is in his room. He's grounded and—uh—not allowed any visitors. You know, like solitary confinement," Mac replied quickly. He toyed with the idea of sending Joanna back to badger Brick—the boy had already implied that would be a real punishment—but adult reason prevailed. "We'll make sure Brick gets plenty of that delicious chicken for dinner tonight," he added heartily, feeling guilty for even thinking of using this eager young girl as a means of retribution.

"Where's Lily? I hope she isn't sick," Tricia piped up. "She wasn't in cooking class again today. Is she all right?" she asked, so sweetly concerned that her father beamed his approval.

"Lily wasn't in class?" Mac was instantly on guard.

"Not cooking class. She wasn't up for it," Kara hastened to explain. "Lily went to bed as soon as she came home. She's sleeping now." She was mentally crossing her fingers as she served up the assorted truths and half-truths. The end result was most definitely a deception, placing Lily in school except for the cooking class. Intimating that she'd come home from school feeling ill.

But what was the alternative? Announcing to one and all that Lily hadn't been in school and her whereabouts for the day remained unknown, not to mention highly suspect? Was what went on within the Wilde family any business of the

Franklins? Kara didn't think so. An inexplicable feeling of loyalty to Lily—and to Mac—kept her silent.

That didn't keep her from feeling guilty, however. Kara was careful not to look either at Will or Mac. Instead she watched Tricia, who appeared displeased. Because her attempt to cause trouble for Lily had been sabotaged?

"Kara, about tomorrow," the reverend persisted. "I will be glad to arrange—"

"I think I'd better stay here with Clay tomorrow, Reverend Franklin," Kara cut in. No, she was not a prisoner here, she assured herself. And she was speaking for herself. She could spend the day in town with the Franklins if she wanted....

Her eyes flicked over Ginny and Tricia. But she didn't want to. It was her choice, her own decision.

Mac smiled, pleased at the outcome. She felt his hand slide over the curve of her hip, his fingers spanning her possessively. Flushing, she tried to subtly step away from him. He did not let her go.

"Tai jumped down and grabbed a piece of chicken and took it back up on the elk head with him," Autumn announced, running in through the den. "Does he like potato salad, too? Can I give him some?"

"That cat!" exclaimed Tricia. "Oh, my throat feels scratchy! I feel like I'm going to sneeze again. Are my eyes getting puffy?"

"Autumn, don't you dare put potato salad on the elk's head," warned Mac.

"Is Brick coming to school tomorrow?" Joanna asked eagerly. "It's Wacky Tacky Day at the junior high. We're supposed to wear the wackiest, tackiest outfits we can find and every homeroom will pick a winner. At the end of the day, there's an assembly and all the winners go up on stage for everybody to see!"

"Wacky Tacky Day?" repeated Autumn, smirking. "Maybe that's why Brick and Jimmy Crow decided to go to Yellowstone."

"Autumn, go into the kitchen and guard the rest of the chicken from the cat," ordered Mac.

The mention of the cat once again, galvanized the Franklins into action. "We really must leave," Ginny said hurriedly. "I know you folks must be hungry and, of course, we can't have our Tricia exposed to cat dander."

The thank-yous and goodbyes were rushed amidst a plethora of parallel conversation and confusion. Ginny fairly dragged her daughters outdoors, and Autumn pulled Kara away from Mac, insisting she come with her to the kitchen.

Mac and Reverend Franklin were left standing alone in the entry hall.

"Are you going to try to keep me from seeing Kara, Mac?" the pastor demanded. "Why?"

Mac shrugged. "I think it's in her best interest to stay here with us."

"Her best interest?" Reverend Franklin snorted his disdain. "You just met her yesterday, Mac. You can't possibly judge what—"

"I'm going to marry her, Rev. It was your idea and it was a good one. But your part of the plan is all over, until it's time to conduct the ceremony. That will be soon, I promise you."

"Mac, this isn't how I anticipated things to be." The pastor was clearly distressed. "I envisioned Kara staying at my house in town while you two became acquainted. I intended her to have a choice as to whether or not she wanted this—this marriage."

"She wants it." Mac smiled a pure male smile of confidence and satisfaction.

The reverend swallowed hard. "Mac, I am well aware that your charm and—uh—skill with women is…considerable. A quiet, sensitive young woman like Kara could be easily overwhelmed by your…attentions."

"Daddy, Mom says we have to go!" Joanna came running

back to stand in the open doorway. "She says we have to let the Wildes eat their dinner now."

"I'll be right there, dear," said the pastor. "Go wait in the car with Tricia and your mother."

Joanna obediently scurried off, and Reverend Will turned to Mac. "Mac, your ranch is one of the most successful in the state, and you've made it that way by using your intelligence and aggression and determination. But to use those qualities, that drive, to hustle an innocent young woman into making a decision about her future while under your—"

"You'd better go, Rev," Mac interrupted coolly. "When it comes to making a choice between your concern for Kara or following your wife's commands, you made it clear a long time ago that you'll do whatever Ginny says, regardless of Kara's feelings."

The reverend blanched. "I know I let Kara down when she was a child," he murmured, his eyes downcast. "Which is why I will not let it happen again. This time I'm going to be here for her when she needs me."

"But she doesn't need you, Rev," Mac said bluntly. "She's not a little girl anymore. I can give her what she needs, what she wants and vice versa. You aren't involved in the arrangement."

"On the contrary, I feel very much involved. I was the one who suggested that you invite her out here, hoping that when you got to know her, you would appreciate all her fine qualities and—"

"I told you I'm going to marry her," Mac cut in. "I don't understand why you're suddenly against the whole idea which was yours in the first place."

"I wanted you to get to know her, to fall in love with her, not rush her into a marriage of convenience to facilitate your problems with the children. You don't know or understand Kara, you couldn't possibly care about her, not in such a brief length of time."

"I don't have the luxury of time, Rev. The kids and I need someone now, and it's going to be Kara."

"It isn't fair to her, Mac." The pastor threw up his hands in dismay. "You don't see her as a unique individual or the special young woman that she is. All you see is a warm-hearted girl whom you can railroad into marrying you to take over this house and those kids. It wouldn't have mattered who got off that plane, you had already decided you would marry her."

"Well, isn't that the whole point of mail-order brides? It's not and never has been a dating service. The objective is marriage for a man who is in dire need of a wife."

"And the woman?" the reverend demanded. "What about her?"

"She gets a husband and a family and a home, all the things you claimed Kara wanted so much."

Reverend Franklin's shoulders drooped. "I just hate the idea of Kara not being valued for who she is," he said with a sigh. "You've made it depressingly clear that you'd take to wife whoever had walked off that plane. It's demeaning for human beings to be viewed and treated as fungible as— as grains of sand."

"Rev, you're overreacting," Mac began, but was interrupted by a long sharp blast of the car horn. "And you're being summoned by your loving spouse. Don't worry about Kara. I'll take care of her."

The horn sounded again, and the grim-faced pastor hurried from the house.

In the living room, Kara stood quiet and still. She'd left the kitchen to talk some more with Uncle Will, hoping it would be less strained with Ginny and the girls in the car, unable to listen and observe them. But the sound of his voice and Mac's halted her in her tracks and their topic of conversation—her—rendered her immobile.

She'd heard her former stepfather express his concern for her. And she had heard the cold-blooded way Mac Wilde viewed her. As a commodity, a convenience. Interchangeable with any other woman.

It wouldn't have mattered who got off that plane... Fungible... Not valued for herself... You'd take to wife whoever had walked off that plane... The words tumbled through her head, mocking her. When she heard the reverend leave the house, a lump swelled in her throat. She wanted to go with Uncle Will, to run away from this place. To run away from Mac Wilde.

Impulsively, she rushed for the door only to collide headlong with Mac in the vestibule.

"Whoa!" He laughed, putting his hands on her shoulders to steady her. "Are you trying for some kind of track record? I think Clay's made it through the house in two seconds flat. You'll have to beat his time."

Kara didn't smile or laugh or even look at him. Quickly slipping out of his grasp, she hurried outside on the porch in time to see the Franklin's car heading down the driveway, away from the house.

"The Rev had to leave." Mac came to stand behind her. "Ginny was determined to get Tricia far away from the dangers of cat fur as soon as possible." He locked his hands around her waist, clasping them on her stomach. "It was nice of them to bring dinner and all, but truth be told, I'm glad they're gone." He nudged her hair aside with his lips, then kissed the curve of her neck.

"Oh, don't!" Kara exclaimed, thrusting his hands away from her. She stormed back into the house, her hazel eyes blazing.

Mac followed her. "What's wrong?"

He looked baffled. It was obvious he had no idea why she was so upset. His total lack of awareness stoked her fury higher.

She whirled to face him. "I was in the living room while you and Uncle Will were talking. I heard everything that was said."

Mac's eyes narrowed. "And?"

"And?" she echoed. *"And?"*

"You said you overhead our conversation, and I want to know why you're suddenly madder than a wet hen. You didn't hear anything you didn't already know. So why the tantrum?"

"I am not having a tantrum!" she fairly choked on the words. "I just can't believe that you could be so—so obtuse and unfeeling to think that I shouldn't mind hearing myself described as a—a—fungible convenience, interchangeable with whatever other woman happened to get off that plane. You don't know me or value me as a person, you just want to use me to—"

"Wait a minute, lady!" Mac seized her around the waist and pulled her into the small room across from the living room, the one whose door had been closed until this moment. She had time to glance around to see that it was an office, complete with desk, computer and other business machines, before Mac pushed her against the wall, pinning her there with his big hard frame. He caught her chin in his hand and forced her head up.

"If you were listening carefully, you'll realize that I never said those things," he growled. "That was your beloved Uncle Will describing you, honey, not me."

"Let me go!" Kara demanded, struggling against him. She was humiliated and furious and, worst of all, hurt. She scorned herself as a naive fool for forgetting, even for a moment, exactly why Mac Wilde wanted her here.

"I've decided to stay with the Franklins tonight and return to D.C. tomorrow." She refused to meet his eyes, despite his efforts to force her to do so. "Tai can spend the night in their garage. I'll fix up a box for him—it won't hurt him for just one night. Now, let go of me! I'd like to start packing."

"You're not going anywhere," Mac growled.

He angled his body forward, and she could feel the hard evidence of his desire straining against her hips. She gulped, startled. How could he be so aroused when they hadn't even kissed, when he'd barely touched her? Except to drag her into his private office, Neanderthal-style. Well, such caveman tactics might turn him on, but she refused to succumb to them!

Automatically, she tried to draw back, but there was nowhere to go, she was sandwiched between the wall and Mac, her hands trapped at her sides.

"I liked having you here to greet me when I came home this evening," he said huskily, his lips brushing hers. "Let's go back to that moment, when I first walked through the door, before all the interruptions and all the people…"

He nipped at her lips as he spoke, taking small sensuous bites after every couple of words.

"No!" She tried to turn her head away but his hand held her chin firmly, keeping her mouth available to him. "Let me go, Mac. I don't want any part of your stupid plan. I just want—" She paused to gasp.

Mac had wedged his knee between her thighs. She uttered a breathless little cry as he rubbed his hard arousal against the softest, most vulnerable part of her in intimate suggestion.

"You want what I want," he whispered.

Six

A tidal wave of heat surged through her. She tried to hang on to her outrage. ''Don't think you can use your—your *charm* and *skill* with women to—''

''I'm not going to waste time arguing with you. Actions speak louder than words.'' He threaded all his fingers through her hair, holding her head captive between his strong hands, and then covered her mouth with his.

Kara moaned, her mind spinning. She was falling for his macho tactics all over again, just like she had yesterday! Just like she would tomorrow if she dared to stick around. She knew she should push him away. Her hands were now free to do so, but a syrupy lassitude was seeping through her, and she couldn't seem to summon the energy to do anything but slump bonelessly against the wall. And Mac.

He thrust his tongue deep into her mouth, and her body arched reflexively. Wildfires of sensation raged through her every erogenous zone, melting her, turning her body pliant and soft, sensuously fitting itself to the contours of his hard male frame.

Kara abandoned any semblance of resistance. The pleasure and excitement coursing through her was too intense to give up. Tension spiraled inside her, growing tighter. Her arms slid around Mac's neck and she kissed him back as wildly, as carnally, as he was kissing her.

His hands cupped her bottom, caressing her and lifting her higher and harder against him. Kara writhed against him, electrified by the intimacy, wanting more. A knot of desire spasmed through her as he moved his thigh between hers in a rhythmic sawing motion, back and forth, applying an exquisite pressure that caused unbearably wonderful sensations to radiate through her body.

And then Mac lifted his mouth, though his lips remained close enough to touch hers as he spoke. "I hope this clears up any idiotic misconceptions you have about me not wanting you. Baby, when I touch you, I go up in flames."

His words thrilled her. Nobody had ever told her that she set them afire with desire, nobody had ever dragged her into a room and kissed her with a passion she'd only seen in the movies, either.

But then, he knew that, didn't he? *A man of his charm and skill...* She could almost hear Uncle Will's voice warning her not to take Mac Wilde's claims of passion seriously.

"You would say the same thing to whoever had stepped off that plane," she said tautly, lowering her eyes. His intense dark gaze made her blush. "You only want a woman to—"

"I only want you," Mac cut in, his voice rough and raspy. "And you want me so much you're shaking with it."

She was trembling, her legs so weak she probably would've fallen if he hadn't been holding her. And he knew it. She was weak for him; his lovemaking made her weak. And he knew that, too. She wanted him, despite knowing that what he wanted from her were her housekeeping and child-care services, not her heart and her mind and her body.

Though he didn't mind taking her body, as long as she was so willingly offering it to him. Helplessly willing.

She had no secrets from him, he knew everything! Tears of humiliation stung her eyes.

Mac studied her, wondering what she was thinking. His body was throbbing with the ache of pent-up desire. She roused him faster and harder than any other woman he'd ever known, and that included his ex-wife, Amy, whom he had always considered the major lust-inducer of his life.

Now he gazed into Kara's limpid hazel eyes, he ran his thumb over her tremulous, slightly swollen lips. It seemed he was going to have to rethink his previous beliefs. Amy was a distant memory who didn't measure up to the passion Kara so effortlessly kindled within him.

"I'm sorry the Rev upset you," he said softly. "You were happy till the Franklins showed up tonight. I think it's best if you keep your distance from them, at least for a while."

Kara stared into his burning dark eyes. He was sincere, she marveled. He actually believed it was Reverend Franklin and his family who'd caused her distress. She was somewhat awed by his ability to miss the point entirely. Maybe those books in the pop-psychology section in the bookstores had it right, after all: men and women really were from two different planets with astonishingly disparate perceptions, language and actions.

There was a racket emanating from the kitchen. Mac draped his arm around her shoulders and pulled her close to his side as he walked her out of the office. "We'll finish this later," he murmured, leaning down to drop a quick kiss on the top of her head. "After the troops have retired for the night."

The sensual promise implied in his words, in his possessive hold, made her shiver. "Mac, I can't. I don't…" She took a deep breath and started over. "I don't have casual flings."

"You know a casual fling isn't what I'm proposing,

Kara.'' Mac grinned. ''Which is a natural segue into what I am proposing—marriage.''

They came to a halt in front of the big granite fireplace in the living room.

Kara gnawed nervously on her lower lip. ''You really expect me to go through with this mail-order marriage, don't you? I mean, Uncle Will hoped it might happen, but he didn't consider it a done deal. You do.''

''That's right.''

''You think that I'm so desperate that I'll marry a man I don't know, a man I've known for less than two days? How do you know that I—I'm not already in love with someone else?''

''You're not, are you?''

The question was posed so indifferently, Kara was insulted. ''Maybe I am!'' she flared.

''Then why did your uncle Will suggest that I invite you out here to be my bride?'' Mac challenged, his sardonic smile matching his tone. ''He hardly would've done that if he knew you were in love with another man.''

''Maybe he didn't know!''

''If you were madly in love with some guy, you'd have told him,'' Mac declared with maddening assurance. ''Women don't keep stuff like that a secret. On the contrary, the moment a woman decides she's in love, she can't wait to announce it to the whole world.''

He was so offhand, so *sure* of her. Kara was seized by an impulse to shake him out of his complacency. ''That is patently untrue. There are times when a woman has no choice but to keep her love a secret.'' His smug grin of disbelief egged her on. ''For example, I wouldn't have told Uncle Will a thing if…if the man I love happened to be married!''

She clasped her hand over her mouth, horrified by her brash outburst. She would never become involved with a married man, not even hypothetically! Flushed with shame and unable to even look at Mac, Kara pulled away from him and rushed into the kitchen where Autumn, Brick and Clay were feasting on the dinner provided by the Franklins.

"Do you mind if I join you?" she asked, casting a quick look at the swinging door. Mac had not followed her. She was both relieved and disappointed.

Kara sank onto the bench behind the table.

Brick slid the plate of chicken her way. "It's not as good as KFC, but it's not bad. And it sure beats Mrs. Lattimore's moose meat casseroles."

"That was moose meat?" Kara felt queasy as she recalled the heaping portion she'd eaten last night.

The kids laughed merrily at her discomfiture.

"It might've been elk," Clay informed her gleefully. "Or rattlesnake or bear."

"Maybe Mrs. Lattimore is a secret cannibal." Brick nudged Autumn. "Guess what kind of meat she'd use then?"

"There are cannibals in prison," Autumn announced seriously. "They look just like regular people—but they're not. They like to *eat* regular people."

Tai meowed a greeting from atop the elk head where he was tearing apart a large piece of chicken. Autumn launched into a long and nauseating tale of imprisoned cannibals, a topic she'd seen discussed on one of the many true crime shows she watched incessantly on TV. Brick and Clay got into an argument about video games, tossing around unfamiliar terms like Game Genies and warp zones.

Kara fixed a plate of food for herself, benignly ignoring her dinner companions who finally settled down to eat with her.

In the living room, Mac stared into the vacant eyes of the moose above the mantel, pondering Kara's abrupt exit.

"I don't know whether to congratulate you or feel sorry for you, Uncle Mac." Lily's voice sounded from across the room. "If you were trying to insult Kara and drive her away, congratulations, you did well. But if you were trying to lure her into marrying you or even into your bed, wow, you blew it!''

Mac whirled to see his niece curled up on the sofa, daintily nibbling on a fried chicken leg. ''When did you come in?''

''I was here when you came in with Kara,'' Lily said blithely. ''You didn't see me, of course. You were too busy putting your great big foot into your mouth.'' She rolled her eyes. ''I'd heard that before the four of us arrived on the scene, you were the most popular bachelor in Bear Creek, with loads of single women chasing after you. But after observing your technique, all I can say is that the single women of Bear Creek are either desperate, or totally uncool. Maybe both?''

''You shouldn't eavesdrop on private conversations,'' Mac snapped.

''Sorry.'' Lily's apology contained not a shred of remorse. ''But what were you trying to do, Uncle Mac? Have you changed your mind since last night about marrying Kara? Are you trying to send her back East as fast as you can?''

''You weren't eavesdropping very carefully, were you? I have *not* changed my mind about marrying Kara as soon as possible. Of course I'm not trying to send her away!''

''No? Well, you sure could've fooled me!'' Lily gave a dramatic shake of her long, dark hair and took a fierce chomp of the chicken leg. ''I bet Kara doesn't know where she stands, either. Men!''

''What's that supposed to mean?'' demanded Mac.

Lily stood and stalked dramatically toward the swinging door to the kitchen. ''It means men don't say what they mean *or* mean what they say.''

''And women do?''

''We would if men didn't force us into playing games and telling lies. But you do, so we have to counter every move with one of our own.''

''Like Kara saying she was in love with a married man? I don't believe that for a minute.'' Mac frowned. ''Do you?''

"Uncle Mac, the point is that you forced her into saying it because *you* said she'd better take you up on your offer because she's desperate and has no other prospects. What woman could listen to such an insult without at least trying to salvage some pride?"

"I didn't mean it the way you said." Mac was indignant. "I didn't say it that way, either."

"Well, that's what I heard. That's what Kara heard. Naturally she couldn't let it pass. Women say and do what we have to when it comes to outmaneuvering men."

"Is that so?"

There was an edge in Lily's tone that Mac found disturbing. He looked at his niece, his gaze assessing. Lily was staring into space, her dark eyes glittering, her expression sultry and calculating and utterly adult. With her beauty and smoldering sexuality, she appeared every inch the woman who could outmaneuver whatever man she happened to choose as her target.

Mac swallowed. "Lily, what's going on with you?"

Lily merely laughed. "Uncle Mac, I'll have to get back to you on that one."

"Honey, I'm worried about you."

"Well, don't be. I know what I'm doing." Lily pushed open the door and strolled into the kitchen. "I think," she muttered under her breath.

Mac, following close behind her, felt a wave of foreboding and stress crash over him.

He stepped into the kitchen just in time to see Clay plunge his hands into the lime Jell-O ring, scoop it up and hurl both fistfuls at Brick. The seven-year-old's aim was right on target. Brick's hair and face were covered with gobs of glutinous green.

"Clay, cut it out!" Mac roared as Clay reached for some more ammunition. "Brick, don't you dare!" Brick had his left hand in the dish of coleslaw, ready to counterattack. "No food fights! I will not tolerate that kind of—"

"Help!" shrieked Clay as Mac strode toward the table, looking like a towering, thundering god of war. The little boy jumped onto Kara's lap and clutched her tightly, hiding his face against her breast. "Don't let him hit me, Aunt Kara!"

Kara, who had watched the food ambush in amazement, was further astonished by her unexpected elevation to kin status. *Aunt Kara?* She gazed down at the child's head, his dark hair soft and tousled. Clay was warm and small and holding on to her as if she were a life preserver in a storm-tossed sea. Instinctively, her arms closed around him.

Laughing and dripping Jell-O, Brick walked over to the sink and submerged his head under the faucet to wash the stuff off.

Mac stood above Kara, glaring down at Clay who kept his face hidden. "Clay Wilde, I want to have a word with you." He grasped Clay's arm.

"He's gonna hit me!" bellowed Clay.

"Mac, no!" Kara quickly turned aside, her grip on the child turning steely. "Calm down! Clay was just—just—" She paused, somewhat at a loss. He was just throwing food at his brother at the dinner table? It didn't seem like a very sound defense. But Clay was clinging to her, he needed her. He was so little and Mac was so big.

"*No?*" Mac roared. "Dammit, I will not be manipulated this way! If there is one thing we're going to get straight, it's—"

"Hey, chill, Uncle Mac," Brick chortled. "Here, I'll help you." Grabbing the spray hose from the sink, the boy aimed it at his uncle, blasting him with cold water.

For a few seconds, Mac stood in place, so caught off guard by the attack he didn't even attempt to dodge the watery stream. And that was long enough for him to be thoroughly soaked by the steady flow of water. Long enough for Brick to drop the nozzle and dash from the kitchen.

The hose twitched and bounced, spraying water everywhere.

Mac recovered and sprang into action. "Brick!" He tore out of the kitchen after his nephew. A door slammed hard, instantly followed by Mac's furious pounding. "Open this door!" he ordered. "Brick, open up right now!"

"Sounds like Brick made it safely to his room," Lily remarked, sauntering to the sink to turn off the water.

"If you don't open the door, I swear I'll kick it in!" shouted Mac.

Autumn, who had been sitting on the bench beside Kara, suddenly let out a piercing scream. "Uncle Mac is going berserk!"

Kara could only imagine how those TV tabloid shows Autumn watched had depicted "going berserk." Plenty of gore, certainly. Terror and horror, a given.

"Autumn, your uncle is not going berserk," Kara firmly assured her. "He's angry but he—"

Autumn let out another scream, this one so loud that Kara's eardrums throbbed. One more scream like that, and they would all be in danger of permanent hearing loss.

Kara rose to her feet, settling Clay onto the bench beside his sister. "Autumn, no more screaming. And Clay, keep your hands out of that Jell-O. I'm going to talk to your uncle Mac, right now."

"Uncle Mac's in trouble," Clay chanted in a singsong voice. The prospect seemed to delight him.

"Aren't you glad you decided to take a walk on the Wilde side, Kara?" Lily was grinning. "Calling this family dysfunctional is paying us a compliment."

"You're not dysfunctional, you're all just…very emotional and expressive," Kara countered bravely. She kept telling herself that as she walked to the door of Brick's room, which Mac was still pounding on while alternately threatening to break it down.

"Mac." She laid her hand on his arm. "Mac, you're all wet. Why don't you change into some dry clothes and then have some dinner?"

Her calm quiet tone was in blatant contrast to his infuriated tirade. She tightened her fingers on his arm. "If you keep yelling, Autumn is going to keep screaming. She thinks you've gone berserk, and heaven only knows what that means to her.... Maybe that you'll mount her head on the wall next to the elk's?"

There was a shout of laughter from behind Brick's door.

Mac heaved a long sigh and leaned against the wall. "That's not the least bit funny," he growled.

At least he'd stopped yelling and pounding. And there were no more high-decibel screams coming from the kitchen, either. Kara felt a giddy surge of relief.

"You think I'm being unreasonable?" Mac glowered at her, and Kara's apprehension level rose again. Was he going to transfer his fury to her? "You think I don't have a right to be upset when those little monsters throw food and—"

"They're not monsters." Kara steeled herself against his anger. "They are high-spirited boys. Didn't you and your brothers ever do anything..." She paused. "Uh, high-spirited when you were kids?"

"Sure. Of course. We even had a few food fights in our day. But we didn't grab a hose and drench our mother when she told us to stop. I have every right to expect—"

"My mother wasn't the type to laugh off a little water play, either," Kara cut in. "I distinctly remember her confiscating the squirt gun I'd saved my allowance to buy, after I squirted it in the house. She threw it in the trash. I was quite bereft because I was left with no money and no weapon."

Mac fought a smile. If she was trying to jolly him out of his fury, he would not succumb. He refused to be charmed!

"Well, rightly so. Spraying water all over the house is anarchy," Mac stated loftily. "Though I don't really remember, my mother probably disposed of our water guns, too, a move I applaud. And I demand—"

"I wouldn't have squirted my mother, Uncle Mac," Brick called through the door. He was obviously listening to every word from his position of safety. "But you aren't my mom. You're my uncle who is cool and likes joking around and who squirted me with that same hose in the summer when I complained about being hot. 'Cool it, Brick,' you said and then you squirted me. I was soaking wet and you laughed your head off, remember, Uncle Mac? We all laughed."

Mac's face reddened. "That was different," he muttered.

"How?" Kara's lips twitched. "It seems to me that water fights are either allowed in the house or they're banned—for everybody."

"It seems that way to me, too." Brick's voice sounded through the door.

Mac ran his hand through his wet hair. "Okay." He gritted his teeth. "From now on, water fights are forever banned in this house, and that ban extends to everyone. Anyone who violates that rule will—"

"Get his head mounted on the wall?" Brick suggested, coming out of his room. "What about food fights? Are they banned, too?"

"Yes," Kara said decisively. "And I think we'd better inform Clay about the new house rules, right now."

"Autumn, too. You didn't see her give Clay a dollar to throw that Jell-O at me," Brick added, flashing Kara a grin.

Mac uttered a strangled sound and stalked into the kitchen. "No more throwing food," he ordered sternly, glaring at Clay. "No more paying someone to throw food, either." This to Autumn. He glanced at the pools of water on the floor and the counters. "Lily, get a mop and clean up this mess."

"In your dreams." Lily tossed her long dark hair. "Brick did it, he can clean it up."

"Mac, you could catch cold in those wet clothes," Kara intervened hastily. "Don't worry, we'll take care of things here in the kitchen. You go change into some dry clothes."

"Achoo!" Brick faked a sneeze. "Poor Uncle Mac might catch the sniffles in those nasty wet clothes."

Kara tensed. That kid just didn't know when to quit. She

quickly stepped in front of Mac, hoping to avert another clash. She placed her hands on his chest to keep him in place, though she half expected him to toss her aside and take off after Brick again.

But he didn't. He placed his hands over hers and pressed them against his wet shirt. She felt his damp body heat under her fingers.

Mac gazed down at her, and his eyes held hers. "Contrary to what you might think, I'm not a tyrannical ogre who goes around hitting kids. I've never laid a hand on any of them. Though I sometimes think a couple of swats on the behind wouldn't hurt either of the boys."

Kara thought of the way Clay had jumped onto her lap, clinging to her for protection. *"Don't let him hit me, Aunt Kara!"* Even the memory of that scared little voice roused her protective instincts. "Maybe your brother James hit them when he got angry," she murmured, horrified at the thought.

"Or maybe Clay knows exactly what to do to activate your protective maternal instincts," Mac suggested.

"That is a very cynical thing to say, Mac Wilde. Clay is just a little boy, only seven years old." She tried to pull her hands away.

Mac's fingers tightened around hers. "You like the kids, don't you?" He watched her thoughtfully. "You care what happens to them."

"Well, of course." His stare was intent, drawing her into him, until she felt lost in his deep dark eyes. She could hardly think, she was beginning to have trouble remembering to breathe. "I mean, they're just kids and they've been through a lot and—"

"I won't throw food anymore," Clay announced, wiggling his way to stand between Kara and Mac. Kara was grateful to him for breaking the spell Mac seemed to have cast on her.

The little boy linked one arm around Kara, the other around Mac. "When can we get my puppy? Aunt Kara said we could get a puppy 'cause we need a pet," he explained to his uncle.

"Oh, we definitely need a pet around here," Mac said dryly. "What about a wolf cub or a baby grizzly bear? They'd fit right in."

"We're not kidding, Uncle Mac," reproved Autumn. "We really are getting a puppy. Aunt Kara promised."

"Well, since she's the one who's going to be around to house-train it and do all those other things a puppy requires, it's okay by me," Mac said lightly. He arched his brows and returned Kara's startled glance with a challenging one of his own.

Try and get out of it, his dark eyes seemed to say. *Go on and tell the kids that they can't have a puppy because you won't be here to take care of it—or them.*

Kara opened her mouth to speak, but she couldn't say the words. Not with little Clay snuggling against her, not with the three older kids watching her and Mac standing so closely together.

"I feel like I'm living in a TV sitcom," Lily remarked, glancing around the kitchen. "The crisis is resolved at the end of the episode, everybody is smiling at everybody else. Our theme song plays. Fade to close."

"I like shows like that," Autumn sighed.

"Well, I think we're more *Tales from the Crypt* than *Full House,*" countered Brick, but he was clearly joking and everybody laughed, including Mac.

Kara felt a surge of warmth flow softly through her. Jokes aside, there really was a family feeling in this room right now, a sense of unity and belonging that she had always longed for but had never been able to achieve. Certainly not as a child, after her beloved stepfather, Will Franklin, had been replaced by her mother's new husband, Drew Ansell. Drew and her mother adored each other, claiming theirs was a magical love of a lifetime, and perhaps it was, but there wasn't much room for a daughter from a previous marriage in such a tight coupling.

Though Drew had never been overtly unkind to her, Kara had always felt in the way, an intruder in their home. She remembered how gladly Drew paid her bills for summer camp, providing it was one that was hundreds of miles away and not the local day camp. "Why not visit Uncle Will in Montana? I'll be happy to pay your way out there and you can stay as long as you like." Drew made the same offer every holiday, every summer, until she was grown and on her own. His offer always had to be refused because Kara knew she was as unwanted in Ginny Franklin's home as she was in Drew Ansell's.

But now, here with the Wildes, a group of similarly displaced misfits, Kara felt the warmth of kinship. Of need. They needed her here; the events of the day proved it. She'd made a difference here today. For the first time in her memory her presence had made a difference to someone. For the first time ever, she had been needed.

Kara looked at each of the kids, then at Mac, who was still holding her hands, keeping her locked in place as he studied her with nerve-tingling intensity. Kara's breath caught in her throat. If she hadn't gleaned the need of sexual desire from the primitive hunger glittering in his dark eyes, the hard heat of his body provided ample physical evidence. Being needed in this urgent, provocative way both thrilled and scared her.

Swiftly, Kara pulled her hands away from his and moved away from him, acutely aware of the flush staining her skin.

"I guess I'll get out of these wet clothes, so I won't be at risk for the sniffles," Mac said drolly, shooting his older nephew a wry look.

Brick snickered and faked a few more sneezes as Mac exited.

To Kara's surprise, when she suggested that Clay, Autumn and Brick go to their rooms to get ready for bed, they did so without offering a single protest or argument. Lily stayed to help her clean up the kitchen, further astonishing her, given the girl's earlier response to Mac's demand to help.

"You did an excellent job of handling Uncle Mac tonight, Kara," Lily said approvingly as she sloshed a mop through a puddle of water on the floor. "You stepped right in when he went nuclear and you smoothed things over." The girl smiled slyly. "And getting him all hot for you was definitely a good move on your part. Not even those wet clothes could keep him from—"

"Lily!" Kara interrupted, blushing and aghast.

"I bet he's taking an ice-cold shower right now," Lily continued gleefully. "So how long are you going to hold out? Not too long, I hope, because Uncle Mac is—"

"Lily, please!"

"You're blushing!" Lily was delighted. "That is soooo cute!"

"Not again!" Kara groaned.

"It seems to me that someone who blushes at the thought of Uncle Mac in the shower is not secretly and madly in love with a married man," Lily declared, staring intently at Kara. "Am I right?"

Kara dropped the sponge she was using to wipe the table. Shame blanketed her. "I'm sorry you had to hear that, Lily. It's not true and I shouldn't have said it. I—"

"Oh, I know why you said it," Lily interrupted grimly. "Like Uncle Mac gave you any choice! I already told him how dumb he was, just in case he didn't know it. And he didn't!"

The thought of Mac and Lily discussing her made Kara cringe. Nor was she comfortable discussing Mac with his teenage niece. But Lily was not about to let the subject drop.

"Why won't men admit what they want instead of always finding some stupid reason to deny it?" Lily continued, her voice rising in agitation. "It can't be an honest, 'I'm crazy about you and want you to live with me.' Oh, no, instead it has to be, 'stay here and watch the kids because you don't have anyone else in your life.' Why can't it be, 'I'm in love with you' instead of, 'you're too young for me and I hate it that I want you so much'?''

Kara was mortified by the first reference, which she knew was about her and Mac, and curious about the second which seemed a likely allusion to Lily herself. ''Is that what—what Mr. 'Paradise' said to you? And what he didn't say?'' she added quietly.

''Mr. Paradise,'' Lily repeated, grimacing. ''Yeah, that's him, all right, and that's what he said. And what he should have said. It's stupid, Kara. We're so right for each other, but he's grabbed onto the age thing...'' She wrung out the mop with a startling ferocity. ''Where are all those new-age guys who are supposed to be so open with their feelings? And how come you and I got stuck with retro-macho types who would rather be branded with a hot iron than admit they need a woman for something besides sex?''

''And child care,'' murmured Kara, in spite of herself.

Lily nodded her agreement.

''This man you're seeing,'' Kara said carefully, ''does your Uncle Mac know him?''

Yesterday the girl had proclaimed her lust for Webb Asher, the ranch manager, Kara recalled. For one paralyzing moment, she wondered if he could possibly be Lily's secret lover.

Kara instantly dismissed the idea. Lily had been playfully teasing when she'd made those remarks about coveting his body, and Webb Asher certainly had not acted like a man enraptured, however unwillingly. He'd tied Lily to a chair, flicked her away from him as if she were a mosquito and stormed from the kitchen to get away from her! No, Webb Asher couldn't be the man. Kara felt a modicum of relief for that fact.

''Yes, Uncle Mac knows him, but that's all I can say.'' Lily shrugged. ''I know we've bonded tonight, but it's better

if you don't know the name of my—of him, Kara. You'd feel
obligated to tell Uncle Mac."

"And he would…go berserk?" Kara nervously wondered
aloud.

"Maybe. Probably." Lily sighed. "Definitely."

Kara winced, imagining the scene. "Lily, I wish I had
some wise advice to give you, something that could—"

"The only advice you could give me that I'd listen to
would be 'Go for it, girl.'"

"Not knowing any of the details, I couldn't, in all good
conscience, tell you that, Lily."

"I know." Lily returned the mop to the small utility closet.
"I guess I'll go to bed now. After all, I have to get up for
school tomorrow." Her dour expression left no doubts as to
how she felt about that requirement. But she paused on the
threshold, before leaving the kitchen and cast Kara a sudden,
brilliant smile. "Hey, Kara, tonight? Go for it, girl!"

Seven

"Go for it, girl!" Lily's inspirational cheer rang in Kara's ears as she checked on Clay and Autumn, and ended up tucking them into their beds. Both of them put their arms around her and kissed her good-night. Their easy acceptance of her warmed Kara's heart. They wanted her here.

She stood outside Brick's and Lily's doors and called a good-night to each. They responded with friendly good-nights of their own. Kara knew that as far as they were concerned, she was welcome to stay.

Mac wanted her here, too, though his motives were unmistakably self-serving. But without Uncle Will around to remind her, his motives didn't seem to matter as much as the fact that she was wanted. And needed. That she'd finally found a place where she felt she belonged.

"Go for it, girl," indeed! Lily's voice echoed in her head again. She and Mac weren't playing a game that required bold moves and tactical strategy. Kara gulped. Were they?

Certainly Lily seemed to see relationships between men and women as something akin to war games.

Well, she did not, Kara assured herself. She was caught in an admittedly strange situation here, but she would behave like the mature and honest woman that she was.

That meant no game-playing, no bold moves or audacious strategy. It meant fixing a plate of food to take to Mac because he hadn't returned to the kitchen, and she knew he must be hungry because he'd missed eating dinner.

Kara carried the heaping plate, a glass of orange juice and a fork and napkin to Mac's room. After bringing him dinner she would turn in, she decided. Though it wasn't very late, she was still adjusting to the time-zone changes. And it had been a very, very long day.

She knocked lightly on his bedroom door.

"Come in."

At the sound of his voice, a surge of fevered blood rushed to her cheeks, turning them scarlet. Her heart began to pound in her ears. "I can't open the door, my hands are full." Her voice was husky and she was suddenly breathless. "I brought you some dinner."

The door swung open. Mac stood before her, wearing a thick white toweling robe. He was rubbing his hair dry with a smaller towel. His eyes flicked over the big plate containing servings of chicken, potato salad, coleslaw, rolls and a piece of pumpkin cake.

"What? No Jell-O?" His dark eyes gleamed.

Kara chuckled. "Since it became a weapon, it's off the menu."

"Good idea. One never knows when the irresistible urge to fling it might strike." He took the plate from her. "I guess I overreacted in a major way tonight, yelling and chasing through the house like a maniac." He shook his head ruefully.

"You had reason to be provoked." Kara found herself defending him. "I mean, after driving all day to bring Brick back, probably the last thing you needed was a food fight in your kitchen.''

''No, that was the next to the last thing. The penultimate. The arrival of the Franklins was the last thing I needed.'' He carried the plate over to the wide armchair and ottoman under the window, and sat down. ''I wondered if you were going to call the Rev and ask him to come back out here and take you into town tonight.''

''No. I decided not to.'' Kara walked over to hand him the glass of juice.

Mac stared askance at the orange juice. ''Isn't there any coffee?''

She shook her head. ''It's too late to drink coffee, the caffeine will keep you awake for hours. And the only other choice of beverage was milk or Mad Cougar malt liquor. I'll go back to the kitchen if you'd rather have milk, but I won't get you that poisonous-looking brew with the rabid wildcat logo on the can.''

Mac grinned. ''The juice will be fine. Will you keep me company while I eat?'' he asked politely.

Kara glanced at the thick closed bedroom door and at Mac, who was balancing the plate of food on his lap. ''All right.'' Her voice sounded wary and hesitant to her own ears. ''For a little while.''

She sat down tentatively on the edge of the bed. Other than the ottoman at Mac's feet, the bed was the only place in the room left to sit.

''While I was in the shower, I was thinking up ways of disabling Reverend Will's car so he couldn't take you into town,'' Mac remarked, biting into the chicken. ''Good thing you didn't call him.''

''Mac, I...really, I...'' Kara twisted her fingers, embarrassed at her incoherence. She imagined Lily observing them and rolling her dark brown eyes in exasperation. ''Go for it, girl!''

Kara bolted to her feet. "I have to check on Tai and then go to bed. I—"

"Later," Mac interrupted firmly. His dark eyes, intense as lasers, held her in place as effectively as solid restraints.

Kara sat back down. "You must be terribly tired, I know I am. And after the day you've had, you must be looking forward to getting some rest. You never did say how long it took you to find Brick and what the sheriff said."

Kara flushed in dismay. She'd gone from inarticulate to babbling. Just sitting here watching Mac was arousing her. She scorned herself. How could anyone look sexy tearing into a chicken leg?

But Mac managed the impossible. She stared as his white teeth bit into the fried batter on the skin, saw his tongue flick at the corners of his lips...his lips, well-shaped and sensual, firm and warm. The taste and the feel of his mouth seemed to be imprinted on her brain, and the sensuous memory was instantly summoned.

Kara pressed her thighs tightly together and crossed her arms over her breasts. Beneath the double layer of blouse and bra, she could feel her nipples tighten into hard little points.

Mac continued eating, devouring his dinner with relish. Kara was grateful he was unaware of her inner turmoil.

"The boys had a couple hours' head start on us," he said, breaking the silence to finally respond to her desperate attempt at conversation. "But Jack—Jack Tate—he's the sheriff—radioed the state police to be on the lookout for the car and warned them not to spook the kids into a high-speed chase. Nothing like that happened, thank God. The state troopers were great with Brick and Jimmy. They took them to the highway patrol headquarters where Jack and I picked them up there."

"I hope there weren't any charges filed?"

"No." Mac shook his head. "Not this time. But whatever the state troopers said made a definite impression on both boys. I don't think they'll pull that particular stunt again.

And, of course, Jack and I added our own two cents' worth on the drive home. He took Jimmy Crow and I drove back with Brick.'' Mac grimaced. "He talked me into listening to some of his tapes. The alleged music kids today are listening to is nothing less than appalling. I've heard car alarms that sound better.''

Kara grinned. "Careful. You sound like an old grouch bemoaning the moronic tastes and witless ways of the younger generation.''

"I'm an old grouch who's speaking the truth. Their tastes are moronic and their ways are witless.''

They both laughed. Mac put the plate and fork on the small table next to the chair. He'd eaten everything but the piece of pumpkin cake.

"You don't want dessert?'' Kara asked, glancing at the rejected piece of cake.

"Not that stuff. Pumpkin belongs in a pie, not in a cake.'' Mac stood and walked toward her, a satyr's grin lighting his face. "I'm interested in a different kind of dessert.'' He sat beside her at the foot of the bed. "And so are you.''

Kara's heart leapt into her throat. Her head snapped up to meet his utterly confident, tempting smile. "I—um—I have to get out of here,'' she murmured. Was she telling Mac, or issuing a warning to herself?

Whatever, she didn't move.

"Thank you for bringing me dinner,'' Mac said softly, reaching over to comb his fingers through her thick, straight, light brown hair. "It was very thoughtful of you.''

Kara's eyes were level with his chest, and she stared at the whiteness of his cotton robe, a stark contrast to his tanned skin. The open V of the robe exposed a swatch of wiry black chest hair. For the first time since she'd entered the room, she became fully aware that he was nude beneath that robe. And here she was, sitting on the bed with him. And still she didn't move.

"Lie down,'' Mac said in a velvety voice.

Kara gaped at him, too rattled to speak.

Gently, yet inexorably, his hands settled on her shoulders and pressed her back onto the mattress. He lay down beside her, his dark eyes sweeping over her with a possessive intensity that sent frissons of fear and excitement through her. But even the fear was exciting, almost exhilarating, and she lay there under his watchful eyes, her body quivering with piercing arousal.

"Such big eyes. They're as round as saucers." Mac's lips curved with amused affection. He bent his head to kiss each of her eyelids:

Kara's eyes dropped closed and she couldn't seem to summon the strength to open them again. She was filled with a hot syrupy warmth that rendered her limbs heavy and turgid, and she had neither the strength nor the energy to move them. Mac solved that problem by positioning her as if she were a doll, lifting her leg over his, then caressing the length of it, from the curve of her buttock along the outside of her thigh to her knee.

"You have great legs," Mac murmured his approval. "Long and shapely. I want to see them. As good as you look in those jeans, let's get you out of them."

The meaning of his words didn't seem to penetrate the sensual cloud enveloping her. It was his tone, a low sexy growl that infiltrated, and she squirmed with pleasure.

Ribbons of desire coiled tightly through her as his palm made a return journey, gliding leisurely along the inside of her thigh, his fingers lightly kneading. When he reached the heated juncture between her legs, he placed his hand there, a bold claiming with no tentative touches or gropes.

This time his intent registered loud and clear. A gasp tore from her throat, and Kara sprang upright. Even then he kept his hand in place. Kara paled, then blushed hotly at the sight of it, holding her so intimately.

"Mac, please." Her voice sounded like a faraway whimper. "This—I—we hardly know each other," she finished weakly. The warmth of his hand was suffusing her woman-hood; she was damp and throbbing and aching. If he didn't move his hand...

He didn't.

Kara lay back down on the bed, mesmerized by the agony of longing streaking through her. The invasion of his hand had shocked her, but now it was not enough. She wanted more than its firm, warm pressure. She wanted, she wanted...

He released her, sliding his hand up and over her stomach. When he quickly unfastened the first metal button of her jeans, she rallied her wits enough to stop him, covering his hand with hers. Their fingers tangled.

He was working on the second button; she was trying to still those deft fingers of his. "Mac, we've only known each other two days," she reminded him breathlessly.

He caught her hand and carried it to his lips. The tip of his tongue touched the center of her palm, and she felt the effects of that simple caress exactly where he meant her to.

He smiled at her. "Honey, in this house one day equals five years. Make that five years of doing hard time in prison."

The moment the imminent sexual pressure eased, so did Kara's protests. The aura of intimacy was so pervasive and alluring that she didn't even consider getting up from the bed, much less leaving the room. It seemed so inordinately right to be lying here with Mac, as he kissed and played with her fingers and watched her with his warm dark brown eyes.

"And since we've known each other two days, that means we've been together the equivalent of...how long?"

"Ten years?"

"You really are a math whiz," Mac teased. "But the fully correct answer is ten years hard prison time."

As if of their own volition, her hands were learning the features of his face, stroking the high cheekbones, the strong line of his jaw, the hard tanned column of his neck. "Being here is not like being in prison, Mac," she admitted softly.

"No?" His own hands were moving over her curves with

long sweeping strokes. "You think you could get used to it here?" He kneaded her shoulders, and her muscles seemed to melt under his strong fingers. The same thing happened when he massaged her back.

"I'm already used to it. I like it here." She had neither the will nor the energy to keep anything from him. Not when his clever hands were rendering her pliant and bonelessly relaxed, not when his mouth was bestowing light, butterfly kisses on her forehead, her cheeks, along the sensitive cord of her neck.

"You really do belong here, you know. It's practically pre-ordained." Mac laughed into her eyes. "Anyone who instantly adjusts to life in this madhouse is definitely a fellow inmate."

He might have been joking, but it was the most seductive thing he could have said to her. She belonged. She'd finally found the place and the people she'd been looking for, waiting for, all her life.

"Thanks. I think," she kidded back. But her eyes were shining.

Mac's heart turned over oddly. She looked so sweet, so warm. She looked happy. He was nonplussed by how much that touched him. He was a take-charge, get-things-done type who'd never spent much time thinking about happiness and how to obtain it. Meeting responsibilities and seeing that necessary tasks were completed were the forces that drove him. And he did what was required without pondering whether or not he, and those around him, were happy.

But the warmth and radiance in Kara's face made him glad. He felt protective toward her, he felt possessive. And he was so aroused he was aching. He wanted her with a ferociousness that might have disturbed him—if he hadn't been so consumed with desire.

He loosened the belt that held his robe closed, and lay one hard thigh over hers. "Don't get hung up on time frames, baby. Some people know each other for less than an hour before a one-night stand. Others meet over a weekend and have a fling. Time is irrelevant, especially for us. We're going to be married.'' He brushed his lips tightly across her mouth. "I like the sound of that. I like knowing that you'll be in my bed every night. Every night, starting tonight.''

One-night stand. Weekend fling. The words swirled around Kara's head. She imagined lying in Mac's arms, holding him in hers, making love with him, only to never see him again. She knew she wouldn't be able to stand it. She couldn't bear the pain and rejection of a transitory here-today, gone-tomorrow tryst. Which was probably why she was still a virgin at twenty-six. And why she needed to hear Mac talk about permanence before they made love.

In his bed every night. Her body trembled with the inborn need to belong completely to him. She was going to do it. The realization struck her sharply. Until that very moment, she'd been confused and floundering, but now she knew. She was going to marry Mac Wilde. And she was going to make love with him for the first time tonight. She felt a rush of sheer virginal terror so thoroughly mixed with urgency and excitement that she couldn't begin to separate one from the other.

Mac could, however. "You look like a scared little girl.'' The perception did not please him. "I know you're not afraid of me, Kara.'' His voice was deep and rough. "And I know you want me to make love to you. That's why you came to my room tonight.''

"At the time, I really did think I was simply bringing you dinner,'' Kara whispered. But her soft hazel eyes signaled her surrender.

"Pure self-deception,'' Mac assured her. "But if that's what it took to get you in here…'' His voice trailed off. He was concentrating on the buttons of her lilac silk blouse.

Kara was astonished at how quickly he undid them. A heartbeat later, he'd unfastened the front clasp of her bra.

"I want you, Kara.'' His eyes were dark with desire as he

gazed at her breasts. They were high and round, small and very white with dusky rose tips. He drew a sharp, shallow breath as another bolt of desire shot through him.

Trembling, flushing, Kara resisted the urge to grab her opened blouse and cover herself. The hot assessing gleam in Mac's eyes as he stared at her bare breasts both embarrassed and excited her.

"You're beautiful, sweetheart," Mac murmured tenderly, and his words flowed over her like a honeyed balm, bolstering her confidence and reassuring her. "And I'm not handing you a line or a generic compliment," Mac added, remembering how his last attempt to praise her had blown up in his face. "I really mean it, Kara."

"I really want to believe you," she said wistfully. But whether she did or not, this time she knew she was not going to storm out of the room.

"Believe it, baby." Mac couldn't wait another second to touch her. Reaching for her, he possessed her breasts hungrily, first with his hands, then with his lips.

He took one nipple and drew it into his mouth, sucking hard. Kara cried out with primitive pleasure as shock waves of sensation crashed through her. His lips and his tongue teased and laved first one breast, then the other until she was moaning, her hips undulating in an erotic rhythm that was brand-new, yet purely instinctive to her.

He wedged his knee between her thighs and angled his body over hers so that she could feel the fully aroused strength and length of him. Kara moved against him in a way that wrenched a groan from deep in his chest. His mouth closed over hers, hard and fierce, and Kara entwined her arms around his neck and kissed him back.

The kiss went on and on, wild and deep and passionate. Kara clung to Mac, boldly slipping her hands beneath his robe to feel the hard warmth of skin and muscle and wiry soft hair. He was all male, taut and powerful and Kara savored the physical difference between them, learning the shape and the texture and the strength of him. Her explorations made him shudder with pleasure and the arousing impact of his hard virility sent her own senses reeling.

Kara uttered a throaty cry. She was weak and hot and her pulses pounded with a strange mixture of panic and desire. Her body was aching with an almost painfully intense need, yet the rampant intensity of his demands and her own wild craving scared her.

"I've never felt like this before," she gasped, when he lifted his lips from hers, allowing both to gulp for air. "I never knew I could feel this way."

She was afraid to be drawn into this whirling vortex of sensual pleasure, afraid of being rendered totally mindless by it. By him. The prospect of completely losing control of herself by surrendering to him was as unnerving as it was enticing. And at this particular moment, as Mac was tugging off her jeans and panties, the unnerving aspect of it all was winning out.

"Relax, sweetie." Mac's voice was both soothing and seductive. "I know you're nervous, but there is no reason to be."

She was naked now, and his eyes feasted on her as he shrugged out of his robe. He tossed it onto the floor, near the edge of the bed, where her clothes had landed in a loosely strewn pile.

Kara stared at him, her mouth growing dry at the sight of his well-proportioned, muscular frame, tanned and hard and breathtakingly masculine. Suddenly, fascination replaced her fear and she reached out to touch him. Her hand closed around the satiny-smooth length of him, feeling the heat and strength and the sheer size of him.

Mac closed his eyes and swallowed a gasp of pleasure, overwhelmed by the delicious rapture sweeping through him, evoked by the exquisite feel of her fingers wrapped around him.

Kara watched him, and a heady surge of feminine power

filled her. He wanted her; his desire and his need were undeniable. She could see it, feel it...

Mac opened his eyes and carefully removed her hand, giving her a regretful grin. "Much more of that and we'll be finished before we've even started."

Kara nodded, recalling what she'd read because it was all she had to draw from. But even the evocative love scenes in the books she'd read hadn't prepared her for this, for the sheer physicality of sex, the intimacy, the feelings of power and helplessness paradoxically joined.

It didn't prepare her for the sweet radiating tendrils of heat as her body melted, turning liquid with the flow of desire as one of his hands slid over her stomach, around the narrow curve of her hip to slip between her legs.

Her body arched and she whimpered with ecstasy as he caressed the soft folds, probing the creamy velvet center of her femininity, exploring inside and taking possession of the most secret, private part of her. Wild, wonderful sensations spiraled through her, building in intensity, a sharp tension rising until the pleasure was almost too much to bear.

"Please," she cried, wanting something she could not name, striving for something she couldn't even comprehend. Hot, honeyed flames licked through her body like radiant, sensual fire.

Mac watched her, his dark eyes glittering with passion and possession. "Just let go, baby," he commanded softly. "Let go and come to me."

"I—I can't," she gasped.

"Yes, you can."

And then she did, giving in to the pulsating tension and rocketing sensation which hurtled her into paroxysms of thrilling rapture, into a dimension of pleasure she never dreamed existed.

He didn't give her time to come down. While her body still pulsed with aftershocks of pleasure, he opened her legs wide and surged into her, filling her with his masculine strength and power. Kara gave a reflexive cry and felt the sting of tears in her eyes.

Mac raised his head and stared at her in shock. His breathing was labored and raspy. "You've never done this before, have you?" he asked, even though he knew the answer.

Kara winced at the incredulity in his voice. "No," she admitted, closing her eyes against the stark amazement in his. The shock waves that had thundered through her virginal body were slowly receding. But his virile presence inside her was burning hot and still hurt.

"I—I'd guessed you were fairly inexperienced." Mac tried to moisten his mouth by swallowing. It didn't work. "But I never expected, I never thought—"

"You sound as if the concept of virginity is beyond your comprehension." Kara tried to play it light and cool. He was already disappointed with her; the worst thing she could do would be to give in to this perilous urge to burst into tears.

Mac gazed down at her and saw the shine of tears in her eyes. "Oh my God, don't cry!" he pleaded.

"Poor Mac. The most sought-after bachelor in Bear Creek, trapped with a weepy virgin in his bed." Kara managed a strangled laugh. "I'm sorry. And sorry for you, too."

"And to think I told you that you had no reason to be nervous," Mac muttered as he silently berated himself. He really was a plague-carrying flea on a rat! And if there were any lower life form, he deserved to be called that, too. "But you did, you had every reason to be nervous and wary of me! You really were just bringing me dinner tonight and I completely misinterpreted, I pushed you into this and you've never done it before. You've never been with a man, you're a virgin—"

"You don't have to belabor the point," Kara interjected with a trace of asperity. "This is humiliating enough without—"

"Humiliating? I thought you were in pain."

"I am." She paused to breathe. Strangely enough, the pain was ebbing. Her body was slowly adjusting to him, sensuously stretching to accommodate his hard male virility. "I—I mean, I was."

He moved slightly. Kara tensed, expecting pain, but there was only a twinge.

"Better now?" he asked huskily.

Kara nodded her head. It was definitely getting better. The burning sensation was gone now, replaced by another one, harder to define. The heat was still there but it wasn't painful, it had been transformed into a glowing warmth. And that tearing, stretching pain had evaporated and turned into a feeling of fullness. She closed her eyes. She felt warm and full, and she liked it. It was as if an empty ache she'd never noticed had been exchanged for this shimmering good feeling.

"I don't want you to feel humiliated because I talked you into bed with me, Kara," Mac said softly.

If he were a gentleman, one of those sensitive beta males, he would withdraw from her immediately, Mac lectured himself. He would let her go to her room and spend the night alone.

He faced the fact that he was neither a gentleman nor a sensitive beta male. He wasn't going anywhere.

"Kara, sweetheart, if you were, uh, saving yourself for marriage...well, I really am going to marry you. It's going to be all right, honey. We can...sort of pretend this is our wedding night."

Kara stared at him impassively. "Your ability to miss the point completely is amazing. Absolutely mind-boggling."

Mac looked so bewildered, she nearly giggled. But she quickly stifled the urge. "I was humiliated because you made me feel like some kind of otherworldly freak because I'd never..." She averted her eyes and blushed, much to her consternation. "Because I hadn't had sex. Yet," she added bravely.

She braced herself for his glib reply. And waited. Finally

she gathered the courage to look at him again. Her eyes met his.

"I'm sorry if I made you feel like a freak," he said quietly. "You're anything but. You're a beautiful, passionate, responsive woman, and I feel privileged to be your first lover."

Kara caught her quivering lower lip between her teeth and blinked back the sudden rush of tears. "Thank you, Mac," she whispered.

He leaned down to kiss her mouth with a controlled tenderness that belied the urgent stirrings of his body, locked with hers.

"And I swear I'm not tossing off some all-purpose line I've used before. I've never said those words to another woman because I've never—taken a virgin." He moved slowly, carefully within her, a gentle thrusting that made her breath catch in her throat. "Tonight is a first for both of us, baby," he murmured huskily.

A delicious shiver ran through her, from the tips of her toes to the crown of her head. Then he kissed her. A long hard wet kiss, his tongue penetrating her mouth in excruciating simulation. Kara moaned softly as a tidal wave of passion built to a crest within her. She wrapped her arms tightly around him and arched sinuously against him.

"That's it," Mac encouraged her, his voice low and raspy in her ear. His fingertips caressed her intimately, delicately teasing her into sensual torment. Instinctively, her knees flexed as she shifted in response to his maddeningly arousing touch.

"Wrap your legs around me," he instructed urgently, and she obeyed, taking all of him deep within her. He rocked slowly, tentatively, barely able to breathe as fiery currents flamed with each gliding movement.

Moments later, she was flowing blissfully with the sensuous rhythm he was creating. "It's good, Mac." Her voice was thick and husky with awed wonder. "It feels so good."

Her innocent proclamation acted like an erotic catalyst,

sending a riptide of pleasure through him. "Yes, baby," he rasped, his teeth clenched. "It's so damn good."

Though he tried to prolong it, nature took over and his thrusts became deeper and harder and faster, finally erupting into an explosive climax. With a shuddering groan of pleasure, he collapsed on top of her.

Kara held him tight, hearing her heart hammering in her ears, feeling her face wet with sweat or tears or maybe both. Her hands stroked the smooth damp length of his back as she savored the unfamiliar, demanding pressure of his male weight upon her.

Mac lay so sated and replete that he couldn't summon an ounce of energy to move a single muscle. The thought of separating his body from hers was anathema. His eyes closed, and he felt himself begin to slide into a satiated torpor.

"Mac?" Kara's voice, soft and uncertain, drew him back.

He pulled himself up to rest on his elbows and gazed down into her wide hazel eyes. "Are you all right?" he whispered hoarsely. "Did I hurt you?" He was still in her and on her, and he quickly pulled out and rolled onto his back. "I'm sorry. I must've been crushing you." He reached over and lazily caressed her cheek. "Can you breathe now?"

"I'm fine," she assured him.

She was much better than that; she felt wonderful, dizzy and giddy, as high as the telecommunications satellite beaming down waves to the round dish in the yard. She felt energized, wanting to laugh out loud, to share her thoughts and her dreams, to talk about the pleasure and the intimacy they'd just shared, dissecting and reliving every moment.

Noticing that he'd been on the verge of falling asleep, Kara restrained herself. She mustn't forget that while making love with Mac had been the most seminal experience of her life, it did not hold the same significance for him. He'd known a number of women, in the most biblical sense of the word, and she was merely an addition to the tally. The acknowledgement sobered her, puncturing the euphoric high she was flying on.

"I should go back to my room," she murmured. "I can't stay here."

"Why not?" Mac reached over to turn off the bedside lamp, plunging the room into darkness.

Kara's heartbeat quickened. "We don't want the kids to find us together. Anyway, I won't be able to sleep—here."

"The door is locked, the kids won't bother us." Mac felt her emotional withdrawal and didn't like it. "And what do you mean, you won't be able to sleep here? It's a much better, firmer mattress than that old feather bed in the other room." He rolled onto his side and hooked his arm around her waist, pulling her back against him, fitting their bodies together, spoon-fashion.

"It's not the mattress," Kara countered. Did he actually think it was? She grimaced. He probably did at that. "It's just that I—well, in addition to never having had sex before, I've never shared a bed before, either. It takes me a long time to fall asleep and I'm a restless sleeper. If I stay here, neither one of us will get any rest."

"I'm willing to take the chance." Mac kissed her temple. "You're staying put, sweetie."

"You're so pushy!" Kara cried, trying to wriggle away from him. Mac's arm was like an iron band, holding her fast. "You're overbearing and high-handed and aggressive and—"

"And those are my good points," Mac agreed congenially. "Good night, baby."

Anger surged through her. Kara told herself it was irrational to feel angry with Mac for sparing her the generic lines he undoubtedly bestowed on his partners, words of praise for a lust well-satisfied, a passion excitingly slaked. But she would've welcomed such phrases, however generic. Even if he didn't mean it, she wanted to hear him tell her that sex with her was good, maybe even terrific. Oh, she wouldn't expect an effusive ''The best sex I've ever had'', that notorious tabloid boast. Right now, even a simple ''Wow!'' would suffice.

But Mac remained silent.

''Mac, it's no use. I can't sleep here,'' she insisted, trying to thrash dramatically around in the bed. His inexorable grip allowed only some minor twitching. ''Mac, I mean it. Let me go.''

''No.''

She tried to hold on to her temper. She shouldn't blame him because he didn't view their sexual union as one of the highlights of his life, though it was certainly one of the highlights of hers. It was *the* highlight, Kara reminded herself strickenly. If a tape had been spliced together featuring the highlights of her life, it would've been blank. Until tonight.

''This is all so easy for you,'' she accused.

She'd been so easy for him. And though she didn't regret his seduction, she did regret her whole-hearted participation. Kara knew herself too well to believe that she would have fallen into bed with just any man, simply because he was willing and available. One did not remain a virgin until twenty-six years of age under those circumstances.

No, she'd made love with Mac Wilde because, in the course of two confusing and chaotic, wild and wonderful days, she had fallen madly, passionately and deeply in love with him.

Kara stifled a sob. She wanted—needed—to hear him say that their lovemaking had meant *something* to him, that *she* meant something to him besides a mail-order convenience.

But Mac interpreted her statement literally. ''Easy?'' He grinned. ''Of course. I just made love to my future bride and now it's time to go to sleep. Together.''

He felt fabulous, on top of the world. Certainly, he hadn't felt this sense of optimism and pure well-being for months. Maybe never. Mac closed his eyes. This was neither the time nor the place for reflective introspection. Not that he had much knowledge of such esoteric pastimes. He'd never been the introspective type, but he was sure of this one thing: Reverend Will Franklin had done him one hell of a favor when he'd suggested sending for Kara.

He would have to thank the Rev with a generous donation to the church bell-tower fund or something similar, Mac decided as he drifted into sleep.

Kara lay still, listening to Mac's breathing grow deeper and slower. She decided a change in tactics was in order. Arguing with Mac about sleeping alone was clearly a lost cause. He had stubbornly decided that she was to spend the night here with him and wasn't about to be convinced otherwise. So she would wait until his *permission* was not needed.

The moment she was certain he was asleep, she would slip out of his bed and this room and retreat to the privacy of the guest room next door. Kara lay quietly, wondering when she should make her move. A glowing languor suffused her entire body. Despite her emotional agitation, her body was inordinately relaxed, and the physical relaxation began to overtake her mind.

The room was dark and quiet. Mac had pulled the thick quilt over them, protecting them from the chill in the air. The furnacelike warmth of his body next to hers was cozily enervating. Her eyelids grew heavy. It took so much effort to keep them open that she finally gave up and let them drift shut.

Kara breathed a drowsy sigh. She would lie here for a few more minutes and then get up. Just a few more minutes....

Eight

The insistent buzz of the alarm clock jerked Kara out of a deep sleep. Beside her, Mac groaned and fumbled with the clock before finally shutting it off. Her eyes snapped wide open as the shocking realization dawned....

She was nude in Mac's bed!

Erotic memories of the night before swept over her, along with her ill-fated plan to sneak back into the other room. Instead, she'd fallen asleep in Mac's arms and slept with him the whole night through. Naked!

"Stay in bed and go back to sleep," Mac ordered huskily. "I've got to call the kids for school, but you might as well—"

"I'll get up." Kara quickly bounced out of the bed and fled to the bathroom. She closed the door behind her. And locked it.

Mac heard the telltale click of the lock, and a small smile played around the corners of his mouth. Her modesty amused him. Certainly, her reluctance for him to see her nude this morning was in sharp contrast to her uninhibited passion last night.

Last night. He smiled in remembrance as the sensual memories of certain unforgettable and irresistible scenes rewound in his mind. And along with the feelings of satisfaction and completion from last night came a powerful surge of tenderness. For Kara. She had been so sweet and innocent, yet so passionate and willing.

He had been her first lover. A possessive thrill ran through him. And he would be her only lover. Her husband. He realized that he was eagerly anticipating their wedding, rather than merely resigned to it.

Mac padded to the window, naked, and opened the thick curtains. It was a dismal day, gray and cloudy, with rain pounding against the glass. But the weather did not dampen his high spirits. Whistling cheerfully, he retrieved his toweling robe from the floor, pulled it on and headed out to begin the day.

Kara slipped another stack of buckwheat pancakes onto Brick's plate, marveling at his capacity for food. This was his third serving. Autumn was still working on her first helping that she'd drowned in maple syrup. Lily desultorily sipped tea and nibbled on a piece of toast. Since Clay hadn't yet fully recovered enough to return to school, he was still asleep in his room.

Tai marched into the kitchen, his tail held high, and announced his arrival with a robust meow.

"Tai slept in my bed last night," said Autumn. "When I woke up, he was in the middle of it. He kind of hogged the bed, but I didn't mind," she added graciously.

Tai demanded and was served his breakfast, and he turned his attention to it, ignoring the humans.

"Isn't this great? Having a real home-cooked breakfast!" Mac exclaimed enthusiastically, as he polished off his third stack of buckwheat cakes. "When was the last time we didn't have something cold or nuked in the microwave for break-fast?'' He smiled at Kara. ''The Rev was right. You really are a good cook, Kara.''

''Judging by that gleam in your eye and that bounce in your step and your ungodly cheerful mood this morning, cooking isn't all she's good at,'' Lily drawled.

Kara blushed scarlet and nearly dropped the electric skillet she was lifting into the sink to wash.

''Lily!'' Mac admonished, but he did not sound angry or condemning. He sounded…ungodly cheerful.

''What does Lily mean?'' Autumn demanded, reaching for yet more syrup.

Mac moved it out of her reach. ''It means we're all very glad that Kara is here to fix us breakfast.''

Autumn lunged for the syrup. Mac moved it even farther away from her. The little girl scowled, then turned to her older brother, an unholy gleam in her dark eyes. ''Brick, why are you wearing a plain old white T-shirt and jeans to school today? It's Wacky Tacky Day, Joanna Franklin said so. You're supposed to wear some weird outfit and be in a geek fashion show today.''

''What?'' Brick nearly choked on the milk he was swallowing. ''What are you talking about?''

''Uh-oh,'' Lily murmured ominously.

Autumn gleefully recounted Joanna Franklin's description of the day's festivities.

Brick slammed his empty glass down on the table. ''I'm not going,'' he announced. ''I'll be damned if I'll dress up like some freakoid and parade around the school! Nobody can make me go,'' he added, sending a challenging glare at his uncle.

Mac instantly rose to the challenge. ''Brick, you have to go to school. You weren't there yesterday and you've already missed too many days.''

''Well, I'm going to miss another one,'' Brick interjected defiantly. ''Today.''

He stood. So did Mac.

"Would you two mind postponing the zany shenanigans for a while?" Lily heaved an exasperated sigh. "It's only seven o'clock in the morning."

Kara glanced from Mac to Brick. Both were bristling with male determination and pride. She saw Autumn's smile of satisfaction as the little instigator snatched the now-forgotten bottle of syrup and poured it over the already soggy buckwheat cakes.

"I don't mind if Brick stays home today," Kara dared to say. It was either cower silently and watch another Wilde chase-and-shout episode erupt, or try to intervene. "He can help keep Clay entertained, you know, play video games with him, help him with the make-up work the teacher has sent home, those sorts of things."

"Okay," Brick agreed, beaming his triumph.

"What make-up work?" Mac asked, momentarily distracted. But only momentarily. "The boy is not staying home, Kara. This is not about making choices or choosing sides." He looked as furious with Kara's intervention as Brick was pleased.

"She said I can stay and I'm listening to her, not you," Brick taunted.

"The always dependable divide-and-conquer strategy." Lily looked bored. "It worked so well with Uncle James and Aunt Eve that they were on the verge of divorce before they decided we weren't worth the use of our insurance money, and sent us out here."

"I don't blame Brick for having strong feelings about this dress-like-a-nerd day," Kara said with a calm she was far from feeling. "There was something similar in the junior high school I attended. It was called Nerd Day and everybody was supposed to dress in their most stupid out-of-it clothes. I was in the eighth grade and new to the school. We'd just moved a few months before, and the clothes they wore were different from what we'd worn at my old school. Well, the inevitable happened on Nerd Day. Some of the girls came to school dressed just like me. I realized that I was the nerd role model.'' She shook her head. "It wasn't a very good day.''

"Wow! It really must have stunk to be you!'' Brick exclaimed.

"Well, I think those girls were mean!'' Autumn cried, indignant. "I hope they get kidnapped, I hope they get eaten by cannibals and—''

"It was a long time ago, Autumn,'' Kara interrupted the hexing. "But the underlying result of those kinds of days is that somebody always ends up getting hurt.''

"There are some serious geeks at school and I bet some of the Snot Brigade will dress up like them today,'' Brick said thoughtfully. His brows narrowed. "But Jimmy and I won't let them get away with it. We'll beat the crap out of those creeps for hurting the poor geeks' feelings!'' His eyes glowed with righteous fervor as he turned to his uncle. "I'm going to school today, Uncle Mac. I have to be there. I'll go get my books.'' He stalked from the room.

"I'll get mine, too,'' called Autumn, rushing after him. "I wish our school had Wacky Tacky Day and I could beat up people to help the geeks, too.''

"Brick the Avenging Crusader,'' Lily said, shaking her head. "Inspired by Wacky Tacky Day. But hey, he's going to school of his own free well. You're good, Kara,'' she added admiringly.

Mac smiled. "She's nothing less than brilliant.'' He crossed the kitchen and settled his hands on her waist. "Coming up with that maudlin story was a master stroke of psychology. Brick's actually eager to go to school.'' He pulled her closer and rubbed her nose against his. "Thanks for keeping me from whipping up another major scene, sweetie. Your way was much more effective.''

"At least until Brick begins bloodying all those wacky, tacky students,'' Lily pointed out.

"They're keeping him on a short leash at the school, he

won't get the chance to fight,'' said Mac. ''Just getting him there today was victory, and we owe it to Kara.''

His hands smoothed over her pink-and-white striped cotton wrapper which she'd pulled on for her flight to the kitchen this morning. The presence of the kids, combined with the mundane breakfast chores, allowed her to keep her equilibrium. After the tumultuous passion of last night, she needed stabilizing.

But here was Mac, gazing down at her with dark hungry eyes, fondling her as if they were lovers. Kara trembled. As of last night, they were lovers. She was no longer a virgin. She had a lover. Her body flared with a hot urgency; she felt as if the world was tipping off its axis.

Mac tried to slip his hands under her wrapper. He would have kissed her, then and there, but Kara deftly slipped away from him. The small intimacies—with Lily as an interested observer—were more than she could handle so early in the day. Especially after such a wild soul-shattering night.

''You thought my Nerd Day story was maudlin?'' she asked lightly, striving to create some very necessary distance between them. Necessary for her. Mac was moving in on her again, seemingly striving to get closer.

''Watch it, Uncle Mac,'' warned Lily. ''What you meant to say was that it was a cute but corny story, right?''

Mac grinned. ''Right.''

Kara was nonplussed that they thought she'd deliberately made up the Nerd Day tragedy to prod Brick into defensive action. That maudlin, cute but corny, story had been true, and this was the first time she had ever related her humiliation to anyone. She'd shared the painful memory to let Brick know she understood his reluctance to participate in the dress-up day, that she'd once been a new student among unsympathetic classmates and had suffered the insecurities of not fitting in.

Apparently not only Mac but *all* the Wildes had misinterpreted her this time.

Brick and Autumn traipsed back into the kitchen, lugging their bookbags. Behind them was Webb Asher, wearing the cowboy uniform of jeans, boots and faded flannel shirt.

"The kids let me in." Webb explained his presence. "Since it's raining, we won't be out on the range. I thought the boys would do some work in the barns today?" At Mac's nod of assent, he continued. "I have to pick up a few things in town, so I figured that as long as I'm headed that way, I might as well drive this gang into school."

"Great!" Brick enthused. "We don't have to ride that dorky old bus!"

"Or sit in the dorky Jeep, waiting for it to come," added Autumn.

"The Jeep isn't dorky," Mac protested. He'd cornered Kara by the sink and pulled her back against him, wrapping his arms around her waist. "The school bus stop is on the main road at the end of the drive. When it rains, I've been driving the kids to the stop, so they can wait for the bus in the Jeep and keep out of the rain."

"That fun job will be yours when you marry Uncle Mac, Kara," Lily said dryly. "Just one of the many perks that comes with the live-in position as Mrs. Mac Wilde."

"I could name a few other perks that she will enjoy very much," Mac murmured suggestively, nibbling on the curve of Kara's neck. She blushed and tried to casually disengage his grip on her. When her efforts came to naught, she twisted and squirmed to deny him access to her neck. He lifted his lips but held her firmly against him.

"I can name a perk, too," Autumn boasted. "The satellite dish!"

Everyone in the kitchen grinned, even Kara.

"Grab your books, schoolgirl," Webb commanded Lily. "You don't want to be late, do you?"

Kara turned her head sharply. There was something taunting, something provocative in the ranch manager's tone which caught her attention.... Her eyes swung to Lily who was strolling across the kitchen, her hips swiveling sexily, her dark eyes locked with Webb's.

"Thanks a million for driving them, Webb," Mac said. "I really appreciate it."

"Oh, so do I," Lily said, seconding him. She was standing before Webb, giving him a smile that was at once sultry and challenging and inviting.

Kara gaped at the pair. Was Lily playfully baiting the man again, or was she more deeply involved with him? Could *he* be her secret lover? Though she tried, Kara couldn't gauge Webb's response to the girl. His eyes were cool and assessing as he held Lily's gaze, but what did that mean?

Kara swallowed and anxiously glanced up at Mac. Did he sense some sexual undercurrent between Lily and the ranch manager? But Mac was studying *her* intently, not even glancing in Webb and Lily's direction.

"Clay is still sacked out," Mac murmured in her ear. "Since neither of us has had a shower this morning, let's save time and hot water and do it together."

Kara's heart leapt to her throat. She was so rattled by Mac's wicked grin and his titillating suggestion, she was scarcely aware that the others were on their way out of the kitchen, heading toward the front door.

Mac, on the other hand, was acutely aware of the exact moment of their departure. He scooped Kara up in his arms and strode from the kitchen, down the zigzagging corridor, into his bedroom.

He closed the door behind him, pausing to lock it before he took her mouth in a deep, hungry kiss. Still held high in his arms, Kara clung to him, locking her hands around his neck, desire spinning through her with tornadolike force. His tongue plunged deep inside her mouth and she rubbed it, teased it deeper. She had learned a lot about kissing since her arrival in Montana, she thought dizzily, as the last vestiges of control slipped away from her.

Kara surrendered to the consuming fire of their kisses. She

was excruciatingly aware of every sensual aspect of her lover: the muscular strength of his arms holding her, the solid pressure of his chest against the burgeoning fullness of her breasts, the coffee and maple syrup taste of his mouth and the penetrating heat of his tongue.

She loved the feel of him, his raw male power, his unexpected tenderness. She loved kissing him, touching him. *She loved him.* The words swirled around in her head as she kissed him with all the love and passion in her heart.

They were both breathless and panting when Mac finally lifted his mouth from hers.

"I've been wanting to do that since we woke up this morning," he said against her lips. He took a small sensuous bite. "But you took off like a gazelle, and then we were surrounded by a bunch of underage chaperones."

"Those underage chaperones are the reason I'm here," Kara reminded him. And herself. It was time for a much-needed reality check here. She was in love with Mac, but it wasn't mutual. To forget that fact was foolishly risky, heartbreak guaranteed. She mustn't ever lose sight of the fact that Mac would be making love to whatever woman happened to get off that plane in Helena. It just happened to be her.

"Let's not get into that again," Mac growled, as if he'd read her thoughts. "We made love and you're mine, Kara. And you are, you know. You belong to me."

He erupted with explosive force, astonishing himself. He was not prone to sexual possessiveness, and emotional outbursts over a woman were not his style. At least, not until now. Now...he slowly lowered Kara to her feet, letting her slide down the hard throbbing length of his body, turning the release into a long, provocative caress in itself.

Now things seemed very different. The thought of Kara with anyone but him was intolerable. It wasn't much of a stretch to reach the corresponding tenet—that Kara and no other woman but her was meant to be his wife. It almost explained the Amy debacle in a mystical sort of way. Amy was not Kara; naturally their marriage had been doomed.

His thoughts spooked him. He was far more comfortable focusing on the physical aspects of their relationship than delving into alarming insights about destiny and cosmic ties.

And focusing on the physical was exceptionally easy when his body was pulsating with a passionate need that grew more urgent with each moment. ''Come on.'' He fastened his fingers around her wrist and headed toward the bathroom, dragging her along after him.

It took him seconds to turn on the shower, adjust the water temperature and the spray, then drop his robe to the floor. He turned to Kara, his dark eyes burning. ''Let's get you out of that and into the shower.''

Kara's eyes widened at the sight of him, nude and fully aroused. She'd seen him last night in bed, but this was different. This was broad daylight and he was urging her to strip and get into the shower with him!

''I—I'd really better check on Clay,'' she hedged, suddenly desperately shy. ''If he wakes up—''

''He'll get himself a bowl of cereal and turn on the TV to watch cartoons. There are cartoons broadcast all over the world, so they're on at any given hour of the day or night. Clay always finds them.'' Mac had already unbuttoned her wrapper and was slipping it off her shoulders. His fingers traced the elastic waistband of her white cotton panties. ''Why did you bother putting these on?''

''Mac!'' Kara flushed, scandalized. And tantalized. She watched him pull down her panties, watched his eyes dilate and darken as he brushed his fingers through the soft brown nest of curls.

He pulled her into the shower and under the warm spray. Kara sputtered as water poured over her head and into her eyes and mouth. Mac laughed wickedly. ''Afraid a little water will melt you, sugar?''

''I don't recall you laughing with joy when you got a dousing yesterday,'' Kara reminded him. ''In fact, you went berserk. Just ask Autumn.''

Mac held the soap and lathered his hands. ''Well, that was then, this is now.'' He grinned rakishly. ''Come here.''

''You're breaking your own rule.'' Her legs were shaking, her body quivering. This was all so new to her, but so exciting, so tempting that her inhibitions and reserve seemed to dissolve like the soap bubbles floating in the air. ''Yesterday, you officially banned all water play forever, remember?'' she taunted cheekily.

''I'm lifting the ban.'' Mac caught her in his soapy hands. ''And making an exception to the rule. Because *you* are exceptional, baby.''

His mouth, warm and wet, opened over hers as his soap-slicked hands roamed over her, washing her as he caressed her. His tongue deep in her mouth, he thoroughly soaped her breasts, fondling, then gently squeezing, using his palm and then his fingers until she was moaning with pleasure.

He did the same with the rest of her body, the hollow of her waist and navel, the curves of her hips, the soft swell of her belly. She was primed and ready, waiting with shivering anticipation when his hands slipped between her legs. She gasped his name, clinging to him. She could hardly stand it. It felt so good, *too* good! Such acute pleasure bordered on exquisite sensual pain and she twisted against his hand seeking the release he had given her last night.

''Not yet, baby.'' Mac's voice was a sexy, teasing rasp in her ear.

Kara whimpered in protest and frustration, but he kept up his lusty play, bringing her to the edge again and again, but not allowing her to go over it. Driven wild and wanton, she blindly reached for the hard male length of him, wrapping her fingers around him.

''That's right, honey,'' Mac breathed. ''You need to be taught what you want, and now you're ready for your next lesson. That this will give you more pleasure than my fingers.'' He lifted her, pressing her against the wall and plunged into her, sinking deep into her velvety softness.

Kara cried out, her soapy slender body so aroused that she was in a fever of need. It burned and spread and intensified until she was aware of nothing else but their bodies, joined together, wet and throbbing and swollen with desire.

And then the tension and fever exploded to flash-point, lifting them to the heights of ecstasy, to a summit of pure sensual rapture....

Afterward, a languid and rather dazed Kara took a turn at soaping Mac, while the water sluiced the suds off her own body. They shampooed their hair, and they flicked soap bubbles and water at each other, thoroughly violating the house ban on water play.

"Appendectomy?" Mac guessed, tracing his finger along the faded white scar on her belly. "A long time ago?"

Kara nodded. "I was six. I got sick in school and was taken to the hospital, and operated on later the same day. I was scared at first, but my dad rearranged his schedule so I wouldn't be alone in the hospital. My mother was very busy—did I mention that she was a buyer for a department store? She was on an important buying trip and couldn't come home, but I didn't mind." Her eyes misted in reminiscence. "My dad was there. He even slept on one of those chair-bed contraptions at night."

"Your dad. That would be Reverend Will?"

"Yes." Kara nodded her head. "I always thought of him as my father back then, and in those old memories, he still is."

"It must've been weird for you," Mac said thoughtfully. "He was your father and then he wasn't. He turned into some kind of faux uncle whom you seldom saw."

"It was weird." The word didn't come close to describing her pain and sense of abandonment but Kara let it stand.

"No wonder you had trouble trusting any man after the

way you'd been dumped.'' Mac was proud of his insight. ''It explains why you stayed a virgin all those years.''

''Please! No armchair psychology,'' Kara said lightly. She pushed open the shower door. She did not feel like being analyzed by Mac Wilde. Nor did she want him feeling pity for her or the child she had been.

Mac followed her out of the shower. ''You're here with me to stay, Kara.'' He caught her water-slick arm, halting her in her tracks. ''You proved it by trusting me enough to sleep with me.''

''Maybe I was just sick and tired of being the oldest living virgin on the planet.''

He laughed. ''Well, now you're not anymore. You're my sweet and sexy fiancée. My passionate little mail-order bride.'' Wrapping her in a thick blue towel, he began to rub her dry.

She closed her eyes, enjoying his ministrations. Too much. ''Mac, I know you need someone to look after the kids for you, but you have to seriously consider what marrying me means to them. If you—if we—decide things aren't working between us a few years from now, they'll be hurt, especially Clay and Autumn.''

''That's not going to happen,'' Mac said stubbornly. ''It will work, Kara.''

It would've been the ideal time for him to tell her that he'd fallen irrevocably in love with her, and that they would never part, sighed a wistfully romantic little voice inside her head. Kara wanted to hear him say it so badly that she almost didn't care if he were lying.

But honest, up-front, blunt Mac didn't lie. And he didn't say it.

Kara told herself she appreciated his honesty, that she could never trust a smooth operator who said things he didn't mean.

Nearly half an hour later, the two of them walked down

the hall together, dried and dressed, Mac's arm draped possessively around Kara's waist.

"It's still raining," he remarked. Raindrops pounded hard and steady against the house, and a glance out a window revealed no break in the sky's gray cloud cover. "Looks like I'll be stuck in my office today. I needed to catch up on the paperwork, but I hate it."

"Hate the paperwork or hate being inside?" asked Kara.

"Both. I'm a rancher because I like the outdoors. I don't know how the pencil pushers in those city skyscrapers take it, being cooped up and inactive, day after day."

"That was me," Kara murmured. "A pencil pusher in the commerce department in downtown D.C."

"*Was* being the operative word. You're not going back there, Kara."

The possessive command in his voice thrilled her when they were in bed, but out of it, she felt the need to assert herself. He had to know that there were times when he could dominate her and times when he most certainly could not. "I'll have to go back, Mac, I—"

"No." His tone brooked no argument. "We'll pay a moving company to pack up your stuff and send it out here. You can submit your resignation to the commerce department and tie up whatever loose ends there might be by phone or fax. You're staying here, Kara. I'm not going to let you go."

"Actually, I don't have to resign. My job was phased out in the last round of budget cuts." It was difficult making the admission, she felt like a flop, but Kara felt compelled to be honest with him. How could she not, after what they'd shared? "I'm taking my week's vacation now, and then I have to go back to wrap up my final two weeks."

"You're not going back. Who cares if you're there for your final weeks? If they were stupid enough to fire you, they don't get the benefit of your presence. We do." He kissed her, hard and long. "Your days as a city statistician are over, honey. Get used to it."

She already was, and she was loving it, Kara thought dizzily.

The sounds from the television drew them into the big living room-den. Clay was sitting on one of the bright floor pillows, eating a bowl of cereal, his eyes glued to the big screen which featured the Roadrunner outrunning his hapless coyote pursuer.

Tai crouched on the deep sill of the bay window, staring as a squirrel dashed from tree branch to tree branch. He ignored Mac and Kara's arrival. So did Clay.

"You see? Cartoons." Mac cast Kara an I-told-you-so-glance. "The electronic baby-sitter is truly a gift from the gods." He dropped a kiss on the top of her head. "I guess I'll head into my office now. See you later."

He was turning Clay over to her, and she accepted the responsibility.

Mac watched her sit down beside the child and strike up a conversation. Thank God she was here! He'd spent some rainy days cooped up in the house with Clay, and felt himself perilously close to losing it on those trying occasions. Today, Kara was in charge. Whistling, he headed into his office to face the hated paperwork.

The phone rang a half hour later as Kara was sitting at the kitchen table watching Clay laboriously print spelling words on a piece of yellow lined paper. She automatically answered it.

"This is Bear Creek High School, calling to verify that Lily Wilde is still sick," came a brisk voice over the line.

"Still sick," Kara repeated blankly, but the attendance officer took it for an affirmation.

"Thank you. We hope she's feeling better soon." The woman rang off.

Kara stared at the receiver in her hand and a chill of apprehension rippled through her. Lily wasn't in school today? In her mind's eye, she saw this morning's scene unfold once again—Lily sauntering across the room to Webb who watched her, his green eyes cool and intent, his hard mouth drawn tight.

Was that how it had been? Or was she letting her imagination run away with her? Webb might be completely innocent. He might've dropped Lily off at the school not knowing that she intended to ditch, to slip away to "paradise" with her mysterious lover.

What if Webb Asher really was that man?

She would ask Lily point blank as soon as she came home, Kara decided. Until then, she ought to keep her suspicions to herself. The prospect of presenting her theory to Mac without any evidence was daunting, indeed. He'd thanked Webb for driving the kids to school today! If he thought that his ranch manager had absconded to "paradise" with his niece....

Kara shivered.

It was still raining when Lily arrived home with Brick and Autumn later that afternoon.

"We didn't have to take the bus home and walk up that long muddy driveway," Autumn said happily. "Webb picked us up at school and drove us right to the door."

Kara nodded in response, but her attention was focused on Lily. She'd become perceptive at recognizing visible signs of spent passion, and Lily's dreamy-eyed face was an unmistakable display of exactly that. The teenager went immediately to her own room, pleading a headache. Kara didn't buy it, but her plans to question Lily privately were foiled by Mac and the three younger children.

They hung around the kitchen, munching on peanut butter bars she and Clay had baked earlier, talking and joking and bidding for her attention.

Mac smiled his satisfaction as he watched the kids consume their snack. Nobody had thrown food or committed any other untoward acts since entering the house. The aura of calm and order was a dramatic change from the chaotic pre-

Kara era. Mac watched her interact with the kids and was filled with a sense of rightness.

And with desire. Just looking at her, watching her move, turned him on.

She was wearing a gray pleated skirt, short but not outrageously so, and a sand-colored jersey and printed vest. He admired her legs as she walked and he ogled her breasts as she stretched and bended. He knew she was wearing lacy peach panties and a matching bra under that tastefully demure outfit; he'd watched her put them on this morning.

And then there were those stockings she wore—not cumbersome panty hose but sheer thigh-high stockings, which miraculously stayed up and on without a garter belt, though he certainly wouldn't have minded her wearing that fantasy-inducing item. But those stockings of hers were the stuff of fantasies, too. She'd shown him the lacy elastic bands at the tops of the stockings which kept them in place, and he'd stroked the silky soft skin, bared between her panties and stockings. He'd been ready to take her back to bed right then and there, though nature should have decreed such a surge of desire impossible after that tryst in the shower such a short time ago. But the desire was there, hot and urgent, and he'd had to exert considerable willpower to hold back, knowing that Clay was undoubtedly up and about.

Mac's thoughts drifted to that passionate interlude in the shower, then back to the intimate ardor of last night. He felt himself growing hard, the blood pooling thick and hot. He wanted to dispatch the kids to somewhere else and carry Kara back to his room....

"I'm going with Courtney Egan now," Brick announced rather proudly. "She's the prettiest, coolest girl in the eighth grade. Maybe even in the whole school."

"Tom Egan's daughter?" Mac was fully attentive to the conversation now. Tom Egan was a local attorney, a guy he'd grown up with. He hoped his friendship with Tom would survive Brick's sudden relationship with the pretty little Courtney.

"Everybody looked so stupid dressed in those geeky clothes today," Brick chortled as he helped himself to his fourth peanut butter bar. "Wacky Tacky Day! How lame can you get? Only me and Jimmy looked cool. Courtney dumped Chad Walters and told her friend Bethany that she liked me and asked me to her party on Friday. I said okay, and she wrote me a note."

"And so now you're going together?" Kara asked. "My, that happened quickly." Her eyes darted to Mac who was watching her with hooded eyes. "A regular whirlwind romance," she added. She felt lighter than air when Mac chuckled at her small joke. It was fun being with someone who shared her sense of humor.

"Brick is as impulsive as I am," he muttered out of earshot of Brick. "Let's hope he's not as fast, hmm?" Mac grinned salaciously and swung out an arm to catch her by the hand.

He lifted it to his mouth and pressed his lips against her palm. Tingles of sensation rippled through her.

Reverend Will Franklin's arrival a few minutes later interrupted the camaraderie. Mac invited the pastor in, but he wasn't pleased by the impromptu visit. He was polite but cool toward the pastor.

Reverend Franklin ignored him. His attention was focused exclusively on Kara.

"You simply must come to dinner tonight, Kara dear," he insisted, taking her hand in his. "Ginny is cooking a wonderful meal, and we all hope that you'll come along with us to the church's fall white elephant and clothesline sale afterward. Tonight is the first night of it, and you'll have a chance to meet some of our friends in town and—"

"Elephants?" Clay piped up. "*White* elephants? I saw white tigers at the zoo one time. How come the church is going to have elephants there? Is it like a circus?"

The reverend frowned. "It's not polite to interrupt when others are talking, son. Let me finish and then I'll explain."

Clay was undaunted. "I want to go see those elephants, too. Can we, Uncle Mac? Please!"

"A white elephant sale has nothing to do with elephants," Mac explained patiently. "People bring things they don't use or don't want anymore and sell them to other people who want and can use them."

"Stuff like clotheslines?" Clay was perplexed.

Reverend Franklin made a clicking sound of impatience.

"People bring clothes they've outgrown or don't want anymore to a clothesline sale." Kara took her turn supplying the explanations. "They don't charge very much for them, so the people who buy the clothes get a good bargain."

"I have lots of clothes I don't want," Autumn exclaimed excitedly. "Can I get money for them?"

"No. The clothes have already been donated and tagged, and the money goes to the church." Reverend Franklin's stentorian tones resonated throughout the kitchen. He cleared his throat and cast the Wilde children a dismissive glance. "We're veering far from the subject at hand, which is Kara coming to town with me."

"I want Aunt Kara to stay here, not go to some dumb elephant clothes sale," whined Clay. "Tell her she can't go, Uncle Mac."

Kara tensed. She saw Autumn and Brick glance from the reverend to their uncle, their heads moving back and forth like spectators at a tennis match.

"Of course, she can go," Reverend Franklin said firmly. "Kara is not a prisoner here, and it is time she visited with her friends in town."

"What if she wants to stay with her friends here at the ranch?" Autumn asked innocently enough. But her dark eyes sparkled with an instigating gleam.

"Yeah," agreed Brick. "She's my uncle's girlfriend, and you can't tell her what to do. Only he can!"

Mac smiled at the boy, a grin of masculine approval that set Kara's teeth on edge. She could not let such unbridled machismo go unchallenged. For herself, for young Courtney Egan and every other woman, present and future, in the Wilde men's lives, she had to take a stand.

"I'm not exactly your uncle's girlfriend, Brick." Kara's cheeks pinked. Well, she wasn't, certainly not in the usual sense of the word. "Furthermore, men don't order their girlfriends around, women make up their own minds. No one tells me what to do," she added resolutely.

"You mean you can do anything you want?" Autumn wanted to know.

"Yes. Well, anything within reason," Kara clarified. "Anything that isn't at odds with the rules and responsibilities and laws that must be followed," she added, attempting to clarify even further. She didn't want the Wilde children believing that adulthood was a barbaric free-for-all!

"That doesn't sound like doing anything you want, to me." Brick smirked. "Uncle Mac makes the rules and you don't break them. See, he does tell you what to do."

"Uncle Mac is the boss around here," Clay declared, sounding as if he was echoing a much-repeated quote.

Apparently he was, for Mac nodded his approval. "That's right, pal. And don't you forget it," Clay chimed in with him on the last part.

"Could we get back to the matter at hand?" Reverend Franklin was impatient. "Kara, I do hope you'll join us tonight. I have been so looking forward to spending some time with you."

"I would like to," Kara said. "I'm going to," she added, more for Mac's sake than the reverend's.

"All right, you may have dinner with the Franklins, Kara," Mac agreed, though he did not look particularly pleased.

"How magnanimous of the boss to grant me permission," Kara said through gritted teeth. She turned to her ex-stepfather. "Yes, I'll come. Thank you, Reverend."

A shadow crossed the pastor's face. "Not even Uncle Will, anymore?"

"That was simply a courtesy title for a little girl to use," Mac said coolly. "'Daddy' was another one, wasn't it? But Kara is all grown up now, Rev, and the title Mrs. Macauley Wilde will be lasting and for real."

Kara's eyes met Mac's and she saw the determination and the challenge there. She wanted to assert herself; she would've if Uncle Will and the kids weren't present.

Mac, however, had no trouble asserting himself in the presence of anybody.

"Did I mention that the kids and I are going to have dinner in town ourselves tonight?" Mac's voice warmed considerably as he turned to the children. "Clay is no longer contagious and he's feeling good. I think he's ready for an outing. How about it, kids? Burger Barn or Pizza Ranch?"

That set off an internal argument among the three young Wildes.

Mac walked Kara and the pastor to the front door. "After we eat, we'll stop by the white elephant sale, since Clay is so fired up over it."

"Fired up?" That was too much for Kara. She felt as if she were being steamrolled, first by her uncle Will, then by Mac. "He doesn't even know what it is! He—"

"Then it'll be a good learning experience for him," Mac said. "We'll meet up with you at the church hall later this evening and I'll drive you back, Kara. No use having the Rev make another round trip out here."

"I was going to suggest that she spend the night at our house," Reverend Will said tightly.

Mac shook his head. "I'm bringing her back here." He hauled Kara against his chest in the most proprietary way, his arms holding her tight for a long moment. He rested his jaw against her temple. "I'll see you later, honey."

"You sound so grim. Are you making her a promise or a threat?" demanded Reverend Will.

"That's for her to decide," Mac said, releasing her.

Nine

"**K**ara, my dear girl, I can't begin to tell you how sorry I am for bringing you to Bear Creek under false pretenses." Reverend Will sounded distraught as he drove his gray Ford along the rain-swept road toward the town. "I can never apologize enough for getting you mixed up with the Wildes. I am so truly sor—"

"Uncle Will, it's okay," Kara interjected. The poor man had been apologizing since they'd gotten into the car.

"No, no, it's not okay, at all. I can see that Mac is determined to go through with this wedding. Though I admire his dedication to his brother's children, I do not think it's fair that he is trying to railroad you into a one-sided relationship, strictly for his own benefit."

Kara stayed silent. She felt uncomfortable confiding just how far her relationship with Mac had progressed in such a short time.

"Mac is a strong man, a dominating man," the reverend continued. "A good man, but he is accustomed to having his own way. I'm afraid of what he'll do to get it. I believe he'd go to any length to make you marry him and stay on that ranch with those *difficult* children.''

"They're just active and high-spirited,'' Kara defended the Wilde bunch.

"My dear, you needn't choose your words with such discretion, you can speak frankly with me. I'm concerned about you, Kara. I don't want you to be trapped out there by—''

"Uncle Will,'' Kara interrupted. "I think I'd better tell you that I am seriously considering marrying Mac.''

The reverend wiped his brow with a crumpled handkerchief. "I would be delighted to hear that news if I thought you knew what you were doing, Kara. But you don't! Mac has kept you out there, isolated you...'' Will swallowed hard. "He's used his undeniable sex appeal and...experience to hustle you into a marriage of convenience. Convenient for him, that is.''

Kara tried and failed to stop the blush which suffused her cheeks. "Mac hasn't hustled me into anything.''

"I'm sure he's convinced you of that. I'm sure he had you believing that you have been a more than willing participant. He's got you so bamboozled you'll think whatever he wants you to think.''

Kara sighed. "Mac's not some kind of villainous cad, Uncle Will. You wanted me to marry him, remember? You were the one who suggested that I would—'' she cleared her throat and stared at the windshield wipers swishing back and forth "—suit his purposes.''

Reverend Will turned crimson. "I hoped you two could make a match,'' he conceded. "But not like this! I intended for you two to become acquainted in the normal way and develop a compatible relationship that might hopefully lead to marriage. Instead, he practically kidnapped you at the airport, held you prisoner at the ranch...''

"As you can see, I'm not being held prisoner, Uncle Will. I'm here with you right now, aren't I?''

"He's allowing you a few hours away to delude you into thinking that you aren't being held captive. Which, of course, you are. You'll notice how insistent he was about taking you back to the ranch tonight."

"Yes." A frisson of excitement heated her. She thought of the glitter of desire in Mac's dark eyes, of his body's tautness when he'd pulled her into his arms before sending her on her way. He wanted her, he hadn't bothered to hide it. He wanted her back in his bed tonight.

Heady stuff for a woman who'd been feeling like the rejectee on the *Old Maid* card only a week ago, Kara thought wryly. But while Uncle Will was right that Mac had used "sex appeal and experience" to his advantage, it wasn't the only lure this mail-order marriage of convenience held for her. By marrying Mac, she would acquire a home and a family.

She cast a covert glance at her former stepfather. She'd felt superfluous and unnecessary since her mother and Will's divorce. They had both gone on to love others who loved them, but Kara hadn't belonged anywhere—until she'd met the Wildes and found that they needed her as much as she needed them.

But how to explain that unexpected, profound bond to Will Franklin? Kara knew she never could.

"Where is your common sense, Kara? Where is your pride?" the reverend lamented. "You used to be such a down-to-earth, practical child. It isn't *you* that Mac wants, it's a keeper for those kids. And while he certainly doesn't mind using you physically, his actions are not based on caring and love and respect. He doesn't see you as an individual. He would be perfectly willing to marry any young woman who agreed to—" he paused and coughed discreetly "—to meet his terms."

"Mac has been honest about why he wants to marry me, Uncle Will. He hasn't tried to dupe me or deceive me. Honesty is a sound basis for a relationship, isn't it? We could have a successful marriage based on—''

"Mac didn't have to dupe or deceive you, Kara. You're doing a spectacular job of doing it yourself. I know from my own personal experience that the kind of marriage you're considering won't work."

He drew a deep breath. "I was deeply in love with your mother and I wanted to marry her so badly, I didn't mind when she told me she didn't love me, that if she married me, it would be strictly because she needed a husband to support her and her child, who, of course, was you. And it all blew up in my face when she met Drew Ansell and fell madly in love with him. I don't want you to suffer that kind of heartbreak, Kara."

Kara didn't say another word during the drive into town. Reverend Will did all the talking. More about how Mac was using her. How he didn't value or appreciate her as a unique individual but viewed her as merely a commodity and a convenience, interchangeable with any other woman.

The longer Uncle Will bemoaned her lot, the worse she felt. Fungible. Unlovable. Undesirable. Replaceable by any woman at any time. Kara was totally demoralized by the time the reverend swung his car into the driveway of a neat frame house on a well-kept, tree-lined street.

"Kara, before we go inside..." He sounded uncomfortable and kept his eyes straight ahead. "Tricia and Joanna don't know that I was married before. Ginny never wanted to tell them. She felt they might be...traumatized, knowing that their father used to, uh, love a woman who wasn't their mother."

"I think Ginny was the one who's been traumatized by that fact," Kara said quietly. "It sounds like she still is. But you don't have to worry about me saying anything to your daughters about your marriage to my mother. I can simply say you knew my family when you lived back East."

Reverend Will nodded, his expression one of regret mingled with relief.

Ginny, Tricia and Joanna welcomed her cordially. As the minister's family, they were quite accustomed to entertaining guests in their home, and Kara knew she was being treated as well as any friend or parishioner. The meal—Montana steaks, fresh fall vegetables and apple pie—was delicious.

Conversation flowed easily enough during dinner, though Kara remained on guard. But Ginny didn't betray a hint of her former animosity. Reverend Will had a seemingly endless supply of amusing anecdotes and, in between, Kara fielded eager questions about Brick from Joanna. The young girl had a whopping crush on Mac's nephew, despite Will and Ginny's tight-lipped disapproval at the mere mention of the boy's name. Tricia made a few catty remarks about Lily, which Kara pretended not to comprehend.

It wasn't until after dinner—when the Franklin daughters were in the kitchen doing their clean-up chores, and Reverend Will was called to the phone—that Kara was left alone with Ginny. Though she knew it was ridiculous—she was no longer eight years old, she was twenty-six!—Kara felt her palms begin to sweat, and apprehension rose like bile in her throat. Now that there was no audience, she half expected Ginny to drop her polite facade and turn into the archetypical wicked faux stepmother before her very eyes.

"How is your mother?" Ginny asked, and Kara nearly dropped the cup of coffee she was drinking.

It took her a moment to gather her scattered thoughts. "She's fine. Thank you for asking." The silence was heavy as lead. "Mother and Drew moved to North Carolina seven years ago," Kara offered, desperate to fill the void. "She's still a buyer with the Miller-Richards department-store chain, and Drew has his law practise down there. They're very busy." She felt herself winding down under Ginny's steady stare.

"Your mother was one of the most beautiful women I've ever seen," Ginny said tersely.

Kara waited for the inevitable "You don't look a bit like her."

Surprisingly, it didn't come.

"I couldn't believe Will would marry someone who looked like me after being married to a raving beauty like your mother," Ginny murmured, her eyes darting to the door, making sure her daughters could not hear. "And I couldn't understand how she could've walked out on a wonderful man like Will. I kept expecting her to come to her senses, to realize what she'd given up and show up on our doorstep to reclaim Will." A dark flush suffused Ginny's neck and spread upward.

Kara felt a swift rush of empathy. Wasn't her own situation depressingly similar to what Ginny Franklin believed she'd faced all those years ago?

She was in love with a man who wouldn't have chosen her but was willing to settle for her for strictly practical reasons. Did that knowledge ever cease to be painful? Surely Ginny Franklin wasn't still hurting after all these years!

"I'm sure Will wouldn't have married you if he didn't love you," Kara said, to be kind. But she wasn't at all sure. She well knew Mac was willing to marry her without loving her. And according to Uncle Will, her mother had married him without loving him.

"I've been wanting to talk to you, woman to woman, to clear the air." Ginny's smile was strained. "From what I hear, you might very well become a permanent resident at the Double R Ranch. As a member of our congregation, we'll be seeing each other regularly."

Kara did not reply. Away from Mac and the children and having listened to Will's and Ginny's views on love and life, a gloomy pessimism had begun to settle over her.

If Mac didn't love her—and she knew he didn't—how long would it take him to tire of her? He was currently sexually interested in her because she was easily available—right under his roof!—and as Lily had so bluntly pointed out, he'd been without sex for quite some time. She meant nothing to him, as Uncle Will had so acutely assessed. Nothing at all. And that being the case…

Suppose that sometime in the future Mac met a woman and fell passionately in love with her? Her mother had ended her marriage without a second thought when she'd fallen head-over-heels in love with another man.

Kara winced. People did not behave rationally when they were in love. She was walking, talking proof of that, willing to marry Mac after knowing him only a few days, fully aware that he didn't love her.

She considered her options. Was living in Washington with her cat and scrambling to pay bills while looking for work any worse than being rejected by the man you love, in favor of *his* new love? As for the kids, well, if Mac wanted someone else, the kids' opinions wouldn't matter, anyway. Kara had learned that sad lesson when she was just a kid herself.

"I was very surprised when Will told me you were out here visiting Mac Wilde," Ginny continued, oblivious to Kara's troubled silence. "I wasn't aware that you two even knew each other, but of course, I suppose it wasn't unusual that your paths would cross, with your stepfather and the Wilde brothers both being active in environmental causes."

So that was how Reverend Will had explained her connection to Mac and her presence in Bear Creek, without involving himself at all. Kara was rather impressed with his inventiveness.

She thought of Mac, unwilling to go along with any ruse to romanticize their relationship. He hadn't needed even to pretend to woo her; she'd fallen for him and ended up in his bed, anyway. To her dismay, tears filled her eyes. She quickly, forcefully willed them away.

"Will your mother be coming out for the wedding?" Ginny asked, a little too casually.

"There are no definite wedding plans." Kara's cheeks grew warm, and she averted her eyes from Ginny's sharply curious gaze.

"I can understand your hesitation. Oh, not concerning Mac himself, of course. He is so good-looking, a rugged and rough rancher that women have been swooning over for years!" Ginny sobered and leaned closer to Kara, lowering her voice to a whisper. "But having to take on his brother Reid's children practically negates Mac's very considerable appeal. Those four are a handful, and that's putting it very kindly."

Kara merely shrugged. She had no intention of discussing the Wildes with Ginny Franklin. But Ginny was bent on discussing them, no input from Kara required.

"As a newlywed, you'll want to be alone with your husband, but those kids will be around," the older woman said, grimacing. "And later on, when you have your first baby, you'll resent having to take time and attention from your own child to give to those other kids. Oh, if I were you, I would do everything in my power to send those kids back to James and Eve, or to either grandparent. Why should you and Mac be stuck with them?"

Kara stared at her, nonplussed. Did Ginny realize she was describing her antipathy toward her husband's ex-stepchild, who just happened to be her? She realized something else, too. Since she knew how it felt to be an unwanted child, she would make a conscious effort never to make any child feel like an outsider in their home. But whether or not she would have a chance to make good on her vow within the Wilde family circle was another matter. Right now she felt too raw, too vulnerable, to even think of a future with anyone but Tai in it.

Reverend Will entered the dining room, his face wreathed in smiles. "I'm off the phone and the girls have finished in the kitchen. Are you lovely ladies ready to go to the sale and hunt for bargains?"

"We certainly are." Ginny rose and planted a wifely kiss

on Will's cheek. "I think you'll enjoy yourself, Kara. Our annual clothesline and white elephant sale has become a fall tradition in Bear Creek. It isn't just for church members, everybody in town comes, to buy or sell or just to socialize. And there are always some wonderful bargains to be found, too."

"And some unbelievably ugly junk." This, from Tricia who had joined them. "Remember that hideous birdbath the Semmlers donated one year? We nearly died laughing when old Mr. Jamison actually bought it and put it in his front yard."

"Don't be unkind, Tricia," the reverend said mildly. "Remember, one man's junk is another man's treasure."

There seemed to be an abundance of junk at the white elephant sale with not much treasure to be found, Kara thought as she followed Will and Ginny through the maze of tables set up in the church basement. The couple stopped to talk to everyone and introduced Kara to some as "a family friend from back East" and to others as "Mac Wilde's young lady friend."

Kara tried to fend off questions about Mac and wished that the Franklins would stick solely to the "friend from back East" identity for her. She met countless people and had trouble keeping all the names and faces straight. Ginny hadn't been exaggerating when she'd said everybody in town came to the fall sale. With all the interested stares and murmurs that surrounded her, Kara felt as if she were on display along with the white elephants, a curious piece of merchandise to be inspected by one and all.

When Will and Kara were cornered by a garrulous elder man, Mr. Jamison—the proud owner of the hideous birdbath, Kara presumed—Ginny continued her rounds. The next time Kara spotted her, she was in earnest conversation with a striking redhead.

Kara noticed that the redhead kept glancing over at her.

Her glances were not at all friendly, and upon being motioned over by Ginny to join them, Kara wasn't surprised to learn that the young woman, named Jill Finlay, had once been "quite close" to Mac.

"It hurt to refuse Mac's proposal, but I told him that the only children I intend to raise are my own," Jill said bluntly. "If you think you can marry Mac and talk him into sending those kids away, you're in for a nasty shock. He is absolutely committed to keeping them with him."

"I told Kara that. She is undecided about marrying him," Ginny added.

"Well, of course she is!" Jill thawed a bit. "What woman in her right mind would want to move in with those brats? When even Tonya turned him down—she is thirty-four, divorced and desperate—I think Mac realized how unrealistic it is to expect a woman to take on the thankless burden of those horrific kids."

Kara had heard enough. "Oh, I like the kids," she said coolly. "I have no qualms at all about living with them. It's the idea of living with Mac that's holding me back."

She walked off, flashing a brilliant smile as the two women gaped at her.

"Aunt Kara! Hi, Aunt Kara! We're here!" Kara was leafing through a stack of old records, from ancient 78s to the currently defunct 45s, when Clay and Autumn came running up to her.

She was so glad to see them, she almost hugged them. But they were bouncing around too much to catch for even a quick squeeze.

"We ate at Pizza Ranch," Autumn exclaimed. "Now I want to buy something. There's a kit that has beads and strings and you can make bracelets and necklaces!"

"Would you buy me that G.I. Joe torpedo launcher over at the toy table, Aunt Kara?" pleaded Clay. "It's four dollars and it's practically brand-new but I forgot my money."

"You haven't played with your G.I. Joes since we came

to Montana, stupid,'' Autumn scorned. ''You said you only like those weird Power Rangers now.''

''Well, I like both! You don't know everything, Aw-dumb!'' Clay gave his sister a push, sending her backward into a table loaded with piles of magazines. At least fifty issues hit the floor.

Autumn burst into noisy tears and rubbed her arm. ''I think it's broken!'' she howled. ''In three different places!''

''You said I was stupid, you said Power Rangers were weird!'' wailed Clay, building up a defense for himself.

Kara noticed that all eyes were on them. And there were so very many pairs of eyes! Was the entire population of Bear Creek watching them? Mac, however, was nowhere to be seen. Ignoring the multitude of onlookers, Kara examined Autumn's arm and pronounced it not broken and then began to pick up the magazines. She quietly suggested that the children help. Neither did. Both of them were crying.

Brick arrived as she placed the last magazine on top of the table. ''Shut up,'' he greeted his sister and brother. ''You look like geeks, crying like little babies.''

''We do not!'' Autumn said indignantly. Her tears, and Clay's, instantly ceased.

''Where are Lily and your uncle Mac?'' Kara asked Brick. She noticed that although the stares were less overt, she and the Wilde kids were still the main attraction.

''Lily said she still had a headache and wanted to stay home,'' said Brick. ''Uncle Mac thought she was faking it so she could sneak out while we weren't around. But he fixed her good! He asked Webb to come up to the house and make sure she didn't leave.''

''Oh, he fixed her good, all right,'' Kara said grimly. If her theory was correct—but oh, she hoped it wasn't—Mac's plan was akin to putting the fox in charge of guarding the chicken coop.

''And Uncle Mac is still with *her*,'' Brick addressed his

sister and brother who both groaned in disgust. "They're outside laughing it up."

Autumn and Clay groaned again.

"Her?" Kara repeated. Her mouth was suddenly quite dry.

"Marcy Tanner." Brick supplied the name. "She sat with us at Pizza Ranch and tried to be all friendly with Uncle Mac. It was sick." He scowled his disapproval.

"She didn't talk to us, she hates us," Autumn added. "Tricia Franklin told Lily about all the women who wouldn't go out with Uncle Mac anymore 'cause we were here, and Marcy Tanner was one of 'em."

"Aunt Kara, if I tell you a secret, a bad secret, will you still buy me that G.I. Joe torpedo launcher?" whispered Clay, tugging on Kara's sleeve.

Kara followed the sudden turning of both Autumn's and Brick's heads and saw Mac enter the church basement with a petite blonde clinging to his arm. She was all smiles and big blue eyes and dimples, and Mac was gazing down at her, smiling, too.

Kara felt a searing stab of jealousy slice through her. It took every bit of her considerable restraint to keep from racing to Mac's side and pulling the adorable blonde away from him, to perhaps bloody those enchanting dimples. And then she would start in on Mac....

The violence of her emotions both stunned and alarmed her. Acting out primitive passion had never been her style. But then, until she'd met Mac Wilde she had never experienced passion in any form. Kara felt a sickening lump in her throat, which seemed to expand and move lower, to settle like lead in her belly.

"Don't worry, she'll be gone soon," Autumn stood on tiptoe to whisper in Kara's ear.

Was she so very obvious? Kara cringed. She struggled to maintain an outward calm.

"Yeah, we fixed it so we'd be rid of her." Brick chuckled

Anxiety slowly penetrated the despair engulfing her. Kara

looked at the children who appeared quite pleased with themselves. "What did you do?" she asked nervously.

"Swiped her wallet!" Autumn exclaimed gleefully. "Brick took it out of her purse and I hid it in the ladies' bathroom at the restaurant."

"As soon as she goes to buy something, she'll see that it's missing." Brick laughed sharply. "Then she'll have to go back to get it. We'll be outta here by the time she finds it and comes back."

Kara was aghast. "That was an awful thing to do. You both know stealing is wrong, and that's what you did—you stole!" Her voice shook. It was getting harder to keep her cool. "What if someone else steals her wallet from the bathroom and she can't get it back? You have to tell here where it is right now."

"Hey, there's Courtney Egan!" Brick's eyes lit up as a cute brunette waved to him across the room. "I'm going to go for a walk with her outside. See you guys later."

"Are you going to kiss her?" Autumn called after him.

Brick flashed a startlingly wolfish grin and dashed off.

"Will you buy it for me, Aunt Kara?" Clay tugged again on her arm.

Kara felt her head start to spin. It was easy to lose focus with so much competition for her attention. Mac and Marcy. Lily and Webb. Brick and Courtney. Clay and Autumn's fight, which had yet to be addressed. And, of course, the loss of the hapless Marcy's wallet. The Wildes were not only formidable, they were relentless.

"Please, Aunt Kara!" Clay begged. "I'll tell you the secret."

"Yes, all right. What secret? But Clay, no more pushing your sister," Kara said distractedly. "Promise?"

"I promise." Clay beamed.

"And no more calling Clay stupid or weird, Autumn. Now you have to tell Marcy Tanner that she doesn't have her wallet," Kara added.

"Marcy Tanner is ugly." Autumn scowled. "And she eats spit."

"Autumn, that's revolting!" Kara shuddered at the imagery. Granted it was less revolting than Autumn's cannibal tales, but not much.

Clay laughed uproariously. "I spit in Marcy's salad!" he boasted, grinning from ear to ear. "And she didn't even notice. She ate the whole salad!"

"Every last bite." Autumn giggled. "It was so gross I almost threw up all over the table."

"That would've lent an appetizing touch to the meal," Kara murmured. Her stomach was still roiling from Clay's gleeful confession. It was definitely time to assert her adult authority.

"You both treated Marcy Tanner terribly and you owe her an apology." She squared her shoulders and gazed steadily at Clay and Autumn.

"After I get my launcher," said Clay.

"After I get that kit with the beads," said Autumn.

"We aren't doing anything or buying anything until you do the right thing," Kara said quietly. "And the right thing is to tell Marcy Tanner about the wallet and apologize for...for being mean to her. You don't have to go into detail," she added. Though she did not feel particularly charitable toward the flirtatious blonde, Kara felt obliged to protect her from full disclosure.

"I'll wait here while you tell her." One thing she was *not* going to do was trot over to Mac like some pathetically eager puppy, Kara vowed. Although Reverend Will claimed otherwise, she had not abandoned either her pride or her common sense.

Autumn and Clay exchanged glances. Kara waited, half expecting them to pitch a tantrum of nuclear proportion. She had no idea what to do if they did. But she did not back down.

"Okay, we'll do it," Autumn said at last. She grabbed

Clay's hand, whispering to him as they ran over to Mac and Marcy Tanner.

Kara, along with everybody else, watched and listened as Marcy Tanner let out a scream and then lunged toward Clay and Autumn. But the children were too fast for her. They ran away, laughing, heading straight for Kara.

Marcy took a swing at Mac but her aim was off, and he dodged the blow. With another shriek, the blonde stomped out of the building. The entire scene unfolded before the avid audience in less than a minute. Kara saw Mac's expression change from incredulity to thunderous. He looked alarmingly bellicose as he strode toward his niece and nephew, now both clinging to Kara.

As the drama shifted her way, Kara felt every eye on her. Her insides felt as if they'd been frappéd in a blender. Stage fright could never be this unnerving!

"We did it, Aunt Kara," Clay exclaimed. "I told her I was sorry I spit in her salad and she ate it."

"And I said I saw her wallet in the bathroom and I was sorry I didn't tell her about it," Autumn chimed in. "She's a bad one, Aunt Kara! She tried to hit us! And she swore, too, right here in the church!" Her brows furrowed worriedly. "Do you think she's going to sneak into our house and kill us?"

"No," Kara assured her. "I think she'll try to stay as far away from you as possible."

"Good! Now let's buy our stuff," cried Clay, tugging on Kara's hand.

"We're leaving right now!" Mac stood before them, looming tall and strong and very, very angry. "Nobody is buying anything."

"We are, too!" Clay faced his uncle, not intimidated by his size or his anger. "Aunt Kara promised."

"I don't care what she said." Mac was flushed with fury. "You kids have gone too far this time, way too far! You are not going to be rewarded for spitting in a lady's salad and stealing her wallet.''

"I said I *saw* her wallet, I didn't say I *stole* it," Autumn argued righteously.

"That's because Brick was probably the one to take it and you planted it in the rest room," thundered Mac. "Don't try to con me, Autumn." He reached out and grabbed his niece by the arm. "We're leaving and I don't want any more back talk." He started toward the door, pulling Autumn behind him, then cast a commanding glare over his shoulder. "Kara, bring Clay and come along. Now!"

"You're hurting my arm!" shrieked Autumn. "The one that almost got broken in three places!"

"C'mon, Aunt Kara, let's buy my torpedo launcher before he gets us, too," urged Clay, trying to pull Kara in the opposite direction.

Still holding on to the howling Autumn, Mac swung back to Kara and Clay. "If you don't come right now, I swear I'll—"

Jill Finlay chose that inopportune moment to join them. "Mac, may I talk to you for a few minutes?"

"We were just on our way home," Mac growled. But he was distracted enough to loosen his grip on Autumn, who immediately stopped yelling and escaped. She ran to safety behind Kara.

"We'll leave you two to your conversation," Kara said jerkily. Images of Mac and Marcy Tanner, so merry and engrossed in each other, were indelibly etched on her mind. She wasn't about to stand around and watch him with yet another former flame. Putting one arm around Clay and the other around Autumn, Kara led them off, leaving Mac facing Jill.

"Well, Mac, as usual, your young charges put on quite a show," Jill said trenchantly. "But from what we've all seen tonight, your new girlfriend has proven she can handle the little psychopaths. If she hadn't been here, they undoubtedly would've taken the place apart by now."

Mac watched Kara and the two kids, both of whom were smiling and talking animatedly to her. "Is there a point to any of this, Jill?" he snapped.

"I just wanted to offer you my congratulations. Ginny introduced me to the future Mrs. Wilde tonight. I think you've met your match, at last. But a word of warning, Mac. However much you're paying her to go through with this marriage, I'm afraid you're going to have to up the ante. She's made it quite clear that she's thinking about backing out, and after that atrocious little scene with Marcy Tanner, you'll probably have to deed the ranch over to her to get her to stay."

"Is that so?" Mac's hostility was so palpable that Jill took a few cautious steps backward and forced a smile.

"I also wanted to let you know that there are no hard feelings on my part," Jill continued, her smiled becoming more genuine. "I'm dating Tom Egan now. His divorce from Mary Jane was final last spring. We're on the verge of becoming serious."

"Tom has two kids, Jill," Mac couldn't resist reminding her. "What about your vow to avoid all children but your own?"

"I never said that!" Jill's smile turned into a frown of displeasure. "I don't want to *avoid* other people's children, I just don't want to live with them. Courtney and Tommy Junior live with their mother, and they are very different from that brat pack you inherited. The Egan children are polite and well-behaved and easy to deal with."

"For now, maybe," Mac said snidely. But not for long, not if Courtney Egan was hanging around Brick. He found an ironic justice in the prospect of judgmental Jill Finlay having to deal with a potential stepchild corrupted by his nephew.

He walked away from his former girlfriend, blessing fate for taking her out of his life. He'd had similar thoughts about Marcy Tanner tonight. His eyes were riveted to Kara as he headed toward her and the kids at the toy table. In a very short time, she'd become an essential part of his life, and he didn't doubt the rightness of that, even though he was currently furious with her.

"However much you're paying her to go through with this marriage, I'm afraid you're going to have to up the ante.... She's made it quite clear that she's thinking about backing out." Jill's words echoed unpleasantly in his head. He couldn't imagine Kara having a conversation like that with anyone. But what if she had?

Clay and Autumn were clutching their prizes. "Thanks, Aunt Kara!" they chorused cheerfully.

"I hope you know that's not a reward for what you did to Marcy Tanner," Kara said, misery and uncertainty plaguing her. Mac's point had registered with her, but then Jill Finlay had slithered up to him, and she'd felt so jealous and confused that the kids' point—that she'd promised them toys if they confessed to their crimes, which they had, seemed equally just.

What did she know about raising children, anyway? Kara ruminated glumly. She'd been a flop as a child herself, shy and quiet and pitifully lacking in confidence and charm. Not that she'd changed much. Compared to Marcy and Jill, two bona fide beauties, she was lacking indeed, proving just how desperate Mac was to even consider marrying her.

She saw Mac approaching them, felt his steady gaze appraising her. He appeared calmer now, but still angry. Suddenly it hurt to breathe.

"We're ready to go home now, Uncle Mac," Autumn chirped, gracious in victory. "I got my jewelry kit."

"And I got my torpedo launcher," announced Clay, holding up the big box for his uncle's inspection.

"I see." Mac glanced at each child before zeroing in on Kara, his dark eyes piercing. "So what does he get when he sprinkles rat poison on someone's plate? A genuine AK-47 assault weapon? And when Autumn holds up a convenience store, let's be sure to reward her with an eighteen karat gold bracelet.''

"Uncle Mac, are you still mad at us?" Clay was shocked.

"Yes, I'm still very mad at all of you." Mac fastened his hand around Kara's neck and placed the other at the small of her back. The moment he touched her, he felt the anger within him begin to dissipate. Tension of an entirely different kind tingled warmly and pleasantly through his body. He couldn't wait to get her home. "We're leaving now," he announced firmly.

"Okay, we'll go outside and look for Brick," Autumn agreed. "Maybe we'll catch him kissing his girlfriend."

"Brick and Courtney, Courtney and Brick," Clay babbled in singsong derision.

The two scampered off, lugging their white elephants.

"God, what a night!" Mac groused, his jaw clenched. "First, a dinner from hell at Pizza Ranch and then we come here, to be the floor show at the annual fall festival. I can't wait to get back to the ranch—where you and I will have a serious discussion about buying presents for juvenile terrorists."

Kara's emotions were churning like a steaming caldron, volatile and hot. "If you don't take your hands off me, I'll let out a scream that will make any of Autumn's seem like a whisper."

"I'm calling your bluff." Mac's hands stayed where they were. "And issuing a threat of my own. If you don't come with me right now, I'm going to pick you up and carry you out of here, and I don't give a damn that half of Bear Creek is standing around watching us."

Ten

Kara whirled around to face him. Her stomach tightened and she lifted her chin to lock her eyes with his. "Now it's *my* turn to call *your* bluff. I am not going to meekly stroll out of here with you, though I'm sure your gargantuan male ego expects me to do just that. After all, you've had quite an evening, haven't you, Mac? Laughing it up with Marcy Tanner, exchanging long, meaningful glances with Jill Finlay."

It was a most un-Kara-like declaration. A week ago, she wouldn't have raised her voice to anyone, let alone initiated a confrontation to express her anger. She would have quietly withdrawn into her shell, which she'd been doing all her life.

"You think I was enjoying myself with Marcy and Jill? Not hardly, honey. You have all the perception of a—of a—" A sudden enlightened smile crossed Mac's face. "Of a jealous lover! That's what you are, Kara. You're jealous because I was talking to Marcy and Jill." He looked so pleased that Kara wanted to pummel him.

"I am not! I don't care what you do or who you do it with.

And if you want to—to flaunt your girlfriends in front of half the town, well, go right ahead!'' Her head held high, she marched purposefully toward the door.

Mac watched her leave. He was aware of his audience, watching him expectantly, wondering if he would ignore her angry departure and stay to socialize, or follow her out. Bear Creek's most eligible bachelor brought to his knees? Squaring his shoulders and pasting a smile on his face, he sauntered out of the church basement, as if chasing after Kara Kirby had been his plan all along.

He found her standing underneath a wide-branched tree, which had shed nearly half of its yellow-gold leaves. They crackled beneath his boots, announcing his arrival. Kara didn't bother to turn around. Mac frowned. Well, why should she? She knew damn well that he'd follow her out here.

''Congratulations,'' he said grimly. ''Everybody saw your irate exit. They also saw me come running after you.''

''I chose to leave. You didn't have to.''

Mac gave a bark of laughter. ''Yeah, sure. I could've stayed inside and chatted up Jill some more while waiting around for Marcy to come back with her wallet. Provided continuing entertainment to the town by *flaunting* my former girlfriends. Thanks, but no thanks, Kara. I don't care for the role of Bear Creek crowd-pleaser.'' Mac took a step closer to her. ''I'd rather please you, exclusively.''

''Don't think I don't know what you're doing.'' Kara's voice trembled. ''You're deliberately turning on the charm.''

''Is it working?'' Mac reached out to finger a strand of her hair. ''Are you anywhere close to being charmed?''

Kara folded her arms in front of her chest and kept her eyes focused straight ahead, on the parking lot where Autumn and Clay were racing from car to car, peering inside each one.

''You're ignoring me,'' Mac persisted. He tucked the silky lock of hair behind her ear, then ran his hand over her shoulder, down the length of her arm. Kara quivered and tried harder to ignore him.

Mac was undeterred. ''Not a particularly good move on your part, Kara. I'm just obnoxious enough to refuse to be ignored.''

Kara was silent. Did Mac actually think she had some kind of planned strategy for dealing with him? The truth was, she was flying blind without a clue as to what to say or do next.

Mac followed her gaze. ''What on earth are those kids doing now? They're zooming around like a couple of Keystone Kops on speed.''

''They're hoping to catch Brick and Courtney Egan in a compromising position in one of the cars,'' Kara said tightly. ''I'm hoping they won't.''

''That makes two of us. He's too young to be making out with girls.''

''Maybe it's genetic,'' Kara said waspishly. ''I'm sure you started early. And you're still going strong.'' The moment the words were out of her mouth, she regretted them. Once again, she sounded like a jealous shrew!

Mac moved swiftly, standing in front of her, toe-to-toe. ''You're wrong if you think either Marcy or Jill means anything to me, Kara.''

''You'd be married to one or the other if they'd been able to cope with the kids. I'd say that means something!''

''Not anymore. Jill and Marcy were okay for a freewheeling single guy but the moment I became a family man, they were all wrong. It was over.'' He cupped her chin in his hand, tilting her face to meet his dark-eyed gaze. ''And I didn't care, Kara. It just didn't matter.''

Just because he wouldn't admit to carrying a torch for either woman, didn't mean there weren't some sparks there. All of Kara's old insecurities rose up to clobber her. What was the use? She couldn't compete.

''You don't have to explain anything to me,'' she said stiffly.

"Apparently, I do. So I will." He gripped both of her wrists and gave her a gentle tug toward him.

Kara resisted, holding her ground and keeping her distance. Her former stepfather's dire laments played over and over in her head like a tape. *Mac would be perfectly willing to marry any woman who agreed to his terms.*

Any woman. Her or Marcy or Jill, whichever happened to be the first to say yes. And if either Marcy or Jill were to change their minds and accept Mac's offer, Kara had no doubts that she would be on the next plane back to D.C. After all, she was at least his third choice.... Jill's mention of Tonya, desperate but not desperate enough to cope with the Wilde kids, sprang to mind...maybe there were candidates she'd yet to hear about. Maybe she wasn't even among the top ten finalists!

Kara conceded defeat. Why wait around for the rejection that was sure to come? Maybe she should take the initiative and just leave. Be pro-active, like all those self-help articles urged.

Mac heaved a sigh. Discussing Marcy and Jill struck him as irrelevant as speculating on the social significance of lava lamps and mood rings. The past had never interested him as much as the present or the future. He studied Kara thoughtfully. She was his present and his future, but she seemed determined to rehash his spurious past. Well, he would indulge her. There wasn't much he wouldn't do to satisfy her, he admitted to himself.

"Look, honey. Marcy invited herself to join us at the restaurant tonight, and when she heard we were coming here, she decided to follow in her car. I don't know why, because the kids were bratty and rude to her all through dinner and—"

"I saw the two of you together, Mac," Kara interrupted, her voice ragged. "She was flirting with you and you were smiling at her as if you were totally entranced."

"No, I was *in* a trance. I was on automatic pilot, Kara.

When a woman chatters and giggles like Marcy was doing, I zone out. Oh, I can smile and even make an occasional one-word response, but mentally I've teleported myself somewhere else. I was contemplating cattle futures when all of a sudden Clay and Autumn ran over to confess their evil deeds.''

He grimaced wryly. ''Not that they were even slightly repentant. They were downright triumphant!''

''Tricia Franklin told them that Marcy hates them and stopped seeing you because of them,'' Kara said quietly. ''I think they were showing loyalty to you.''

''Maybe they were, in an Addams Family sort of way. But I think it more likely that they were showing their loyalty to you, Kara. Their credo goes something like this—no woman but you hangs with the Wildes, and all interlopers will be prosecuted to the fullest extent of the kids' abilities. Which are considerable,'' he added ruefully.

His fingers tightened and he tugged her a little harder. ''Now come here and kiss me and then we'll go home and—''

''No.'' Kara backed away, as far from him as the length of her arms would permit. Reluctantly, Mac dropped her wrists.

''I'm sorry, Mac,'' she said breathlessly. ''I thought I could go through with it but—''

''Moving on to Jill and those alleged meaningful glances,'' Mac interrupted, his voice resolute and unwavering. ''Boy, did you call that one wrong! Jill thinks I'm an idiot but she's impressed with you. I think she'd be willing to act as your agent in drawing up a killer prenuptial agreement.''

''Prenuptial agreement?''

''Jill thinks you should make me cough up a big bundle of cold hard cash before the wedding. Is she right, Kara? Is that what you're holding out for?''

''No! I never said—I don't understand why she would say such a thing to you. I never told her I wanted money, I...''

Kara paused to catch her breath. She was so off-balance she could hardly remember what she'd said during her brief conversation with Jill. But she knew it hadn't involved a cash payoff!

There was an unholy gleam in Mac's eyes. "If you insist on a prenuptial agreement with a chunk of cash going into a bank account bearing your name only, we can talk to Jill's new flame, Tom Egan, tonight. He's a local attorney and an old friend of mine, and I'm sure he would be willing to draft a—"

"I don't want your money!"

"So you'll marry me without a prenup?"

"Yes! I mean, I would if I was going to marry you but I—I need some time to think, Mac. We both do."

"I don't agree, but you can think at the ranch if you insist."

"No, I need some time alone. I can't think clearly when you—"

"And I are making love?" Mac arched his brows. "Good. I don't want you to be able to think clearly when you're in bed with me. Save all that clear thinking for dealing with the kids and working on the books."

Kara steeled herself against the seductive images of herself in Mac's bed, rendered mindless with desire, then drowsily satiated and replete. Neither state was conductive to analytical thought.

"I can't stay at the ranch. I want to fly back to Washington tomorrow." She swallowed hard. The way he was looking at her, intense and possessive and utterly determined, made chills run down her body.

"I'll ask Uncle Will to drive me back to the ranch to get my things tonight and I'll stay in town with the Franklins." She remembered Tricia's grievous allergies. "We'll pick up Tai tomorrow and drive to the airport, if—if you don't mind letting him stay with you tonight."

"Sure, the cat can stay," Mac said coolly. "In fact, he's not leaving the ranch."

Kara's eyes widened. "What do you mean?"

"Exactly what you heard me say, sweetie. I'm holding the cat hostage. If you want to live with him, you'll live with him in my house."

Kara suppressed an irrational urge to laugh and to burst into tears at the same time. "You can't hold Tai hostage!" She tried for derisive defiance and was dismayed by how nervous and uncertain she sounded.

"No?" His smile was a challenge. "Who's going to stop me?"

Kara stared at him, debating whether he was serious or not. "I am. You—You wouldn't really keep Tai from me, would you?"

Mac tilted his head and appeared to consider it. "I'm willing to negotiate," he said at last.

"How big of you!" Kara wanted to shake him, to wipe that self-confident arrogance right off his face.

"Do it, Kara," Mac taunted, his voice low and deep. "Go ahead and slap me. You know how much you want to. I'd rather have you fight with me than retreat and withdraw. In fact, I won't allow you to do it. I'll keep provoking you until you're so damn mad, you'll attack me instead of detaching yourself."

He was close to achieving that particular goal. Kara imagined smacking his hard cheek, playing the scene like she'd seen in hundreds of movies and TV shows. Her palm actually tingled in anticipation.

But she restrained herself, her civilized reserve prevailing. "You are not going to incite me into an act of physical violence, Mac Wilde."

"Then I'll incite you into another kind of physical act." Mac yanked her into his arms.

His mouth was hard and hot and strong. He crushed her against him, as if he couldn't hold her close enough, molding her softness to the unyielding male planes of his body. His tongue went deep inside her mouth, and Kara moaned as a shiver of pleasure swept through her. Her body was so conditioned to the ecstasy of their lovemaking that he had only to touch her to rekindle the need and the hunger within her.

Kara's self-control, always so formidable, was not strong enough to keep her from responding, and she gave in, leaning heavily into him as he held her tight. Her arms encircled his neck. Her middle rubbed his as she arched against the burgeoning pressure of his thighs.

It was a tempestuous, carnal kiss that swept them instantly into the hot urgent throes of desire. Kara felt his heat and his hardness and clung to him, the empty ache inside her making her whimper because it was an ache only he could fill, and she knew how good it felt with him full and deep inside her.

She wanted him now; nothing else mattered but being with him. Common sense and pride, words of advice from well-meaning others and the specter of past lovers ceased to exist. In this timeless vortex of passion, only the two of them existed.

"Wow!" A third party suddenly was catapulted into their own private world. It was Autumn's voice that shattered the sensuous spell secluding them. "That's how they kiss on soap operas!"

Mac groaned and lifted his mouth from Kara's, but he didn't loosen his grip on her. He held her tightly against him and pressed his lips against her temple. Kara felt the rigidity of his erection fiercely against her and her whole body throbbed in response. Neither she nor Mac were capable of conversation quite yet, but Autumn didn't mind, she carried on a monologue.

She recited a garbled version of several plot lines running on one daytime soap, then added curiously, "Do you think Brick and Courtney are kissing like that?"

"Lord, I hope not," Mac finally managed to rasp.

Kara slipped out of his arms, and he closed his eyes and

clenched his jaw as a wave of unbridled frustration roared through him.

"Lily and Webb kiss like that," Clay said conversationally. He was kneeling beside Autumn, delving into the box and taking out pieces of his new used toy.

Kara drew a sharp breath and looked at Mac who seemed to have been turned to stone. "What did you say, Clay?" he asked, his tone deceptively calm.

But Clay was not deceived. He dropped a plastic wheel and covered his mouth with both hands. "I forgot! It's a secret. I'm not supposed to tell!"

"You knew a secret?" Autumn was indignant. "How come you didn't tell me?"

"I didn't tell anybody," Clay said proudly. "I saw Lily and Webb kissing in the barn and Lily bought me a Gameboy game if I didn't tell." His face fell. "Till now. It just kind of slipped out. Lily will be so mad! She'll run over my Gameboy and all the games with the car. She said so!"

"Webb Asher?" Even in the moonlight, Mac's face was visibly pale. "And *Lily?*" He went even whiter. "My God, I asked him to stay with her tonight! We've got to get home right now!"

His angry urgency alarmed Autumn. "Is Webb going to kill Lily if we don't stop him?" she cried, clutching at Kara for reassurance.

"No." Kara stroked her silky black hair. She didn't add that Webb was the one at risk for homicide—at Mac's hands. No use truly scaring the already anxious child.

Mac was already headed toward the Jeep Cherokee, parked at the far end of the parking lot. Kara scrapped her plans for staying at the Franklins. If anyone could bring some sense of order to the Wildes' house tonight, she knew it was her.

"Mac, wait," she called, and he stopped in his tracks. "You can't leave without Brick."

Mac came striding back. "I forgot all about him." He gripped his head with his hands. "God, I'm a basket case.

Lily and Asher? How long has this been going on? I swear
I'll—"

"Have a serious talk with both Lily and Webb," Kara cut
in, nodding toward the wide-eyed Autumn.

Mac took the hint automatically. It wasn't wise to speak
of killing, even metaphorically, around the crime-obsessed
child. "Yeah, that's right." He caught Kara's hand and
squeezed it, and their eyes met in perfect understanding.

"Hey there, Mac! Jill and I were just talking about you."
A tall, thin man in a dark suit approached them, his arm
draped loosely around Jill Finlay's waist.

Mac looked pained and didn't bother to disguise it. "We're
on our way home, Tom," he said brusquely.

Jill frowned, but Tom Egan didn't take offense. "So are
we. I'm looking for my daughter, Courtney. I have to drop
her off at her mother's. Have you seen her? Her friends said
she came out for some air because it was getting too hot
inside."

Kara exchanged glances with Autumn and Clay. They
shared another one of those moments of wordless, yet un-
equivocally clear, communication.

"We'll find her for you, Mr. Egan," Autumn volunteered
at once. "C'mon, Clay." The two of them ran off bellowing.
"Courtney! Your dad is looking for you," at the top of their
lungs.

Mac paced back and forth like a restless, caged cougar,
unresponsive to Tom Egan's attempt at small talk. Kara
picked up the slack, discussing Montana weather with Tom
and Jill until Courtney appeared with Clay and Autumn.

"Hi, Daddy," Courtney smiled at her father, then shot Jill
a cold look of dislike. She carefully stood between the couple
and took her father's hand. The three walked away.

"Courtney hates Jill," Autumn whispered to Kara. "She
wants her mom and dad to get back together."

"She said Brick told her he'd help her get rid of Jill,"
added Clay importantly.

Who better than Brick to advise a teen on how to conduct a reign of terror? Kara thought wryly. It seemed that Courtney was going all out to sabotage her father's romance with Jill. One could almost feel sorry for the finicky redhead. Almost.

Brick joined them, seemingly materializing out of nowhere. But Mac didn't question him on his whereabouts; he was too preoccupied with the specter of Webb and Lily. Grabbing Kara's hand, he strode toward the Jeep Cherokee, the three kids trailing behind.

"If we go any faster, we'll qualify for the finals of the Indy 500," Kara murmured, clutching the armrests of her seat. She glanced at the children who were quiet, apparently listening to the country song wailing on the radio. But Kara saw the apprehension in their eyes.

A muscle twitched in Mac's cheek but he didn't say anything. Kara found his silence more unnerving than his usually vociferous anger. She remembered what he'd said about her retreating into herself and decided he was right. Even angry communication was preferable to silent withdrawal.

Traveling as they were at the speed of light, the drive back to the Double R took less than half as long as her trip into town earlier that evening. Kara's trepidation grew as they rounded the bend, and the house came into view.

Mac braked to a stop in front of the house and flung open his door. Kara reached over and clutched the sleeve of his shirt. He paused, turning to look at her. "What?" he snapped.

"I want to talk to you for a few minutes," she said, keeping her voice firm. It wasn't easy to sound confident and in control when he was staring impatiently beyond her, at the lighted house a few yards away.

"Kids, why don't you go inside?" she suggested. "Uncle Mac will put the car in the garage, and he and I will be in shortly."

"Sounds like a plan to me." Brick gave her the thumbs-up sign, signalling that he was in cahoots with whatever her plan was. Autumn and Clay followed his lead, tumbling out of the vehicle and racing to the house.

"With Brick working on the case, I give the Tom Egan-Jill Finlay romance about another week," Kara remarked wryly.

"Look, I know you sent the kids in to warn Lily and that snake Asher that I'm on to them and now you're going to try to reason with me." Mac scowled fiercely. "Save your breath, Kara. Asher deserves to be shot for messing with an innocent little schoolgirl and as her guardian, I'm the one to—to…" His voice trailed off. His face, his body, were taut with fury.

"Mac, in case you haven't noticed, Lily is nobody's idea of an innocent little schoolgirl, not even yours," Kara said softly. "Furthermore, I *am* going to stop you from charging in there and smashing Webb Asher to smithereens. What good will it do? Haven't the kids been through enough without watching you attack a man in their own home?"

"What would you like me to do, Kara? Give my blessings to the happy couple? Lend Asher my car so he can take Lily to the Bear Creek High football game on Friday night?"

"For now, I'd just like you to put the car in the garage," Kara murmured. Her eyes darted to the front door of the house. The kids had had time to warn Webb and she fully expected him to come dashing out the front door.

Mac followed her gaze and her thoughts. "The weasel wouldn't risk running into us. He's undoubtedly gone slinking out the back."

His voice was colder and harder than she'd ever heard, and for a heart-stopping moment, Kara feared he was going to storm inside and dismember both Webb and Lily on the spot.

But Mac pulled his door closed and drove the Cherokee to the garage, opening the door with remote control. The heavy door closed behind them. It was dark in the big garage, the only illumination being the shaft of moonlight filtering through the building's upper window.

Kara didn't realize that she was still clutching his arm until Mac tried to remove her restraining hand from his shirt.

Instead of lifting her hand, she linked her fingers with his. "Mac, this probably isn't the best time to tell you this but—but I have to say it."

Mac whirled in his seat, scowling. "No!" His voice boomed. "Don't say it. I will not listen to another word about you leaving tomorrow or any other time. I don't know what the Rev said to you to convince you to leave tonight, but whatever it was, he's wrong. You're mine, damn it! You belong here with me and with the kids. I'll do almost anything to ease your adjustment to living here with us. I'll do almost anything to make you happy. But the one thing I won't do is to let you go, Kara."

"Because you need me as a keeper for the kids." She quoted Reverend Will, whose words were ringing miserably in her ears.

"Because I want *you,* Kara. You can't pretend not to know that." Mac's voice was low but explosive in its intensity. "Whenever I'm near you, I can't take my eyes off you. I watch you move, the way you smile, everything you do and say, and it makes me want you even more. I think about how it is between us in bed and I get so hungry for you I think I'll come unglued unless I have you again."

"You don't mind using me sexually. I'm available and convenient and you've been deprived of sex since the kids arrived. But it won't last. It can't because none of it is based on caring and love and respect." Tears glittered in her eyes and she tried desperately to blink them back.

Mac's jaw dropped. "You don't really believe that?" His eyes narrowed, his face hardening. "Is that the kind of garbage you had to listen to tonight at the Franklins? Damn, I knew I should never have let you go there tonight. I broke one of my most important rules—to follow my own instincts—and every one of them told me that sending you off with your ex-stepfather was a bad idea."

"I wanted to go," Kara countered. "And I make my own decisions, I don't follow your rules." She remembered little Clay's pronouncement, *"Uncle Mac is the boss around here."* Well, he was not her boss!

Mac merely shook his head, lost in thought. Which he voiced aloud. "The Rev is on some guilt trip because he wimped out all those years ago when his wife insisted that he remove himself as your dad. So he's decided he has to protect you from being abandoned by me. Which is insane because I am *not* going to leave you, Kara. I'm not going to let you leave me, either."

He moved closer to her, lifting the armrests of the bucket seats which were between them. Swiftly, deftly, he scooped her up and then took her seat, sitting down on it with her on his lap.

"I'm surprised that the Rev has such a low opinion of me and I'm damn well furious that he has the nerve to even think that you're *fungible* with any other woman. That I could be with you and not value you as unique and sweet and loving and smart and funny..."

He cleared his throat. "I know we haven't known each other very long, but now I can't imagine not knowing you, Kara. It feels as if you've always been in my life because you fit in so naturally, so perfectly. And I admit that the way we met was ridiculous. Mail-order brides? Give me a break! But how we got together doesn't matter anymore, only that we are together."

Joy flooded her, pulsing through her with every heartbeat. The wonderful things Mac was saying negated Uncle Will's hurtful words of caution. And the way he was saying them, his voice deep and huskily earnest, touched her deeply. Her limpid and moist eyes met his.

"Let's stay together, Kara," he said softly.

"Yes," she whispered. "I love you, Mac. I don't care if it's too soon to say it or that we haven't known each other long enough. I know that I love you and I want you to know it, too. *That's* what I was trying to tell you, not that I was going to leave. It took me a little while to come to terms with the inevitable, but I can't leave you or the kids, Mac.''

"You're not going to,'' he assured her.

Instead of raising her ire, his characteristic blend of confidence and arrogance made her smile.

"I want to make love to you, Kara.'' Mac drew her to him for a deep, slow kiss that had Kara clinging to him.

"Here? Now?'' Her voice was thick with desire, her eyes dilated with passion.

"Yes, here and now.'' A faint smile curved his lips as he lifted her and jumped onto the bench-style seat behind them, and then his mouth came fiercely down on hers.

Her body surged against his, and a small soft moan escaped her lips. She was exactly where she wanted to be, in Mac's arms, holding him, kissing him. His big warm hands stroked her back, sliding around her rib cage and moving up to cup her breasts.

Raw pleasure filled her. Kara responded with all the love and desire brimming within her, her hands and her lips as ardent as his.

She felt his long, hard fingers slide under her skirt, smoothing along her stockings until he reached the soft bare skin of her thighs above the lacy bands. He caressed her there until she was twisting beneath his hands, her lips desperately seeking his, while her fingers fumbled with the buttons of his shirt, the buckle of his belt.

"You want me,'' Mac laughed softly, triumphantly. "You love me.''

"Yes, yes,'' she gasped, overwhelmed by her own raging need for him. And his for her.

They kissed again, their movements eager as they pulled at each other's clothes. But they were too impatient to wait and made do with removing the minimal essentials. Frantic for him, aching for him, Kara tried to recline on the seat, pulling him down on top of her.

His dark eyes gleamed. "We're going to try something new tonight." His fingers caressed her intimately, making her shudder with pleasure and urgency. "You're definitely ready, but are you willing?"

She nodded, but her eyes widened with surprise as he positioned her on his lap, facing him, straddling him.

"I've taught you everything you know about making love," Mac said, his voice possessive. "Now it's time for another lesson." His hands held her hips and he eased into her, his eyes locked with hers.

With a sense of awe, Kara felt him enter her, felt her body sheath his. She clutched at his shoulders as her breath came in unsteady gasps.

"Relax." Mac's voice was soothing and commanding and thoroughly arousing. He nipped at her lips, coaching her between kisses. "We'll take it slowly. Move with me." His body rocked hers, erotically, masterfully, and she moaned as her own body matched his rhythm, accommodating his full deep thrusts.

Kara was consumed with a wild recklessness, a fierce need to possess and be possessed. She moved with him and for him, desire knotting tighter, building and burning until she teetered on the edge of ecstasy, finally crying aloud when she went tumbling into a mindless realm of sensuous rapture. Mac joined her there seconds later.

She collapsed against him, burying her face in the hollow of his shoulder. He cradled her in his arms. His chest rose and fell unevenly as his breath rasped in and out. They stayed like that, their eyes closed, holding each other in a state of languid bliss.

Finally, they began to stir. His fingers tangled in her hair and he nuzzled his cheek against hers. "You amaze me," he said huskily.

"Because I'm such a fast learner?" Kara kissed him playfully. Here in his arms, their bodies still linked, she felt exquisitely feminine and confident and loved. Even if Mac hadn't said the words, she felt loved. "It's because you're such a fantastic teacher."

"Mmm, I believe in a hands-on approach to learning."

They laughed softly together.

"I can't believe this…in a car!" Mac smiled into her eyes. "You lured me into the garage and seduced me!"

"Are you objecting?"

"Not at all, baby. I think I'd like to make a habit of it."

Slowly, reluctantly, they drew apart, retrieving certain discarded garments and straightening their clothes. Mac turned on the interior light and Kara combed her hair and pulled out her compact and lipstick trying to make herself presentable. She was surprised at the face of the woman staring back at her in the mirror. It was the face of a lovely woman, sensuous and well-sated, light years away from the shy, inhibited Commerce Department statistician who'd arrived in Montana such a short time ago.

When she was ready, Mac opened the door for her and helped her out of the car. He was being a chivalrous, protective lover and Kara felt cherished as she cuddled against him. They walked to the house, their arms around each other, talking softly, pausing to exchange quick light kisses.

It wasn't until they were on the porch that Kara broached the subject they'd been avoiding. "Mac, about Lily and Webb," she began hesitantly.

"Don't worry, I'm not going to go ballistic." He gave her a sexy smile. "I don't have the energy—you made sure of that."

"Lily is probably in her room pretending to be asleep and Webb's gone back to his trailer," Kara speculated. "Could we leave it like that for tonight, Mac? I think it'll be better for everybody if we discuss this in the morning."

"Okay." Mac nodded in agreement. "I'm going to have to fire Asher, Kara. Too bad, because he was a good manager. He worked hard and came highly recommended. He used to work in Texas for a very wealthy rancher who's married to some senator's daughter.''

Mac shook his head. "I never suspected a thing was going on between him and Lily. I thought she got on his nerves. She acted like such a brat around him, mouthing off to him, taunting him.''

The house was quiet. Not even the television was on. And then Autumn and Clay came running down the hall toward them. They were both in their pajamas and Autumn was carrying a rather disgruntled-looking Tai.

"Can Tai sleep in my room again tonight, Aunt Kara?" Autumn asked eagerly, and when Kara nodded, the little girl turned and ran back down the hall with the cat.

"'Night, Aunt Kara, 'night Uncle Mac.'' Clay gave them each a smacking kiss and then disappeared after Autumn.

Kara and Mac exchanged glances.

"Something's up,'' Mac said ominously. "Those two have just taken themselves out of the line of fire.''

"What they *think* will be the line of fire,'' corrected Kara. "There won't be any fireworks tonight, we're all going to bed.''

"Let's amend that to, the only fireworks tonight will be in our bedroom.'' Mac smiled and leaned down to kiss her.

"I can't wait,'' Kara whispered. She took his hand and started to lead him down the hall.

She uttered a shocked gasp when Webb came out of the living room to stand before her and Mac in the hall. He was literally the last person she'd expected to find in the house. She felt Mac tense and then lunge at Asher like a mountain lion springing on its hapless prey.

"Mac, don't!'' she cried, clutching at him.

"Uncle Mac, stop!'' Lily was on Mac's other side, trying to pull him away, too. Brick was with her, making a half-hearted effort to hold his uncle back. Kara could tell by the hopeful look on the boy's face that he wouldn't mind a good old-fashioned brawl one bit.

Webb offered no resistance. "Go ahead and pulverize me, Mac," he said, his voice a deep rumble. "I have it coming."

His defeated self-condemnation effectively defused Mac's rage. He shoved the other man away from him. "Get out of here, Asher. I want you out of the trailer and off the ranch by morning. Hell, I want you out of the state! I'm going to—"

"No, Uncle Mac!" Lily interrupted. She left her uncle's side and went to stand by Webb, slipping her arms around the man's waist.

Kara watched Mac's face flush with sheer rage. Nervously, she slipped her hand into his. She happened to glance over at Brick, whose eyes were glittering with anticipation.

"Brick, go to bed," she ordered. "This doesn't concern you."

"Uncle Mac might need me to help him *pul-ver-ize* Webb Asher," Brick pronounced the new word carefully and with undisguised relish.

Mac heaved a sigh. "Nobody is going to get pulverized, Brick. Go on to bed."

"Webb is going to tell Uncle Mac how much we love each other," Lily said, smiling up at the ranch manager, her dark eyes glowing. "And we do," she added softly, snuggling closer to her lover. "Don't we, Webb?"

"Ugh!" Brick was disgusted. "I'm not hanging around to listen to that lovesick garbage. I'm going to bed." He marched off in disgust.

The two couples faced each other.

"Why don't we go into the kitchen and I'll make some coffee or tea or something," Kara suggested uneasily.

"I think Webb and Uncle Mac could use something a lot stronger than that." Lily smiled, amused. "Maybe a bottle of hundred-proof whiskey apiece."

Kara marveled at the girl's poise, her own was practically nonexistent. Mac was still gripping her hand, but she felt the tense energy emanating from him. He was furious, and she wasn't sure how much he felt like controlling his rage. Certainly, the sight of Lily clinging to Webb didn't please him. Nor had the young woman's breathless declaration of love.

But when Kara gave Mac's hand a gentle pull, he allowed her to lead him into the kitchen. Webb and Lily followed.

"Why in the hell are you still here, Asher?" Mac growled. "If you had a lick of sense, you'd be halfway back to Texas by now."

"He loves me too much to run out on me, Uncle Mac," Lily interjected.

Webb looked at the floor, then lifted his eyes to meet Mac's flinty-eyed glare. "It's true, Mac. God knows, I tried to fight it. But I couldn't, damn it! I really do love her. I felt like a rat sneaking around behind your back, and when the kids came running in here tonight, I knew I had to face you. I finally admitted to myself how much I care for her, and it's time you knew, too."

Kara paused in her frantic search for tea bags to stare in astonishment. No matter what Lily claimed, she really hadn't expected the tough ranch manager to admit to loving the boss's niece.

"She's just a kid, Webb," Mac exclaimed, exasperated.

"I stopped being a kid a long time ago, Uncle Mac," Lily said softly. "I had to grow up fast, and I did. I'm a woman in every sense of the word."

Mac choked and sank into a chair. Kara crossed the room to lay her hands supportively on his shoulders.

"I wanted Webb from the moment I met him when we moved here this summer," Lily persisted. "Oh, he tried to fight it, he tried to fight me. He tried to keep away from me but I wouldn't keep away from him. I'd sneak out of the house at night and into his trailer—"

Mac uttered a particularly descriptive epithet.

"Nothing happened then, Uncle Mac, honest!" exclaimed Lily. "I tried to seduce him, but he wouldn't let me. We sat around and talked, we listened to music. Webb kept telling me he was too old for me, but I didn't care. Because he's not! I need a man, not a boy, Uncle Mac."

"And Webb Asher is the man you need?" Mac asked sardonically.

Lily ignored the sarcasm. "Yes." She nodded her head vigorously. "All this summer I went after him, I spent hours with him and he never even kissed me, Uncle Mac. Not till September. And he felt so guilty after that and really tried to stay away from me, but we wanted each other too much. I wouldn't let him avoid me."

"You *are* relentless," Mac agreed darkly.

"It seems to be something of a family trait," Kara said wryly, massaging Mac's taut shoulders with her fingers. He'd been so relaxed out in the garage a short time ago, and now he was tense and stressed out. She wanted to comfort him, to provide herself as an outlet to relieve all his tension and stress. She brushed her lips against the top of his head.

Mac responded to her gesture of tenderness by reaching up to cover her hand with his.

Lily's dark eyes took in the scene and she sent Kara an appreciative smile before picking up her narrative. "Anyway, I knew I loved Webb and I was sure he loved me, even though he'd rather be shot than admit it. I had to take drastic action. So I went to the Rustler the day Kara arrived in Montana. The sheriff called Webb and he came to pick me up and got really mad at me. I deliberately provoked him by being unbearably obnoxious, you know, teasing him and trying to run away again and—"

"We came in on that scene," Mac growled. "You were tied to a chair here in the kitchen."

Lily nodded. "And the very next day, the stalemate was broken and we—"

"That's enough, Lily," Webb interrupted firmly. To Mac's and Kara's surprise, Lily actually obeyed him and stopped talking.

"Mac, I know it's crazy," Webb said ruefully. "If anybody would've ever told me I'd end up wrapped around the finger of a pretty little girl half my age, I would've said they were certifiable. I never wanted a serious relationship—I've actively avoided them for years. Back in Texas, my boss's younger sister fell for me. I ended up leaving because she wanted more than I cared to give. When I came here, the *last* thing I ever expected—"

"—was to fall victim to my niece's wiles," Mac concluded. "I realize that you're not fully to blame, but Lily is still in high school, Webb! I can't sit by and condone this—this affair of yours."

"I know." Webb nodded his head. "But it's more than an affair, Mac. I'm going to marry Lily. I realized tonight, when the kids came in to tell me that I'd better get the hell out of here, that I couldn't give Lily up. I have some money saved and my great-uncle is going to sell me part of his horse ranch in Colorado. It's a nice piece of property, and I know how to work it. I'd always intended to go there someday, and the time is right now. I'll leave as soon as you hire a replacement for me, and Lily is coming with me. She can finish school there and—"

"Marriage! You and Lily?" Mac exploded. "That's the stupidest, craziest idea I've ever heard!"

"I can think of a stupider, crazier one, Uncle Mac," Lily said tartly. "You mail-ordering a bride and then falling in love with her and rushing her into marriage before you've known her a week."

"That's different," Mac snapped.

"*We're* different, Uncle Mac. It's the Wilde way to do things—differently from other people."

Mac leaned his head back against Kara's breasts and closed his eyes. "Since I fail to see any way out of this, I have no choice but to wish them luck," he said, more to himself than Kara. "I don't want to alienate my niece or force her into running away."

"Which I'd do in a minute if you tried to keep me from

Webb,'' Lily assured him. She crossed the room to hug her uncle and Kara in turn. "Be happy for me,'' she ordered. "This is the happiest I've ever been my whole life. You don't have to worry about me, Uncle Mac. Webb and I will be fine. It's going to work between us.''

Kara was struck by Lily's determination, a blend of that same self-confidence and arrogance that her uncle possessed. She looked and sounded just like Mac pronouncing that marriage to his mail-order bride couldn't possibly fail.

Mac hugged Lily and manfully shook Webb's hand, though his face was wooden. But fire flared in his eyes when Lily attempted to leave the house to go with Webb to his trailer.

"You're not spending the night with him until you're legally married,'' he said firmly.

"Don't be so retro, Uncle Mac,'' Lily pouted. "I'm going with Webb.''

Kara held her breath. She'd spent enough time with the Wildes to recognize that yet another battle-of-wills was brewing.

Apparently, so had Webb. "Mac is right, Lily. We won't spend the night together until we're man and wife.''

"Isn't that like locking the barn door after Clay has let the stallion out?'' Lily demanded. "I can do what I want and if I want to spend the night with you, I will, Webb Asher.''

"Not until you're Mrs. Webb Asher.'' Webb's tone and hard stare were unyielding.

Kara and Mac exchanged uneasy glances. And then Lily stunned them.

"Oh, all right,'' she said crossly. "I'll stay here.'' She turned to leave, holding her head high and haughty. "I'm going to my room now. Good night!''

Webb caught her and wrapped a proprietary arm around her. "First walk me to the door and kiss me good-night,'' he ordered, grinning.

Lily hesitated for a moment, as if debating whether or not

to argue. Finally, she gave in with a sigh, slipping her arm around Webb and leaning against him as they walked down the hall.

"Well, he seems able to handle her," Mac remarked as he and Kara walked hand-in-hand back to his bedroom. "But I feel like I've failed Lily, and Reid and Linda, too," he added dispiritedly. "Lily getting married so young—"

"Has nothing to do with you, Mac," Kara injected. "I think Lily needs to belong to someone, she needs to have somebody all her own. A need like that is too profound to be bound by conventional rules about age and—"

"—the length of time required for falling in love." Mac gave her a knowing look.

Kara nodded. Her love for him was no longer a secret to be concealed from him. "Lily must have instinctively known that Webb could provide her with the security and the love that she craved, and she went after him. She wasn't about to let you or anyone else interfere. You Wildes are hard to stop when it comes to getting what you want," she added, a smile tugging at the corners of her mouth.

Mac looked at her, and something hot and intense sparked in his eyes. "I guess the word relentless is an apt description of both Lily and me." He carefully locked the bedroom door behind them.

Kara's heart jumped. When he reached for her, she went eagerly into his arms.

"Lily was determined to have Asher, and she got him. Just like I was determined to have you."

"Well, you have me," she admitted softly.

He began kissing her again, deep drugging kisses that stoked the flames between them all over again. Mac picked her up and carried her over to the bed, laying her down with infinite tenderness. It was in his dark eyes as he gazed at her.

"I love you, Mac," Kara breathed on a sigh.

"I know, baby. I love you, too." He lay down beside her, reaching for her.

"You don't have to tell me what you think I need to hear, Mac." She gazed up at him, her hazel eyes solemn and sincere. "I know you want me and—"

"I also love you," Mac insisted. "I realized how very right Lily was when she said I'd fallen in love with you. I think it started the moment I met you at the airport. By the time we'd arrived back at the ranch, I knew I was going to do whatever it took to keep you here. And that was something I hadn't done before," he added, grinning.

At her droll look of disbelief, he grew more insistent.

"It's true! After each woman refused my lukewarm suggestion to move in to take care of the kids, I simply shrugged and didn't bother to pursue any of them. They said 'no' and I said 'okay.' Until you, Kara. I didn't shrug off your refusals. And I certainly pursued you. All of which refutes the Rev's fungibility charge. You are one of a kind, Kara, unique and irreplaceable. You're the woman I love, and I'll spend the rest of my life proving it."

"Beginning right now, I hope," Kara whispered, wrapping her arms around him.

"Beginning right now."

* * * * *

HARLEQUIN®
INTRIGUE

WE'LL LEAVE YOU BREATHLESS!

If you've been looking for thrilling tales of
contemporary passion and sensuous love stories
with taut, edge-of-the-seat suspense—then
you'll love Harlequin Intrigue!

Every month, you'll meet four new heroes
who are guaranteed to make your spine tingle
and your pulse pound. With them you'll enter
into the exciting world of Harlequin Intrigue—
where your life is on the line
and so is your heart!

THAT'S INTRIGUE—
ROMANTIC SUSPENSE
AT ITS BEST!